PRAISE FOR THE
HARRY CON

The three novels of THE GREAT WAY

The Way Into Chaos
The Way Into Magic
The Way Into Darkness

"Connolly pens one hell of a gripping tale and kicks Epic Fantasy in the head! Heroic in scope, but intimately human, and richly detailed. *The Way Into Chaos* intrigues and teases, then grabs readers by the throat and plunges them into desperate adventure related through the experience of two extraordinary narrators. The story never lets up as it twists and turns to a breathless finish that leaves you crying for the next book of *The Great Way*. Fantastic!"

—Kat Richarson

"One hard-hitting, take-no-prisoners, breathtaking holy moly of a book."

—C.E. Murphy

"Complex world, tight action, awesome women as well as men; Connolly was good right out the gate, and just keeps getting better."

—Sherwood Smith

TWENTY PALACES

"Connolly's portrayal of magic—and the hints he drops about the larger supernatural world—are as exciting as ever."

—*Black Gate*

CHILD OF FIRE

"[*Child of Fire*] is excellent reading and has a lot of things I love in a book: a truly dark and sinister world, delicious tension and suspense, violence so gritty you'll get something in your eye just reading it, and a gorgeously flawed protagonist. Take this one to the checkout counter. Seriously."

—Jim Butcher

"Unique magical concepts, a tough and pragmatic protagonist and a high casualty rate for innocent bystanders will enthrall readers who like explosive action and magic that comes at a serious cost."

—Starred review from *Publishers Weekly*, and one of PW's Best 100 Books of 2009

"One of the few urban magic books—for lack of a better term—novels I enjoyed last year was Harry Connolly's *Child of Fire*. And I loved it."

—John Rogers, writer/producer *Leverage*

"Every page better than the last. Cinematic and vivid, with a provocative glimpse into a larger world."

—Terry Rossio, screenwriter (*Shriek, Pirates of the Caribbean*)

GAME OF CAGES

"*Game of Cages* is a tough, smart, unflinching urban fantasy novel."

—Andrew Wheeler

"This has become one of my must-read series."

—Carolyn Cushman, *Locus Magazine*

CIRCLE OF ENEMIES

"An edge-of-the-seat read! Ray Lilly is the new high-water mark of paranormal noir."

—Charles Stross

"Ray Lilly is one of the most interesting characters I've read lately, and Harry Connolly's vision is amazing."

—Charlaine Harris

SPIRIT OF THE CENTURY PRESENTS: KING KHAN

"An exuberant romp that distills all the best of pulp fiction adventure into one single ludicrously entertaining masterpiece."

—Ryk E. Spoor

BAD LITTLE GIRLS DIE HORRIBLE DEATHS AND OTHER TALES OF DARK FANTASY

"Connolly writes tales of magic and mystery in more modern times incredibly well. His work reminds me a lot of Tim Powers or Neil Gaiman. I highly recommend this collection."

—Jason Weisberger at *Boing Boing*

THE WAY INTO
MAGIC

Book Two of The Great Way

Harry Connolly

RADAR AVE
PRESS

Interior art by Claudia Cangini
Map illustration by Priscilla Spencer
Cover art by Chris McGrath
Cover design by Bradford Foltz
Book design by The Barbarienne's Den
Copy edited by Richard Shealy

Printed in the United States of America

For Roger Zelazny, my favorite author during my teenage years.

THE WAY INTO
MAGIC

THE
WASTES

TEMPEST
PASS

LAKE
WINDMARK

SALTSTONE

WHITE C.

FREEWELL

BENDERTUK

ESPILETH

BESCOS
SEA

SIMBLIN

OF

UM

SHELTERLANDS

FORT
PISKATOOK

FORT
SAMSIT

EAST
FORD

THE STRAIT

INDREGA

IMWOOD

RADAIN

BAY OF
STONES

RIVERSHELF

LANDS

BY PRISCILLA SPENCER

CHAPTER ONE

CAZIA FREEWELL NEEDED SEVERAL DAYS TO ADJUST TO THE PRESENCE of a second mind inside her own. She still hadn't seen the Tilkilit queen—even though she'd been close enough to spit on it . . . her . . . *it*—but her thoughts were constantly under watch. Whenever Cazia thought about freedom, home, escape, her Gifts, the weapons the Tilkilit warriors carried, or even how ugly the creatures were, the queen sent a wave of disapproval so powerful that it was indistinguishable from self-loathing.

At first Cazia stubbornly fought, just as she'd always fought. The queen was an Enemy, and while she had *retreated* from many of the Enemies she'd grown up with, she had never stopped *resisting*.

Except that retreat from the queen was impossible. It had invaded her thoughts just as the Tilkilit had invaded her homeland of Kal-Maddum. The creature was listening to her thoughts, and whether Cazia was down in the lightless tunnels or out in the thick, mist-shrouded forests of the valley floor, she could not escape.

And she hated it. Cazia may have been young, but she'd had a lifetime of practice nursing her resentments; unfortunately, this time she could not hide her feelings behind a stoic expression. She could not retreat to the solitude of her room. She could not do anything but endure the presence of an Enemy's thoughts inside her own. Worse, the queen's thoughts and hers were so mingled that Cazia sometimes struggled to separate the queen's opinion of her from her opinion of herself. It was almost like going hollow again, expect without the increase in magical power and insight.

She hated that creature more than she had ever hated anyone in her life.

"I am a free human being," Vilavivianna had whispered to her one morning, perhaps twenty days after they'd been captured. They were sitting together in the mist-shrouded meadow the Tilkilit had claimed as their own. There were steep mountains to the west and south, and ocean far to the east, but she had not seen them in many days. The Tilkilit swarmed in the lowest dry spot in the Qorr Valley, hiding in the trees and the never-ending fog.

"I am a free human being," Ivy said again. "I am no one's property." The little Indregai princess looked pale and exhausted; she had been fighting against the queen's mental control as hard as Cazia had. They clasped hands and repeated the words together. "I am a free human being."

The creature's counterattack was so furious, it overwhelmed them. Their minds went blank and they fainted into the grass.

They woke together, almost as though the queen allowed it. Before Cazia could even remember where she was, a Tilkilit warrior pressed one of their strange smooth stones against her hand. She felt her magic being drawn out of her. Again. Every day, they did this to her.

But she didn't dare resist. Each of the Tilkilit were about the size of the princess, who was only twelve years old, but they were tremendously strong and well armed. They could throw stones with the power of a man with a sling, and had already taken down Kinz, the third member of their expedition. She had been taken away; hopefully, the Tilkilit were repairing her injuries, but a small part of Cazia's mind was convinced that she'd already been eaten.

Poor little Ivy looked miserable. Cazia shouldn't have let her come with her over the mountains.

The earth rumbled. One of the Tilkilit's worms was passing nearby, but thankfully, it was deep below ground. Cazia most definitely did not want to look at one of them ever again. The creatures were colossal, large enough to shatter the gates of the Palace of Song and Morning simply by laying the weight of a front end against them, and Cazia had seen the Tilkilit riding them into battle.

Cazia had helped Vilavivianna destroy one, and the memory—just a fleeting image of the beast writhing and burning—brought on a flood of recrimination that she was certain was not her own. Fairly certain.

The rumbling shook the branches of a nearby tree. Cazia realized she'd never seen one like it before: the bark was like tin, and the blossoms it bore were as white as fair-weather clouds, with shiny metallic tips.

She scowled at it. This plant was not native to Kal-Maddum. It was another invader in the Qorr Valley, just like the Tilkilit.

Only a few days' journey from this spot, a portal to other lands sat open, allowing anyone or anything to pass through in either direction. The connection at this end was constant and unwavering, but the other side changed to a new location every ten days. Anyone and anything might pass through, and did. Some invaders were Enemies, like the insect queen that had declared that Cazia was her property, or the gigantic eagles that soared above the mists overhead. Some were the seeds of harmless plants like . . .

Then she noticed a ring of bare earth around the base of the tree, and brown grass at the edge of that. Apparently, this tree was poisonous to native life.

A powerful wave of revulsion ran through Cazia. That portal needed to be closed or destroyed in some way, so that no more horrors like the poison tree or the Tilkilit queen could invade her Kal-Maddum. Her home.

The queen knew her thoughts instantly and overwhelmed her again, driving her unconscious.

It continued that way, day after day. The warriors used their anti-magic stones to deny Cazia the use of the Gifts. The queen monitored their every thought and made them regret even the most casual thoughts of discontent. After fifteen more days, Kinz was permitted to rejoin them. Vilavivianna leaped at the older girl to hug her, but Kinz did not seem to mind. After the princess released her, she rotated her shoulders and declared herself completely healed. Her time inside a Tilkilit cocoon had repaired her broken bones as if she had never been injured.

"I'm glad they didn't eat you," Cazia said.

"I am made glad, too. What has been happening?" Kinz asked. They sat in a little circle. The mists were thick that day, but the girls could not even pretend they could talk in secret. Tilkilit warriors moved at the edge of the clearing, just within sight, and the queen never seemed to sleep.

"Nothing," Vilavivianna answered. "They keep us prisoner here in the forest, moving us only when the mists become so thin that they fear one of the Great Terror will attack from above." The *Great Terror* was the Tilkilit name for the gigantic eagles that nested in the cliffs above and hunted them ruthlessly. "We are not even allowed to relieve ourselves in private."

"It is not like they make to peek, Ivy," Kinz said. Her voice was thick with exhaustion. The three of them glanced up as a nearby warrior passed close by. Its reddish-black, hard-shelled body was as narrow as a man's thigh, and its tiny eyes were sinister and opaque. It wore nothing more than a green sash—apparently a signifier of rank—and carried a short spear, pouch of stones, and tiny mace it carried in lieu of a dagger.

The Tilkilit could leap surprising distances and were deceptively strong. Cazia knew she and her two companions could escape from the Tilkilit if they could get a decent head start; while the warriors were quick, they had no endurance. Unfortunately, the Tilkilit knew that, too.

"They are careful," the princess said. "And they are waiting for something."

Cazia tore a few blades of grass out of the dirt and threw them back down. "They're waiting for us to surrender."

Kinz looked at them both. "Do they know everything? Ivy?"

Vilavivianna lowered her eyes. "They do. The Alliance, the five peoples, the serpents, the giant eagles, and . . . and the tunnel Cazia dug to bring us over the mountains."

"They also know the tunnel is blocked," Cazia said, "although I doubt it worries them much. I think the only reason they haven't already scaled the mountains on this side and started down the tunnel is that we can't really remember where it is."

"No," Ivy said decisively. "They will not climb above the mists, not with the birds circling above us. It would be a slaughter. And what would the queen do? Set up the holdfast here in Qorr? No, they want another way out."

Cazia felt herself flush. Of course they wouldn't expose themselves to the birds. What's more, their riding beasts could never escape over the mountains. They were simply too huge.

The queen was getting the better of her. The thing was inside her head, listening to her every thought, and she had no space to plan a counter attack.

Cazia ran her fingers across the stiff, broken grass beneath her. Did the queen know where she was at every moment? Certainly not, or they wouldn't be watched so closely, even when they went behind a tree to relieve themselves. Could the queen see out of her eyes or hear what she heard?

If so, she must have been as bored as Cazia was, spending day after day in this meadow, with nothing to look at but the same few trees and the white mist, which never completely cleared even during the warmest hours. It was one of the few aboveground places where the Tilkilit could hide. Worse, late at night, when the wind blew strongly out of the east, Cazia could hear the terrifying sound of crashing surf.

Ivy sniffled. "I miss home," she said. In that moment, the princess looked like the little girl that she was, although Cazia was just three years her elder, and Kinz two or three older than that. "I hate sleeping on the wet grass. The food they give us is disgusting and I am always thirsty. Why can they not let us relieve ourselves in private!"

"Little sister," Cazia said, but Ivy didn't want comfort. She stood and stamped off into the mists. Warriors followed her. Warriors followed all of them.

Kinz's expression was pinched and unreadable. The Tilkilit queen might have been able to read the older girl's thoughts, but Cazia couldn't.

They both glanced at Ivy. While she was the youngest, the princess had been raised with private tutors who had taught her about the wider world. She spoke several languages and had negotiated for the supplies they needed for this trip. Kinz was mostly good for catching fish and carrying their packs. Cazia herself had merely blundered along, misusing her magic until she had driven herself to madness. It was Ivy who had saved their lives, more than once, with her common sense.

I should never have let her come along.

::You are my property.:: The Tilkilit queen's "voice" was loud and sharp in her mind. Cazia felt a sudden revulsion at the intruding thoughts. The creature hadn't used language since that first meeting. ::You are my property. You will accept this. As I obey the voice of the god in the air, you will do as I command. If you do not, I will take away your little sister.::

A white-hot fury run through Cazia. She hated everything about those oily, red-sharp thoughts. The queen's mind was flat and hurried and utterly alien to her own. And she'd just been stupid enough to threaten Ivy.

If she'd still had her magic, Cazia would have started burning every Tilkilit in sight, and Fire could take the consequences.

If you do anything to hurt that little girl, if you or your people put so much as a bruise on her, I will kill myself and leave you stranded here.

Cazia could feel the creature's shock. She could feel the way it grappled with the concept of suicide as though it was a new and unimaginable idea. Risking death it understood, but ending life voluntarily?

Clearly, the queen wanted to dismiss the idea as an empty threat, so Cazia recalled the few suicides she'd known in her life in the palace—two servants who had hung themselves, a guard who had fallen on his sword, a young scholar who leaped from the top of the tower. The queen was right there in her thoughts and understood that this was truly something her kind did.

Confusion flooded them both. Cazia was as alien to the queen as it was to her.

A wave of censure washed over her, and the queen's anger was so intense that Cazia blacked out.

The scream of an eagle woke her in the middle of the night. The fog was so dense that it blocked out all starlight and she could not see her own hand when she held it up to her face.

However, she could hear the beating of huge wings and the panicked clicking of the Tilkilit warriors. There was another piercing scream, and she heard the Great Terror flapping away. Kinz and Ivy grabbed hold of her and they clutched each other in the darkness, waiting for silence to return.

Kinz led them toward the trees. Cazia crawled after them, trying to be as quiet as possible. There was no way the giant eagle had targeted its prey by sight; it had to have located it by sound. Once they found a narrow space between two large trees, they wrapped their arms around each other again, and they did not shiver from the chill wet air alone.

The Tilkilit queen wanted a tunnel. Cazia wasn't just supposed to surrender to the queen's authority; she was still alive because the queen wanted her to dig a tunnel through the Northern Barrier that was large enough for the giant worms. The Tilkilit would have passage into the rest of the continent while the queen . . . Could she be moved? She lived in utter darkness; the one time Cazia had been near her, she could not see anything but she had the unmistakable sense of hugeness and immobility. Maybe the queen wanted to rule from her burrow in Qorr, or maybe she planned to create a second queen to make the trip into the Sweeps.

Not that it mattered. Cazia had no intention of—

She blacked out again.

It was not quite dawn when she came around again. The same night? At first, she couldn't tell, but she didn't feel thirsty enough to have missed a whole day.

"Are you well, big sister?"

Ivy's hand was cool against the side of her face. Cazia sat up and clutched at her head. She'd had worse headaches in her life, but she wasn't sure if the queen had caused it or if she was merely parched. "I'm thirsty."

"Take this." Ivy pressed a bowl of water into her hands. The Tilkilit drank from wooden bowls, for some reason. "They brought us double rations of water today. Perhaps they're not trying to kill us after all."

"I'll believe that when they set us free."

She drank deeply from the bowl, gulping the chilly, slightly salty water. Great Way, but it felt good to wet her throat. Then she noticed two more in the grass beside her and gulped them both down greedily. It wasn't enough, but she felt better.

Kinz approached them with a pair of apricots. She handed both to Cazia. "We have eaten."

"Kinz," Ivy said. She laid her hand on the older girl's shoulder. "Kinz."

Cazia noticed the servant's face was pale, and there were dark, puffy circles beneath her eyes. "Kinz," she said with none of Ivy's gentleness, "why have you been crying?"

"I am not free," she said. "The Poalos are no longer made free. Ever since I was old enough to run beside the herd, I have known the day might come when I would make to lose my freedom. The bad marriage. The sudden sickness. Grabbed in the night by slavers out of Indrega—"

Ivy gasped. "My people are not slavers! How could you say such a thing!"

Kinz gave her a withering look. "Raiding parties make from your lands to skulk into ours. My own cousin was taken when I was seven. She is probably still making to scrub pans in some minor chief's kitchen, assuming she has not been whipped to death." Ivy opened her mouth to protest, but Kinz cut her off. "You might have had all the best tutors, little princess, but there is still much you do not know."

At that, Ivy fell into a resentful silence. Kinz looked guiltily back at Cazia, as though she knew no one really wanted to hear her. She continued anyway. "But I always thought it would be soldiers out of Peradain. Whenever their spearmen and -women made to approach our camp to collect their tribute—"

Taxes, Cazia thought automatically, but she kept her mouth shut. What did it matter now if the Poalos and other herding clans had been part of the Peradaini Empire? The empire was gone.

"I was sure they would take us all away," Kinz finished. "Turn us into *servants.*"

"You are a servant," Cazia blurted out. "You're my servant, and Ivy's, too. You swore service to us on the day we left the Ozzhuacks."

"I think the Queen of the Tilkilit has made to take my contract by force."

Cazia wouldn't accept that, not when—a sudden bloom of censure began to crowd out her thoughts. It wasn't enough to make her black out, though. The queen wanted them all as her servants.

All they needed was a chance to put some distance between themselves and the warriors. Cazia didn't know what it would be, but it had to come sometime, in some form.

The queen's censure grew stronger. Cazia saw spots before her eyes.

"Has the queen stopped the attacks on you?" Ivy asked.

Kinz shook her head. "It is not enough to make a surrender to her," the girl said. "She wants us to love her, too."

It took all the willpower Cazia had not to bark out a derisive laugh. She held her anger and outrage inside, squeezing it down until it was as smooth and hard as an iron coin. Love? The Tilkilit? Did the queen understand anything about her?

"She doesn't just want us to surrender," Cazia said. "She wants us to be part of her swarm . . . hive, whatever she calls it. And we can't be part of her hive unless we are as devoted to her as her warriors are. Only then will she trust me enough to order me to dig a passage through the mountains into the Sweeps."

Kinz and Ivy stared at her, openmouthed. "A tunnel that lets her people out," Ivy said, "would let The Blessing in. Has she not read our minds?"

Kinz shook her head. "Do you think she believes us?"

The question startled Cazia. Of course the queen believed them. The queen was a bug. She and her insect people thought bug thoughts; they were orderly and dense. While the queen could insert her thoughts into the minds of others, most of the complicated conversation that took place among the rest of her people was done by smell.

The Tilkilit didn't arrange discrete words into a long caravan of sounds that revealed meaning. They spurted out bursts of odor. It was very short and very complex, and if Cazia was any judge, it was *not* well suited for lying. Confusion bubbled through her thoughts, and of course, it belonged to the queen. Dishonesty seemed a more difficult concept for the Tilkilit mind than suicide was.

But Cazia's people—and it was only since she'd seen the city of Peradain fall to The Blessing that she had begun to think of the Peradaini as hers—were famous for their song, storytelling, and theater. What's more, none of their performances were meant to be literal; everything was coded. Flooding stood in for the devastation of war. A man who risked all for some ambitious goal "built a tower too high." A duel between two enemies was a bloody, punishing footrace.

In fact, the spells Cazia had learned—the ones the Tilkilit's anti-magic stones prevented her from casting—affected the physical world only. They couldn't change a person's mind or make them fall in love any more than the queen's mental bullying. But art could. And the Tilkilit didn't seem to make art.

They don't lie.

"I love it here," Cazia said suddenly. The other two girls stared at her in mute surprise. "I love everything about this and I'm so glad I don't get to make my own decisions any more. If there's anything a girl my age likes, it's to have someone else tell her what she ought to be doing."

Kinz and Ivy glanced nervously at each other. "Cazia," the little princess said, "is that you talking?"

They don't understand me, she thought. *No, they do. They understand me perfectly.*

She turned directly toward Kinz. "How do you think your ugly brother is doing?" Just mentioning Alga made tingles run up Cazia's back. The way that beautiful, arrogant jerk had smiled at her . . . "I can't help but wonder how someone so physically repulsive is doing out in the world all alone."

Kinz blinked twice. "Yes. Yes, he is made very ugly. Humble, too. If only girls would make to show the interest in him, he might lose some of his humility."

"What are you both talking about?" Ivy asked, annoyed. "Alga was not ugly at all. I thought your brother was quite handsome." This last was delivered to Kinz with an air of kindly reassurance.

Cazia took Ivy's hand. "I'm only sorry that we don't have more meatbread for you. I know how much you liked it." Ivy wrinkled her nose, but before she could complain yet again about how salty meatbread was, Cazia pushed on. "The Tilkilit queen is really powerful, don't you think? She can obviously push her thoughts into all of her people's minds at once."

"Yes," Kinz agreed. "It was obvious that she knew when we made to capture one of her people, and that she had warned all those other soldiers where we were."

Ivy knitted her brows. "No, it wasn—"

Cazia squeezed her hand. "If only The Blessing could be here. I miss having them close."

The little girl's mouth made a little circle, then she looked back and forth between them. "Oh! Oh, yes, I wish The Blessing could be here, too, so I could ride the shoulders as we ran through the wilderness."

Once the princess understood what they were doing, she took to it like a flower to sunshine. She chattered endlessly about their conditions and the things she would rather be doing, all while saying the exact opposite of how she felt.

Cazia did her best to make sure they both understood words weren't enough. They had to think opposite, too. If the queen figured out what they were trying to do—

No. The queen is in complete command of our thoughts and understands them perfectly. There was no way to fool or confuse her.

When their first meal was brought to them, they chatted amiably about how much they enjoyed the uncooked tubers and sticky resin the Tilkilit fed them. Their praise and enthusiasm became so absurd that they actually laughed. Cazia could feel the queen's thoughts growing calm.

At midday, a warrior still laid an anti-magic stone against her bare neck, and the shock of it made her collapse into the grass. *These stones are killing me.*

The queen felt more remote for the rest of the day, and a tiny hope that they were pleasing her kindled in Cazia's thoughts. Still, she turned her concentration toward the game in the same way she had drilled her thoughts down into Gifts when she was learning spells.

They spent the day lying on the grass in the chill, blowing mists. The little warriors circled them in steady, unceasing patrols just within the treeline. The girls ate, sang more songs, and whiled away the hours.

It surprised each of them how quickly the game became second nature.

That night, Cazia did not have her magic taken away by the anti-magic stone. She fell asleep wondering if they would come to her in the morning. They didn't.

"I'm disappointed to feel my magic returning," she told the other girls. "Just a little so far. It's been so good to be free of it. Still, if the queen has need of it, I'm ready to serve."

It was two more days before the warriors moved into the center of the clearing, spears at the ready. Bags of food and skins of water were cast at their feet, then they were prodded until they stood.

The ground trembled, rustling the leaves in the nearby trees. All three felt the meadow beneath them rise slightly, then settle down again. Another of the Tilkilit's massive worms had passed beneath them, this one much closer to the surface.

::You will make a tunnel through the mountains to the south. It will be broad enough for all of us.::

Doing your will is my deepest wish. The queen seemed satisfied by this, and the group set out.

The mists were so thick, it was difficult to be sure which direction they were traveling. All Cazia could be certain of was that they were going uphill. "I hope," she said, "that we're so close to the base of the cliffs that we can start digging for the queen without any distractions."

That didn't happen. The Tilkilit lead them over a hill that was thick with young oak trees. For a moment, the mists were thin enough to see the Northern Barrier looming above them. There was a two-day march ahead of them if they kept a good pace.

"That fast-moving river is dangerous," Kinz said, pointing far out toward a low place on the valley floor ahead of them. The fast-swirling mists were thin there, and they could just barely see a low, wide river with white water at the edges. "We could easily drown if we fell in."

"We should definitely not do that, then," Ivy offered.

"But if you do," Kinz said, "the best possible thing you can do in a fast-moving river is to put your feet down. Always, always try to stand in a strong current."

One of the warriors prodded them in the back, forcing them onward. Cazia glanced upward and saw an eagle floating on the updrafts. It appeared to be quite close, but she knew that was an illusion created by the colossal size of the thing.

They went down the hill, staying under the cover of the trees until they were safely back inside the concealing mists of the valley floor. The ground trembled again—that worm was moving with them, which didn't bother Cazia at all. There were about three dozen warriors in their escort, but there might have been more ahead or behind in the column. Boy, was she glad to see so many of the queen's soldiers around them.

They didn't reach the riverbanks until midmorning of the next day. The mists were thin here. The Tilkilit skirted the shallow, gradual banks, turning west to head upriver. The churning river was surprisingly loud.

When they made camp that night, Cazia couldn't help but imagine the source of the river—how close was it to the portal at the westernmost part of the Qorr Valley?—and its outlet. Like all sensible Peradaini, she had a well-earned horror of the sea, and the idea that she might fall into the river and be swept out beyond the shore made her stomach flutter like a cage full of moths.

The Tilkilit woke them the next morning before dawn. Of course. The eagles were least active at sunrise and sundown, so if there was a safe time to cross the river, it was before the start of the day.

"Look at this," Kinz said.

The trees nearest the river were looking ragged and sick. Stone spikes had been driven into the trunk and a clear liquid dripped from the tip of the spike into wooden bowls hanging below. Tilkilit warriors emptied the bowls into their skins.

Now that Kinz had pointed it out, Cazia saw the little spikes everywhere. Was the nasty resin the insect people ate drained from trees? If so, they were killing this forest.

Those poor insect people, trapped in a valley too small to hold them, especially with the queen laying so many eggs. Why, if they didn't escape soon, they might even suffer famine.

The queen's thoughts were faint but still present. How powerful she was!

By dawn, they came to a narrow part of the river. A minor rockslide on the far bank made the water narrow enough that it had been spanned by a felled tree.

As they climbed up the exposed roots, Cazia said, "You know what I hate? Those black stones the Tilkilit carry. The ones that take away my magic. I hope I never have to travel with them again."

Kinz glanced at the warrior just ahead of her on the trunk. The sack of stones was hanging from his sash on the left side. Cazia noticed for the first time that his sash was edged with black. Was he a commander of some kind? "Be careful," Kinz said. "Stay close to me so I can show you the part you where you really don't want to make a fall."

Once they'd reached the top of the trunk, the three girls stayed close together. The warriors around them paid more attention to the awkward curve of the tree and the skies above them than they did the girls, and why not? The girls were friends of the Tilkilit. *Loyal friends*.

They were barely at the midpoint when Kinz cried out—in the least believable way you could imagine—as though she was losing her balance. She clutched at the nearest warrior and dragged him over the side of the trunk into the churning water.

As they fell, Cazia saw Kinz grab hold of the Tilkilit's pouch of stones.

Ivy went over the edge before Cazia even had a chance to realize this was the moment. Warriors surged toward her and she leaped outward just beyond their reach.

At the last moment, Cazia changed the angle of her fall so she landed on the Tilkilit in the water with both of her knees.

Chapter Two

Tyr Tejohn Treygar woke in terrible pain, but it was not as terrible as he'd expected. His legs, his back, his pelvis—they felt as swollen as risen dough and were blooming with raw agony, but considering the fall he'd taken . . .

He was facedown in the dirt. Dry dirt, too, like a hard-packed floor, not the wet river silt of the banks of the Wayward River. No, it was called the Shelsiccan now. The old Peradaini names were being thrown away in favor of the even-older Finshto ones.

"He didn't cry out," someone said. Tejohn wanted to turn to see who had spoken, but flexing his neck muscles to lift his head intensified the agony in his shoulders and back. Great Way, his mouth was parched.

"Because he was still unconscious when he hit," another voice said. Tejohn recognized that voice immediately. Tyr Finstel's men had captured him a second time, but this time, the tyr himself had come to question him.

No, not "Tyr," he reminded himself. The old imperial ranks had also been cast off. No longer a tyr, a tyrant, or a chief, he'd declared himself *King* Shunzik Finstel, lord of Ussmajil and all the lands that holdfast protected.

But where were they? The flickering light suggested a lantern. They were indoors, somewhere, or it was nighttime.

Something pressed against his left calf, and the agony became so intense, Tejohn thought it must be a white-hot iron or maybe a dull knife. The urge to turn and *see* what was happening to him was almost as strong as the pain itself, but he couldn't manage even that. He was helpless. Fire and Fury, the pain grew so huge that he had to cry out with all his strength. His voice sounded dry, hoarse, and weak.

"No more is required," King Shunzik said. "Just my hand on your flesh. No more than this."

Was that just the touch of a man's hand? Despair flooded Tejohn. This much pain would destroy him, and however overwhelming it felt, inflicting it was trivially easy. Worse, Finstel sounded as if he was enjoying himself. Tejohn almost asked why.

"Where is Lar Italga?" the king asked.

Tejohn could see nothing but hard-packed black dirt as his mind raced through a clash of images. Nothing came together; the pain was too great for him to think clearly. He could see Lar's face before him, laughing. Lar Italga was the uncrowned king of Peradain, the Morning City. He was the last of his royal bloodline, bereft of soldiers, palace, everything . . . even the empire he had been born to rule.

I have plans for this empire, Tyr Treygar, plans that would end much of the misery and injustice my people endure, plans I have nursed since I was a small boy. But Lar was gone now, vanished like the empire, and all of Kal-Maddum had fallen into misery and injustice.

Tejohn's wife and children would never see him again, and they would never know how he died. Someone touched him and he screamed again. The pain, once increased, never subsided. Should he answer this question? Did he know the answer? Did it even matter any more?

"My king," the first voice said. "He's still too damaged to get trustworthy information from him. He should have more time on the sleepstone. Then, when the pain begins again, he will tell all."

"The man is a traitor to his family, his lands, and his king. To me! I don't want to see him hale and hearty. I want to see him crippled." The pressure against Tejohn's shattered leg stopped, but the pain did not. When the king spoke next, his voice sounded very close. "The spikes outside Ussmajil are decorated with the heads of Italga bureaucrats, but you will never be so lucky. You will spend the rest of your days in darkness, alive but broken. For what you have cost me, for the attempt to steal my uncle's glory, for entering my lands like an assassin, no man's pain will last as long as yours."

He was so close that Tejohn could have crushed his throat with a sudden blow, except Tejohn could not even turn his head.

Hands grabbed him roughly and lifted him up. The pain was so intense that he blacked out.

He awoke in utter darkness, feeling himself swaying and jolting as though floating through turbulent waters. After a moment of panic, he realized that someone had placed him on a litter and lifted him off the sleepstone. Why could he see nothing? Had the Finstel's interrogator blinded him?

Someone hissed at him to be quiet. He pressed his parched lips shut, only then realizing he had groaned in pain and fear. Fire and Fury, did they expect him to go meekly to his own execution?

But that seemed wrong, somehow. He didn't believe Finstel torturers would work in hushed, hurried secrecy. "What—"

"Ssss," the voice said. "This is the only chance at rescue you will get, so be silent."

Tejohn was carried up a long stair, but he could see none of it and knew he wouldn't have recognized his surroundings even if a lantern had been lit. Someone had wrapped a cloth beneath his neck to brace his head. A rescue? He didn't believe it. This was some trick Finstel had arranged to bring him hope and then steal it away again.

It's what Tejohn would have done. Pull the injured prisoner off a sleep-stone when he was almost healed. The darkness and pain would keep him disoriented, and he might spill his secrets to his pretend rescuers.

Except Tejohn didn't have any secrets. At least, none that would interest the Finstel king. Did Shunzik really care about the rightful heir of Peradain? Or the ring he'd given to Tejohn that proved he was regent over the empire?

He felt his hard litter slide onto a long wooden platform. A woman leaned close to his ear and whispered, "This next part will be painful, but if you make any noise at all, you will doom everyone in this cabinet."

He didn't believe it for a second, but he played along. As long as he didn't allow himself to hope, they could only inflict physical pain.

Someone placed a box over his head. A rough wooden notch had been cut on one side so the edge would not press against his throat, and he could feel the raw splinters against his skin. Then, someone began to dump something over his body. Fire and Fury, how it hurt.

The smell flooded through the slats in the box and he knew what they were piling over him: garbage. His stomach soured and grew tight; he tried not to breathe through his nose, but it did no good. Tejohn imagined rot seeping into open wounds on his legs and felt his despair grow stronger.

He welcomed it. The weight of the garbage on his ruined body pressed against him, making his pain swell, but he kept silent. Let it happen. Let it all happen. The days when he could have affected his world were long past. Let death come.

Soon, he felt wheels rolling heavily down a rough dirt ramp. He'd been placed on a cart, not a platform. Every jolt against a stone or rut was like white fire through his legs and back, but he clenched his teeth and kept silent. The box blocked his view of his surroundings, of course, but he felt a cool, wet breeze blow through the slats against his face. Outside. Had he really been taken outside the holdfast? There was no light to suggest daytime, but somewhere, he felt a spark of hope. Perhaps he really was being rescued after all . . .

He swept that thought away with a wave of self-loathing.

The sound of voices startled Tejohn so much, he almost cried out. Someone was scolding someone else, and that someone else was responding with weary assurance. Tejohn couldn't make out specific words, but it sounded like a conversation they'd had many times before, probably over some obscure rule. The cart didn't even stop completely while they spoke, only slowed a bit, then resumed its normal thumping pace.

Downhill they went. Always downhill. After a long while, Tejohn could no longer resist the urge to believe he was truly being rescued, although it began to dawn on him that a rescue now, while he was still a broken man, would leave him crippled. Better to have slid a knife between his ribs or dosed him with poison.

Maybe the people involved in this rescue were no friendlier to him than the Finstels. He felt himself wavering between hope and despair like a slender stalk in a storm. If he could have emptied himself of one or the other, he would have. *Monument sustain me.*

Eventually, the downhill slope became so steep that the weight of the garbage piled atop his legs shifted against him, and it took all his willpower not to cry out. Then he heard the scrape of a wooden shovel against the wooden planks of the cart, followed shortly by a splash. They were shoveling the garbage off—

Before the thought had even finished, a shovel struck against his knee, and the flare of pain was so great he had no hope of remaining silent. His cry echoed inside the box, and no sooner had he stifled it than someone had snatched the box off of his head.

"You Fire-taken fool," a woman said, her voice low and harsh. "Don't thump a broken man's broken body!"

Tejohn was absurdly grateful that he was not the fool, but there was no apology forthcoming. He looked up at the night sky, as bright with stars as he'd ever seen. Laoni had once described it as a vast array of pinprick lights, sparse in some places, clustered in others. Tejohn was too nearsighted see that himself.

To him, the starlit night was a blur of darkness and gray light, and it was beautiful. Laoni had always thought it was sad that he could not truly appreciate stars or mountain ranges, but for Tejohn, this was enough. He'd seen one more night sky before the end of his life, and he hoped his wife and children, hiding far away in the east, slept peacefully beneath it.

Grateful am I to be permitted to travel The Way.

A pair of men hurried to the cart. One took hold of the litter handles beside his head and slid him off, letting the garbage fall off him. The second wiped the far end clean, then took hold.

Tejohn tried to look at the nearest man, but it was too dark to see anything but silhouettes. All he could see of the man's face was a fringe of unkempt hair. They carried him down the muddy river bank with extraordinary care; if one of them slipped, he would certainly drown like a helpless babe.

He wanted to turn, if only to see how close the water was, but the bundled cloth still held his head in place. The footsteps of the two men as they waded into the water sounded as loud as shouting in the cool night air, but the shovel loads of garbage helped mask the noise.

"Hold your breath," the man beside his head whispered, and Tejohn barely had time to inhale before he was lowered into the current.

Great Way, it was cold, and that cold was so welcome. His pain did not vanish but did ease. A hand brushed at his chest and legs, and he realized they were cleaning the garbage off of him.

Then he was raised into the air again. Someone sliced at his tunic—not his, he thought, something the Finstel torturers had put on him—and pulled it out from beneath him. Fire and Fury, that brought his pain back again, but before he could make his displeasure known, he was plunged under again, before he could take a decent breath. This time, he thought he would drown.

They lifted him out of the water and carried him to the bank. There was another quiet conversation, but without the box, he could hear it clearly.

"Thank you. We will not forget what you've done."

"And we will not forget the debt you owe us." Tejohn recognized that voice as the woman who had not called him a fool.

"As ever," the first man said. "Come."

The litter was borne up the riverbank into a street. Tejohn could still only see directly upward, but the eaves above him showed that they traveled narrow alleyways rather than broad streets.

Always they were silent. Once, the man holding the foot end of the litter slipped in something, and the shift gave Tejohn a jolt of pain so powerful that he gasped. No one criticized him. No one apologized. They simply kept going.

When they finally went indoors, they entered a great open passage with no door on it. The roof was a broad stone laid across two columns, and the walls were unadorned. It took only a moment for Tejohn to realize that he had been carried across the threshold of a temple, and that he had not said a prayer.

"Grateful am I," he croaked, "to be permitted to travel The Way."

The man holding the head end of the litter glanced down at him, but Tejohn could not see his expression.

They carried him through a doorway, down a long stone stair, then through another doorway and across a room filled with loud snores and gentle whispers. People, Tejohn thought. Probably refugees.

Soon, they came to a stone room deep within the earth. The dungeon of the Finstel holdfast had a dirt floor, but even the secret rooms of the temple were made of stone. That pleased Tejohn for some reason he wasn't ready to understand.

The litter was set on the floor and the bearers left. Someone lit a lantern, and the unexpected glow of it made Tejohn catch his breath. Light was as welcome as an old friend.

"Drink this," a man said. The fellow gently lifted Tejohn's face and pressed a cup of water to his lips. Great Way, it was so good!

He drank as much as he was permitted, but it was slow. Very slow. The man was dressed as a priest, with a robe the color of fresh blood and the mild, flabby face of someone who does little more than sweep. He was old, possibly the oldest fellow Tejohn had seen in his life, with outsized ears and nose, and deep, deep wrinkles down the side of his face.

"That is better, yes?" the priest said.

"Yes." Tejohn's voice had begun to sound normal again. The cup was refilled and offered again.

"You must wonder why we freed you," the old man said. "I would, if I were you. Let me explain: it is the duty of the Temple to care for the people, and it is impossible to care for them if we do not know what ailments they suffer. Am I clear? You have been abroad in the world, Tyr Tejohn Treygar. You have attended the councils of kings and have traveled with the meanest of refugees. What's more, you have met our foe in battle."

The priest paused, as though he expected an answer. Tejohn only pursed his lips toward the cup. He was given more to drink.

"It is not just the fall of Peradain that worries us." The old man sounded profoundly tired. "Rumors suggest that the demon Kelvijinian stirs in the eastern mountains, and Boskorul rounds the Indregai peninsula toward the

Bay of Stones. These are troubled times, my tyr. We would know what you know."

The cup was empty. "And why should I tell you anything?" Tejohn croaked.

Someone nearby gasped and muttered unhappily. His litter bearers? "We did just save you from King Shunzik's torture chamber at no small risk to ourselves."

"It seems to me that it was the servants' cabinet that took all the risk. You were just the ones who prompted them. And for all I know, this is a Finstel trick."

The old priest looked at Tejohn with an expression of unabashed surprise. Then he filled the cup again and raised it to Tejohn's lips. "You are a cautious man. I respect that. Song knows, you have little reason to trust any within Finstel lands. We must, perhaps, do more to earn your favor. Do you see where we have brought you? We know your vision is poor, but surely you can see that far?"

The priest nodded toward the other side, but Tejohn couldn't turn his head to see. The priest tilted it for him.

Great Way, it was a sleepstone. Somehow, this temple had a sleepstone hidden deep inside it.

"Always, we have a terrible need to heal those who can not afford to pay Finstel prices. Right now, they must wait for you."

"Sir," one of the litter-bearers said, "his wounds are too old."

The old man nodded. "I was afraid of that." He drew something from inside his robe. It was a long steel needle. "My tyr, have you seen one of these before?"

Tejohn was about to say no, but then he recognized it. "In Samsit, when I was healed on the sleepstone, the medical scholar jabbed my knee before I lay down."

The priest seemed pleased. "Ah, yes, to remedy an old injury, yes? Something that went unhealed for too long and caused lingering pain? I regret to tell you that the new injuries you suffered are the same. They will never heal correctly unless they are renewed."

"No," Tejohn croaked, but hadn't he allowed a medical scholar to do the same thing to him? And what choice did he have?

"It will all be for the best, I assure you. Before we start, look at the lantern hanging on that wall, if you would, my tyr."

Tejohn tilted his head back as far as he could and looked "upward" in the direction the priest was pointing. There was no light source visible; was the man pointing out an unlit lamp?

Then there was a sharp exhalation from one of the litter-bearers, and Tejohn felt some sort of grit fall into his eyes.

Immediately, they began to burn. He blinked at them, trying to let his tears wash away whatever the men had blown onto him, but the tears only made the pain worse. He cried out, unable to raise his arms or his legs, as his eyes began to feel slimy and scorched.

"It will only hurt for a short while," the old priest said, and someone began to plunge the needle into him.

It was a long time before they put him onto the sleepstone and allowed unconsciousness to claim him, but when he awoke, the entire world was new.

Chapter Three

THE WATER WAS BRUTALLY COLD. ANY SATISFACTION CAZIA FELT WHEN the carapace of the Tilkilit warrior cracked beneath her weight was spoiled by the icy shock of her plunge.

Save us! We're going to swim to the northern bank. Send help! Cazia's heart wasn't in the game any more, and she doubted the queen would be fooled much longer. She waited for some sort of response—a scream of rage, a wave of hatred that would make her black out and drown—but if the Tilkilit queen knew what was happening, she was silent.

Always try to stand in a current. Right. Cazia pulled her heels up to her rear end and rolled onto her back. Her hiking skirts were already soaked through but the water was fast and turbulent enough that it pitched her above the surface where she could gasp for air.

Cazia had expected the warriors to attack from the banks and the tree trunk, but now that she was in the water, she had no idea if they were. The river was so loud and churning so crazily that a full-grown okshim could have fallen in beside her and she wouldn't have known. She swept by something huge and unyielding—she didn't touch it, but she felt the way it broke the river's flow—then sank deep into the turbulent waters.

There was no choice; Cazia stripped off her jacket. Her Fire-taken skirts ought to go, too, but the knots would be impossible. She kicked off her boots and struggled to the surface.

As soon as she reached the air, the water swept southward around a bend and grew calm. She'd survived, somehow, despite everything. Elation rushed through her, then panic. Ivy! Where was Ivy!

Cazia kicked, raising herself as high out of the water as she could. There was Ivy, floating downstream with Kinz. They were shoulder to shoulder, leaning back as if lounging on a couch. Cazia resolved to do the same.

After one glance behind her, of course. She couldn't resist one glance.

The fallen tree was out of sight behind the stones and trees at the bend of the river, but there was something back there. Cazia squinted toward the northern bank and saw something moving in high, bounding arcs. The Tilkilit were coming after them.

Cazia rolled over and kicked toward Ivy and Kinz. They were only twenty or thirty feet ahead, but she couldn't close the distance. Worse, the effort was exhausting.

"They're coming!" she yelled, a splash of river water garbling the words and nearly choking her. She lay back, her legs stretched in front of her, the way Kinz and Ivy were, while the older girl turned to look at their pursuers.

The Tilkilit were fast, but they didn't have stamina. If the girls stayed afloat for long enough, they would outpace the warriors and be free.

As long as they didn't drown. As long as they didn't freeze. As long as they weren't thrown over a waterfall or—Great Way, keep us on your path— swept out to sea.

No. Cazia drove those thoughts from her mind. They would escape or they would die. She was not going to fall under the Tilkilit's power again.

So, escape. As the river turned eastward again around a massive boulder, she began to plot out their next move. Assuming all three of them survived, they would have no food, no clean water but what she could conjure, no way to make a fire except by her magic. Their clothes would be soaked through and they would have no weapons. Not even knives, Monument sustain her. Her dart spell would work on stones and wooden stakes, if it came to that, and she hoped it wouldn't. Kinz, accustomed to her flint hatchet, would probably be satisfied with a sharpened stick.

But they would need to find another column of vines that went as close to the top of the Northern Barrier as possible, and then they would need to make their way back down. Of course, if they could find the tunnel she dug on the way in, that would be best.

Cazia glanced to her right, peering through the mists. The cliffs were over there, but she could not see them. She had no idea how far away the mountains were or how to find their entry point. Not that it mattered, as long as Kinz still had that bag of Tilkilit stones.

It wasn't long before the water didn't feel cold at all, which was probably not a good thing. She tried to loosen the knots holding her skirts to her hips, but her fingers were too numb to make much progress, and wet knots were always harder than dry ones. They had to get out of the water as soon as they reached a safe distance from their captors . . . whatever that was.

The current swept them around bend after bend, but always they continued generally eastward. The river widened and the water slowed. The banks receded from view on either side and the sky above them showed a lot of blue. It was a beautiful blue of the sort that makes families put aside an hour's chores to walk through meadow or just to thank The Way for a beautiful summer day.

But it was dangerous for Cazia, Ivy, and Kinz, because it meant they were exposed to the eagles. Cazia couldn't see any of the raptors floating above them, but it was only a matter of time before one spotted them.

Kinz was already stroking toward the southern bank, with Ivy clinging to her back. Cazia felt a twinge of guilt that she'd left Kinz to care for the girl, and began to paddle after them. She'd always considered herself a strong swimmer, when she got the chance, but she couldn't help but envy the older girl's long, steady strokes. Worse, she realized the current had already carried them out of the river into a lake as large as Peradain itself.

Then she looked down. The water was cold and clear, and the slanting early sunlight allowed her to see all the way to the bottom.

There was a skull of a gigantic creature below her. It was lying on its side, its eye socket empty of everything but a few wriggling fish. It was long and flat like a sword's blade, and its mouth was jagged with impossible teeth. Each of those teeth was as long as an Ozzhuack spear.

The sight made Cazia gasp with terror and she nearly choked on a mouthful of water. The creature had massive ribs that came near the surface of the water but no limbs that she could see. Fish clustered around the last few strips of flesh clinging to the bones, slowly tearing it away to expose the white. Was this creature some sort of serp—

An eel. A surge of raw terror rushed through Cazia. They had come much, much closer to the ocean than she had thought. Suddenly, the Tilkilit no longer mattered. The monstrous eagles above no longer mattered. All she cared about now was that they not be swept out to sea.

She swam as hard as she could, doing her best to mimic Kinz's style, but it didn't seem to matter. The flow had her and was driving her eastward. The river, which she had thought would save her, was quickly becoming her Enemy.

Or maybe not. The current flushed her into a backwater on the southeastern end of the lake, and when she finally crawled through the stony shallows toward the shore, she saw Kinz and Ivy had already collapsed onto the grass.

"I thought you could make to swim," Kinz admonished, and really, Cazia was not in the mood.

"Not drowning is swimming," she snapped. Her teeth were chattering and her limbs numb. The stones should have been painful against her bare feet, but she couldn't feel it. She scrambled wearily off the shore and wrapped her arms around Ivy. The princess's lips were blue and her eyes were half closed. Cazia pulled her close and held on, hoping her own shivering body would warm the girl, even if just a little.

Kinz's lips were blue, too, but she had the strength to move around. "One of those little fish bit me. I—" An idea caught hold of her and she hurried into the trees, emerging a short time later with a long, rough wooden branch. With a flattish piece of flint she found near the water, Kinz shaved branch and leaf off of it, then created a rough point.

Then she went down into the shallow eddy, going deep enough that the small bloody bite mark on her calf was below the surface. She stood utterly still, makeshift spear at the ready, waiting for her own blood to draw in a fish.

A sharpened stick. Cazia had been right, and the image made her laugh weakly. Kinz gave her a flat look that Cazia couldn't read, but she looked away. Ivy shivered against her and Cazia began to rub the girl's arms and hands to warm them.

If only they had a fire—

"Inzu blesses us," Kinz said. She strode into deeper water and pulled from the water the strangest white fish Cazia had ever seen. No, it was her jacket, then both of her boots. The current had driven them into the eddy, just as it had driven her. Kinz carried them up onto the shore to dry.

There was more flint scattered around the water's edge, along the steep banks of gray silt. Grass grew just beyond that, lying atop the hills around them like a rough blanket. Black-barked trees with yellow-green leaves stood even farther back from the water, casting heavy shadows on the ground around them.

Cazia hissed and pointed out into the deeper water. A brownish hump with little splashes at its edges floated toward them like a cautious predator. "Get back!" Cazia whispered harshly, but Kinz ignored her, moving forward with the spear held at the ready.

Everything was quiet, and Cazia heard the distant crashing of ocean waves upon a shore.

Kinz, now thigh-deep in the water, stabbed toward the brown hump and lifted her spear. There was a wriggling fish on the end. With a flick, she slung it onto the grass, then struck four more.

Eventually, she cried out and backed sloshing from the water. Cazia suddenly recognized the brown hump; it was the Tilkilit warrior she had jumped onto, and the splashes around it had been fish feeding on the corpse. Kinz's loud rush to shore had frightened them away.

"I can start a fire," Cazia said. She could feel her magic inside her; it wasn't strong, but it was enough to light kindling.

"Sit. You have the deep chill," Kinz said. Her lips were returning to their natural color. "It is making your thinking weak. We are being hunted from the west and from the sky above. No fire."

"That doesn't make sense," Cazia insisted, certain that her thinking was completely logical. "How are we going to eat fish without—"

Kinz laid the largest fish on a rock and bashed its skull with a second rock. Then she dug her fingers into the gill and tore the head off. After splitting it open down the center with a piece of flint, she offered the raw wet flesh to Ivy.

Under normal circumstances, Ivy and Cazia would have recoiled in disgust at the idea of eating raw fish, but the cold water had stolen their strength. Ivy tore into the flesh with all the energy she could bear, and Cazia did the same. After they'd chewed every morsel from the skin and spit out the scales, then stripped the bones down, Kinz held out a little red organ to the princess. "The heart," she said. "It will give you strength."

Ivy took it and swallowed it down.

Kinz glanced at Cazia as she reached into the other guts. "You should have the lungs to make calm your breath."

"Ugh," Cazia said. "Don't ask me to eat lungs."

Kinz poked Cazia's forehead with one bloody finger. "See? Weak thinking. Fish do not have lungs. Now, sit."

Kinz gave them a second fish to share, and she ate one herself. Cazia was sure the others had cheated her out of her fair portion, but she knew better than to make the accusation aloud. *Weak thinking.* Kinz and Ivy would never cheat her. Cazia was simply hungry, cold, and confused.

They ate everything off those fish that Kinz would allow, but it wasn't enough. It was still summer, and as the day grew warmer, Ivy's color returned. Cazia walked to the lake's edge to look for more fish, but the warrior's body had been swept back out into deeper water and there were no more fish to be caught.

"We should get moving," Ivy said. "I want to see the ocean."

"What?" Cazia exclaimed, her voice so loud that she slapped her hand over her mouth. "No, we can't go near the *ocean*. We're trying to get out of this valley alive, remember?"

"We can make a detour," Ivy said. "I have never seen this part of Boskorul's realm; none of my people have."

"It's dangerous."

"As an Ergoll, I am expected to make religious pilgrimages to parts of Boskorul's realm. It is a sacred tradition. None of my people will have seen this part of the sea before today, and it would be an unforgivable insult to spurn the chance. It would offend our god."

Kinz shrugged. "I vote against making offense to the gods, even the gods of your folk traditions."

Cazia wasn't sure which girl she should be more annoyed with. Actually, yes, she was. The oceans teemed with monsters; everyone knew that.

Kinz stepped toward her. "Stop scowling, Scowler. I have something that will make you feel better." She held up a bag that Cazia recognized immediately.

"You still have them!" She peered down as Kinz fumbled with the leather strip holding it shut. Great Way, she'd completely forgotten about the bag of stones.

"That is not all I got," Kinz said. "I made to follow that particular warrior across the bridge for one reason." She opened the pouch. Inside was the blue translation stone that Cazia had made so long ago.

"You didn't!" A flush of relief washed through her. Hers. That magic was hers.

Kinz smiled in a crooked way Cazia had never seen from her before. "I did."

Cazia wanted to reach into the pouch to grab it, but there were four anti-magic stones inside. And, she suddenly realized, they were touching the translation stone. "Did the black stones drain the spell from it?"

Kinz's smile faltered. She took the blue gem from the pouch, saying only "Tingles" as her fingertips brushed the other stones. Translation stone in her fist, she turned to Ivy.

The princess said something in her native language. Ergoll, she'd called it. Whatever she said, it was short and guttural, like trying to get someone's attention with a mouthful of pebbles. Cazia didn't think it was the same language she had spoken at the edge of the ruined Indregai camp. Kinz seemed pleased. "Thank you."

Cazia accepted the gem and slipped it into her pocket. It felt absurdly good to have something of her own. Sure, she could have made another with a bit of effort and the right sort of mineral, but those minerals were hard to find and the spell was exhausting. Why should she have to? The gem would have been worth a small fortune back in Peradain—before, of course—but the Tilkilit didn't even know what they'd had.

Ivy turned toward the east just as a heavy bank of fog topped the hill to the east and rolled over them. The slow, rhythmic crash of the surf was louder in the wet air. "You can't mean to drag us there," Cazia said. "We have no food, no shelter, and an actual army hunting us. Do either of you know how long it will take to find a way over the mountains? Because I don't. We have to escape the valley with what we know. We have to bring these stones back with us."

Cazia pointed toward the pouch in Kinz's hand, and she tucked it into her belt.

Her pleas could not sway the other two, no matter what she said. She was tempted to threaten to leave them, but she couldn't bear the thought that they'd call her bluff. She'd been so horrible to Ivy after she'd gone hollow, she was not sure where they stood. The princess had *said* she wanted to put that behind them, but if Cazia pushed too hard, she might make an Enemy of the girl. Of both of them—it had been Kinz who looked after Ivy in the water, after all.

So they set out eastward without packs or supplies, their boots squishing in the mossy mud. Once on the move, they were quiet by mutual unspoken agreement, climbing uphill in the mists. The sun was a bright white spot against the bright white sky, and they followed it through the morning. The fog was awful; they could have seen farther with torches on a moonlit night. Cazia knew that somewhere to the north, the lake would be flowing into the ocean, but she was glad not to be near it.

She wondered, though, at the way Ivy and Kinz calmly approached the water. Were imperial shores the only ones troubled by sea giants and other monsters? It was possible that Ivy's ocean god—Boskole, or whatever she called it—kept the eastern side of the Indrega Peninsula safe, but only if it were real, and Cazia wasn't ready to accept that. As for Kinz, well, Cazia had underestimated her before, but she seemed to have been created to be underestimated. Maybe she really did understand the dangers. Maybe she was just brave.

As the morning grew late, the fog finally thinned again, and the other girls picked up the pace. Cazia followed, trying to convince herself the others knew what they were doing and that this would be a safe detour. She'd only seen the ocean once in her life, after all, and that from a distance. Maybe the Ergoll and Poalo peoples took family picnics on the beach.

They finally topped another hill. The fog had burned away more than expected, and they could see a fair distance.

The ocean rolled and surged just at the foot of the hill. She could have reached the beach in two hundred paces, maybe three. From there, it would have been another fifty before the water touched her feet. The waves crashed and rolled in toward the shore, over and over, in an endless assault.

On the right, to the south, was a jagged ridge of rocks that ran out into the water. It must have been the end of the Northern Barrier, battered down by the endless waves. The ridge was slick black stone and made nearly vertical cliffs, except in the places the waters had worn an overhang.

To the left was another ridge and smattering of black stones, but these were more sparse and didn't extend as far from shore. Many of them stood like irregular towers amid the crashing waves. Both ridges served to narrow the bay and blunt the force of the surging ocean.

That first time Cazia had seen the ocean, she had stood within a tower at Rivershelf and watched the waters churn. Three great eels had battled a great hulking thing that floated just below the waves. The battle had been terrifying, even at a distance, and the sounds that echoed through the city had chilled her blood. The stones of Rivershelf's waterfront had been awash in red and black fluids, which servants had collected at terrible personal risk. Two had been snatched from dry land by a tentacle that had dragged them down into the sea while she watched.

Monsters. The ocean was full of monsters, and human beings did not even dare to approach it, except in a few select places like Rivershelf or the Bay of Stones, where the shallows stretched far from the shore.

Here, though, she saw nothing. Her brother—and how the memory of him pained her—had said they'd seen a rare sight that day in Rivershelf, but she'd never really believed him. She had always suspected that that sort of massive combat was a daily sight. Yet here they were, looking over the churning waters with no idea what might lie beneath.

"That is unexpected," Kinz said. They turned southward to follow her gaze.

Low against the cliff wall, right at the edge of the beach, was a squat stone tower. It was the same color as the black ridge behind it, and Cazia was embarrassed not to have noticed it herself. Still, there it was just the same, with a conical roof and short, wide windows.

"We should go back," Cazia said.

"It is too late," Ivy said. "The way we are standing out on this hill, they are sure to have seen us."

Then we should run, Cazia wanted to say. Kinz spoke first. "Assuming anyone is there. Does it not look abandoned to you?"

It did. Cazia had to admit that it did.

Ivy turned toward her. "Big sister," she said, with surprising warmth, "I know how you feel about the ocean—I know how the Peradaini people feel—but we have risked so much to search for answers, have we not?"

"We have our answers," Cazia said quietly.

"Not all of them," Ivy said. She glanced back at the tower. "This seems like it could be important, does it not?"

"Yes," Cazia answered. "Little sister, you're right. It might be important. But we have learned so much that needs to be shared with your people and mine. And yours, too," she said to Kinz.

"I am glad you made to include me," the older girl said with a sardonic smile.

"Sorry. Listen, it is not just about the Tilkilit, the eagles, and the portal. It is those stones." She pointed to the pouch Kinz was wearing. "I can't carry them but you two can. They could change the way magic is done. They could turn the war against the grunts in our favor."

"In your favor," Kinz said. "For your empire."

"Monument sustain me," Cazia spat, because she didn't want to wish the girl Fire-taken. "Would you take the grunts over the Peradaini people?"

"I will *take* neither," Kinz answered, bringing her open hand down like a chopping ax. "I want them to destroy each other so I can make again my clan and live like free people."

Goose bumps ran down Cazia's back and her face grew warm. "You're talking about women and children, too. You're talking about lives lost while we dawdle. With these stones, our scholars could save lives."

Kinz glared. She pushed her dark hair out of her face—she needed to re-braid it, but Fire take the idea that Cazia would touch that oily mess. Let Ivy do it, if they were going to ally against her.

Then the older girl turned away and marched across the slope of the hill toward the tower.

Cazia lunged forward and caught Ivy's elbow. "Little sister," she said, half afraid the younger girl would object. "Let her go ahead. She's got the only weapon, such as it is. And she's . . . " Cazia wasn't sure how to finish that sentence. *She dislikes me because of things I didn't do and had no control over. It's not fair.*

"Cazia," the princess said, her tone annoyingly patient. "Kinz has buried the family. She has seen the family killed by Peradaini soldiers because they objected to the size of the tribute—taxes, I meant to say. Do not argue; I will call them taxes while talking with you. However, you should understand that whatever Peradaini kings say, the herding clans of the Sweeps consider themselves free people. If you do not want her to treat you like an enemy, do not treat her as though you have the same desires. She is not a subject to either of us."

"I don't have subjects," Cazia snapped. "I'm not a princess."

"You would be if you had been born among my people," Ivy answered placidly. "She knows this."

Cazia glanced across the hill at Kinz's retreating form. "She signed on as our servant. She was revealed to be a spy. She asked to remain a servant but—"

"She is not a servant," Ivy said.

"She swore an oath—"

"I would not take a Peradaini-style servant into this kind of danger. Kinz is our companion. Please understand: *I must do this.* It would be blasphemy if I did not 'dawdle' here. When we are done, we will take your stones back over the mountains. Now we must catch up to her."

Ivy turned her back on Cazia and ran after Kinz, her boots making squashing noises on the mossy hillside. Cazia reluctantly followed, feeling terribly alone.

Chapter Four

Kinz marched in the lead, moving across the slope with as much care as if she was walking at the edge of a precipice. Ivy was close behind. Cazia followed even more slowly. The loose, mossy stones were slick; if she fell and sprained her ankle, here within sight of the ocean . . .

He skin prickled at the thought of being dragged beneath those icy waves, breath bubbling out of her. She looked out at the water and saw nothing dangerous there. The churning, roiling ocean appeared to be mindless and uninhabited. The black, stony beach showed no signs of sea giant footprints or nests. But Great Way, did it have to be so loud?

The squat stone tower did not appear damaged—there were no holes in the roof, no collapsed stonework, not even a rotted wooden spar—but it still gave off an undeniable sense of abandonment. As they came closer to the structure, they discovered that there were more structures behind it: a second, smaller tower, a shiny black pier that protruded out into the waves, a pit filled with water, and a blockhouse at the base of the cliff.

There were no burning lamps visible inside, no discarded cloths, no stacks of baskets by the entrance. High seas had washed the stony beach up against the bottom of the doorway. It was as if the towers had been shaped from the rock by the wind and sea and still waited for their first occupants.

Kinz stood a respectful distance from the tower door and shouted a greeting. Then she did it a second and third time. No one expected an answer and none came. She advanced toward the door and pressed against it.

Cazia was sure it would be barred or at least stuck, but it swung open easily. Kinz and Ivy disappeared into the structure.

That left Cazia alone. On a beach. She ran down the last part of the slope toward the door, half convinced that the wet crunch of her tread on the moss-covered gravel would draw the attention of something horrifying in the water.

The walls were smooth. The towers had not been built from stone blocks. There were no seams, no mortar, no joins at all. The walls were as even and featureless as water in a still pool.

She went inside, noting that the door was made of the same smooth black stone, but it was as thin as a wafer. There was no furniture, no broken crockery, or evidence of a fireplace. Ivy and Kinz stood at the bottom of a flight of stairs, but they no longer seemed keen on exploring. Cazia had to move closer to them to see why: while the ceiling in the room was twelve feet from the floor, the stairs were practically a tunnel. The space was no higher than Cazia's belly button.

"Little people?" Ivy said, but Cazia had no idea what she meant. She knelt to look up the stairs. It was pitch dark.

Cazia walked a circuit of the room. There were no other doors, only shutterless windows. A black stone core supported the tower the way a center pole held up a round tent, but there were no doors in that, either. The choice was simple: leave, stay huddled in this insecure room, or crawl up the stairs.

How did we get to this madness? Grunts rampage on the far side of the mountains while we satisfy our curiosity. Still, Cazia had to admit that she was curious, too.

Cazia took a little gray stone from just beyond the door. Her magic had not fully returned, but she had enough for a small spell. She rubbed the mossy stone clean and cast a light spell on it. After so long, casting one of the Gifts felt like going home, like she was studying to be a scholar again. For a moment, as she held up the little glowing stone, she remembered the Scholars' Tower, the map room, Doctor Twofin, and all the other parts of her life that were now lost.

She smiled anyway. Whatever she had lost, she still had this.

Then she glanced at her companions and saw Ivy's furrowed brow and Kinz's stony, hostile expression. Fire and Fury, they hated her *and* her magic.

Cazia wished she could think of something to say to the little princess to reassure her, but she couldn't, not while the older girl was standing right there. *She swore to be our servant, but she lied.* Cazia wasn't sure why that mattered so much, but it did. All three of them had lied during their time together—and Ivy's plan to turn Cazia over to an Indregai military commander had been the most serious.

So, why did it bother Cazia so much that Kinz had been their servant and then, quite suddenly, stopped? Now she wanted to be treated as an equal—a companion—and that bothered Cazia for reasons she couldn't articulate at the moment, but she was sure they were solid, good, excellent reasons.

Kinz wanted to lead the way up the stairs, but Cazia pushed by her and climbed on her hands and knees. The stone steps were painful, but not as bad as the rough passage she'd dug up the Northern Barrier. "Be careful," Ivy whispered from close behind. They were following her through yet another tunnel.

The stair-tunnel curved around the stony core of the tower. Cazia felt goose bumps run down the length of her body. Anything could be up ahead. Ivy's little people, armed with little spears and little bronze knives, might charge at them, screaming. A grass lion might have made a den on the top floor. A sudden flood of water might wash them all the way into the ocean.

She shut her eyes and did her best to clear her thoughts. It occurred to her that to be extremely brave, a person ought to have no imagination at all.

Nothing attacked them on the stair except for a horrifying stench that grew thicker as they approached the top. Cazia reached the second floor after approximately one half circuit of the tower. It resembled the first: the only light came from narrow, unshuttered windows and the floor was bare smooth stone without a stick of furniture.

There were other differences beside the smell. Rows of cubbyholes had been built into one of the walls. At one spot, the stone wall protruded to form a bowl. At another, there was a wide, flat stone shelf—almost as large as a bed—with a white stone lever above it. As best Cazia could see, the lever did not do anything; it was a length of stone bent midway at a right angle as though it had been carved from the corner of a block, nothing more. The lower end of the lever was oddly shaped, like an oversized setting for a now-missing jewel.

Then they found a depression in the stone floor full of putrid water. It might have been a bathing tub at some point, but the water was covered with a noxious scum with nasty gray and green lumps floating in it.

Ivy waved her hand in front of her nose. "Oh, that is revolting! How long has this stood here?"

"Too long," Kinz said. "Let us make to move on quickly."

Cazia set the glowing stone into a cubby nearby and began to move her hands, beginning the preparations for the Fifth Gift. She heard Ivy call her name, but ignored her. All her concentration was focused on the filthy water below.

Having gone hollow and been cured of it, Cazia had a new, deeper understanding of the way her thoughts and motions controlled the Gifts. It was a new level of knowledge and power, but she had not yet been given the chance to truly explore it.

The Fifth Gift was one of the first she'd been taught. She'd been casting it since she was nine years old, but today, it was an incredible strain. Creating lightstones was easy—had always been easy, although the one she'd just made barely glowed at all. Other Gifts were not so simple.

Calling up her magic for this spell was like trying to inhale with a hand clamped over her mouth. She pushed outward, feeling the magic pass through the water like a net, purifying it.

But she didn't have the strength to do the whole tub. With nearly two-thirds left undone, the thought structures in her mind collapsed and the noxious scum sloshed through the cleaned part of the tub, undoing her work.

"I'm not ready yet," she said. "I just need a little more time."

She didn't have to look at the others to know what their expressions would be, but she did it anyway. Of course, they were unhappy to see her casting spells again, but really, what did they expect?

Ivy found and pulled a small stone lever. The nasty water drained out through a tiny drain in the wall. Cazia went to the window beside it and saw the ocean churning below. It gave her a sick, prickly feeling, especially knowing they had just dumped garbage at the water's edge like bait in a nonexistent trap.

Even with the water drained away, the tower room still smelled so horribly, it made her want to retch. At least she wasn't hungry any more.

"Big sister," Ivy began warily, "maybe it would be best if there was no more magic. At least, not unless we all agree it is truly necessary."

Despite herself, Cazia was surprised. "You expect me to ask permission? Am I the servant now, little sister?"

That seemed to surprise Ivy. Cazia turned away from them to avoid saying anything that might infuriate them, and noticed another low entrance. She approached it and held up the lightstone. It wasn't a stair this time but a corridor. Who would build a structure where the rooms were high enough to stand in but everyone had to drop to their hands and knees to move between them?

Cazia began to crawl. The others followed her, and this time, there were no frightening flights of imagination. This time, her thoughts were consumed by what she would say if Kinz and Ivy demanded a veto over her spellcasting.

The idea of it soured her. She needed them if she was going to get back over the mountains—and they needed her even more—but how were they going to make it if they didn't trust each other?

The corridor opened into another round room of black stone. This one did not have the massive circular core at the center, but it did have another flight of tunnel-stairs leading down. Along the walls were another series of flat, broad shelves, none higher off the ground than knee height. They had been arranged in groups of three or four with open spaces between.

"What do you think?" Ivy said. Her voice sounded strained. "Are they beds for families to sleep together or couches for elders to discuss the plans?"

Ivy sat on one and Cazia sat across from her. Her hiking skirts were still damp from the river and the cold stone chilled her. "More like punishment."

Cazia began to string together the thoughts that would let her cast the Eleventh Gift but she did not move her hands. The spell would never work without gestures, but the stone began to reveal itself to her in a way she didn't quite understand, as though she could feel the inside and outside of it without touching. The beds were hollow. Very sturdy, but hollow.

"Ooo!" Ivy said, pointing.

There was a row of cubbies along the floor behind Cazia, but these were not empty. Cazia rushed toward them.

The nearest held a jumble of odd wooden tools: charred, slender skewers, fat wedges, and twisted things that might have been scrapers of some kind. Backscratchers? It didn't matter. Cazia tossed them aside.

The cubby beside it held a small stack of mud-colored cloths folded into odd, five-sided stacks. Shaking one out, Cazia found it was circular and only a little musty.

In the next, she found something astonishing. It was a finely-wrought semicircle of intricate ironwork. Kinz gasped when she saw it, and Cazia spun around. Kinz had her hand on Ivy's elbow, holding her back so Cazia could search the cubbies alone. Were they expecting her to disturb a snake or something? Cazia felt a sudden tingle of nervousness. Whatever danger they were expecting, they were letting her face it alone.

Cazia tossed the iron circlet to Kinz. "Take it. If we ever get out of here, we're going to be going to Indrega, right? That ought to pay for a meal or two."

Kinz blinked at it, her hand absent-mindedly rubbing at a spot of rust. Now that she didn't have a hand on her arm, Ivy rushed forward to join Cazia on the floor.

Cazia didn't want to look at either of them. Was Kinz trying to freeze her out and win the princess over? Probably not. She was almost certainly trying to protect the girl from Cazia. Hmf.

"Look at this!" Ivy pulled a small stack of square mats from one cubby. They were as long as Cazia's hand, and had been dyed in six, no, seven colors. "Look at that blue."

The little girl was right. Blue dye was precious and difficult to use, but this blue was as vibrant and even as the sky on a cloudless day.

All the mats had the same design, with minor differences: each had a yellow circle at the center, with six yellow rays shooting from it all the way to the edge of the cloth. In each of the wedges formed by those rays was a different design. One had a bird in a blue sky. Another showed black monoliths against a white background. Another looked like stormy water beneath a gray sky. Another showed a glowing mountain against a red sky. The last two were harder to recognize. A yellow forest, maybe? Brown desert beneath an orange sky?

"It's the portal," Cazia blurted suddenly. "The Door in the Mountain."

"Do you think so?" Ivy answered. "It looks more like the sun."

"Remember what Chik told us? He said his people came from a place where the soil, grass, and trees were orange. From another land."

Ivy examined the design skeptically. "A red sky? An orange sky?"

Cazia held the mat close and examined the fibers. They were some kind of hair, but she couldn't recognize it. "If they have different lands, they might have a sky different from ours."

"It is possible," Ivy said indulgently.

"Little sister, don't condescend," Cazia admonished, and the little girl blushed.

As Kinz came close to them, Cazia held up the mat in her hand like an empty platter. "Let me keep one of the Tilkilit stones. You can have the others, but I want one, just in case."

Kinz made no argument but she clearly tried to think of one. She drew one of the smooth black stones from the pouch at her waist and dropped it onto the mat.

At the last moment, Cazia realized it was a mistake. The first time she'd had her magic stolen away, the stone had affected her through her skirts, and this strange mat offered her no better protection. She cried out and dropped it when Kinz placed it into the mat, but not fast enough. Her magic was gone again.

"Fire and Fury," she spat. "Now I have to wait for my magic to come back again."

Looking slightly relieved, Ivy held another iron circlet in her hand, but this one was meant for fighting. It was plain and sturdy, with two finger-long spikes protruding from the front. The ring, though, was very large. Cazia thought it might fit her thigh just above her knee, but who would make such a thing? And why?

Ivy passed the spiked ring to Kinz, who accepted it with a quiet "Thank you." The older girl tried to find a way to wear it, but it wouldn't go around her arm or her leg. The decorative circle rested on top of her head like a child's crown.

Ivy cleared her throat. "Do you think the Tilkilit built this place?"

"No," Cazia said immediately. She ran her hand over the smooth stone. "This place was made by magic, and the Tilkilit would have made more if they knew how, if only to protect themselves. Whoever did this is strong with magic. Plus, they built it by the sea, so they must have done it quickly."

"But would that not affect them?" Kinz asked warily. "The way you were 'hollowed out'?"

"I assume . . . " Cazia jumped up and rushed across the room. "Follow me." She led them back through the low tunnel toward the bed with the lever above it. "Kinz, fit one of the stones there."

The Tilkilit stone fit perfectly into the oddly hollowed end of the white lever. Then Cazia lowered it to the bed and lifted it again.

"Then this *is* a Tilkilit building!" Ivy said.

"No," Cazia said. "No, it just means that the Tilkilit have their own version of the Evening People."

Kinz snapped up the stone and returned it safely to her pouch. "What does that mean?"

"The Tilkilit empire was built with the help of a more advanced people. Just like the Peradaini, someone with powerful magic has been helping them. And whoever these benefactors are, they're here, in Kal-Maddum."

CHAPTER FIVE

WHEN TEJOHN AWOKE, EVERYTHING ABOUT THE TINY ROOM HE WAS in seemed different. There was very little light, but it seemed to be pressing in on him in a way he couldn't quite understand, as though he were under water.

A deep breath assured him that his back and ribs had been fully healed and he could move his arms and legs freely. The priests had healed him; it hadn't been a trap at all, unless the Finstel king was waiting outside the door with a sledge.

As he swung his legs over the side of the stone, he heard tiny bells jangle. Someone had tied a cord of ceremonial chimes to his ankles. Sure enough, in the room beyond the door, he heard wooden chairs scraping against stone, then shuffling feet.

A young, clean-shaven fellow stepped into the doorway but came no closer. The light from the other room—the only light there was—lit only his edges, and there was something strangely vivid about him. His mussed hair and the folds of his robes were so clear, they appeared to have been cut out of the universe with a razor. "Tyr Treygar," he said, halting in the doorway. "Do you need me to get you something?"

"Water," Tejohn croaked. He wanted light, too, and food and news and weapons and freedom, but water would do for now.

The priest left the room and returned shortly with a bowl of water. He admonished Tejohn to drink in sips, which he did. When the bowl was empty, the priest went to the other room to refill it.

Tejohn looked around. He looked to be in the same underground chamber, but the rough stone walls were oddly detailed. The firelight from the other room made them a complex arrangement of contour and shadow. The priest returned.

Tejohn took the bowl. "How long?"

"Ten days, my tyr," the priest said. "I have clean clothes for you, and a bowl for washing. Let me set the water by the fire to warm. Stay here, please, for the moment. The next room will seem painfully bright to you. I'll bring more water, too."

Tejohn watched him hustle from the room. The young man's tone and body language held an earnest desire to please that Tejohn had never seen from a palace servant, who were usually creatures of chilly efficiency. Of course, now that Tejohn had spent a short time as a servant, he knew chilliness was a mask for raw hatred.

Ten days? He stripped off the robe they had draped on him. Someone had kept him clean during the long healing process: a servant, or was that priest's work? And how had they prevented him from dying of dehydration?

Tejohn drained the second bowl more quickly than the first, then was given a bucket of water and a rag. If the water had been warmed in some way, it wasn't evident, but he wiped himself down, then put on the robe the young man brought him. His was pale gray where the priest's was red.

"Let me refill your bowl," the priest said.

"Thank you." That seemed to surprise him. Tejohn continued, "What's your name?"

"Beacon Javien, my tyr."

"That's not a Finshto name, is it? Where are you from?"

The young priest glanced around the room as though he was being trapped. Tejohn knew how he felt. "My tyr, my family were Redmudds. I was an acolyte at the temple on Red Hill when the grunts attacked. We thought we were safe on our islands, but no. The beacons put me on a northbound boat, and I received my final initiation from Beacon Veliender. He's Redmudd, too, although . . . "

He stopped there and his face flushed with embarrassment. He must have thought he was rambling.

"Thank you for looking after me while I healed," Tejohn said.

"It is our duty to aid and guide those who travel The Way," the priest answered. "If you feel strong enough to climb stairs, my tyr, Beacon Veliender would like to break her fast with you."

Tejohn felt weak and famished, but Fire take the idea that he would be carried again. "I would like that as well. Lead the way."

The young priest was correct. The fire in the hearth of the next room wasn't large, but it was painfully bright. His eyes, shut for ten days, watered and ached as though he was trying to look directly at the sun.

The room was still full of people, which Tejohn had not expected but should have. They were so quiet, like parents sitting beside a babe in a cradle, or mourners beside a deathbed. Were they waiting their turn on the sleep-stone? Fire and Fury, he hoped all those people hadn't waited ten days for him.

The stairs were dark. The light from the candle Beacon Javien carried cast strange shadows around them. Tejohn began to suspect it was enchanted. Everything beneath the temple seemed alien.

At the top of the stair, Javien knocked at a heavy oak door, then entered at the command of a woman inside.

The room was much larger than Tejohn had expected, almost as large as his indoor practice gym at the palace and full of fresh air. There were day beds, desks, and tables set around the room in no particularly sensible arrangement. And there, at the far side, was an older woman, her gray hair tied back into a bun, working at her desk by candlelight.

She was so far away—perhaps twenty paces or more—but Tejohn could see her so clearly! There was so much detail that Tejohn felt a moment of disorientation, as though he were standing directly in front of her instead of across the room, and he swooned momentarily. Javien caught his elbow to steady him.

"My tyr, this way," Javien led him to a wooden bench and practically shoved him onto it. "You should have told me you felt weak. If you had fallen on the stairs—"

"I'm fine," Tejohn said. The gray-haired woman hurried toward them. "I don't feel weak, just disoriented. My eyes . . . My vision has changed."

Javien looked alarmed, but the woman's expression softened as her concern turned into understanding. She addressed the young priest. "Along with his injuries, Tyr Treygar was treated for extreme nearsightedness."

"Ah," the fellow answered. "I was not informed." There was a hint of reproach in his voice.

Tejohn looked around the room. Every desk, every candle, every wax tablet . . . It was all so elaborate. For his entire life, most of the world had been little more than colorful blurs, but now . . . It was as though a mist had blown away.

Everything was so detailed and specific. The grain of wood on a bench, the way a stylus and tablet lay beside each other, unique and discrete . . . Tejohn hadn't imagined that the world contained so much *information*.

"I understand it can be disorienting," the woman said, her voice deep and soothing. "You aren't the first."

"I could have done this years ago," Tejohn said, unable to keep the resentment from his voice. "I knew my eyes were weak, but I had no idea the world was so . . . " He couldn't finish that sentence. He wasn't even sure what he wanted to say. *Full.* He had no idea the world was so full.

"There aren't enough scholars or sleepstones to fix everyone's vision or hearing, and with the way things have gone, it looks like there never will be."

Movement off to the right caught Tejohn's eye. An old fellow roused himself off a day bed and, after a quick glance at Tejohn, shuffled out through a side door. For a moment, Tejohn was embarrassed to have woken him, but he quickly realized that none of the other priests had hushed their voices. "I don't remember waking up," Tejohn said in the same tone. "I was on the sleepstone for ten days, but I don't think anyone woke me for water."

"You're correct, my tyr," the woman said. She had watched the old fellow step out of the room but now turned her attention back to Tejohn. "In fact, medical scholars will sometimes refuse to treat someone with injuries as extensive as yours, or will let them die on the stone. Severely injured patients can not be woken and moved during their sleep without harming them further. At the temple, we've developed a clever machine that will drip liquid, ever so slowly, into the sleeping person's mouth. Water, diluted fruit juice, thin broth, it doesn't matter. It's never enough to drown or choke the patient, but it does wet their lips."

"Why not share this clever machine with the Scholars' Guild?"

She smiled. "That could be awkward, since they do not know we have sleepstones nor the skill to create them. As priests of the temple, we have tried to guide them toward the idea, but without success."

Doctor Twofin, the scholar who instructed the prince in magic, had admitted that the Scholars' Guild had secrets they kept from everyone, even the royal family. That was right before he had betrayed Tejohn and dropped him from a flying cart, leaving him broken and at the mercy of his enemies. The servants had secret societies of their own, he had also learned, that they called *cabinets*, because they were a source of necessary things. And now the priests of the temple as well?

Tejohn began to think he was the only person without a secret agenda . . . but no, that wasn't true. The prince had given him a mission to complete, one Tejohn was not always free to talk about.

The old fellow returned through the side door again and moved toward the wall. No, there wasn't a wall there. Tejohn hadn't noticed it before, but where the wall should have been was open space.

As if his return was a cue, the older woman suggested they have breakfast together on the eastern deck. Sunrise would begin soon. Tejohn agreed, waving off Javien's help. She turned to the young man. "Soup first, I think, considering. The rest when the kitchen is ready. We're starting the day so early. And wake Ulmasc; we need her now."

Beacon Javien hurried down the stairs, and the woman led Tejohn onto the terrace. "I would like to know the name of the person I'm speaking with," he said simply.

"How unspeakably rude of me," she said. "I was so caught up in worrying about you that I forgot my manners. My name is Beacon Veliender."

"Ah," Tejohn said. They had reached a table at the edge of the terrace. Veliender gestured to a seat that would allow him to have the best view of the coming sunrise. "That's another Redmudd name, isn't it?"

She gave him a crooked smile. "You could say that. It is, in fact, even older than the name Redmudd. Many, many years ago, when my clan surrendered their broken spears to the Peradaini, the . . . tyrants showed their fealty by changing their names to the Peradaini translation."

"So, Veliender means 'red mud'?"

She spread her hands. "Actually, it means 'dirt soaked with blood,' but the days when my people thought of themselves as deadly warriors are generations past. Battlefield losses will do that."

Tejohn glanced at the old man, who was sitting at the next table. He stared off into the distance as though deaf to everything they said, ignoring them. Could he hear what they said and would he join them to break their fast? Tejohn had always heard that the priests had no hierarchy within their temples; everyone was a "Beacon" and no one was in charge. Of course, he didn't believe it really worked that way for a moment, but this was the face they presented to the world. Perhaps the old fellow was the head of the temple.

A red glow had appeared over the horizon. Tejohn stared out into it, watching it spread across the sky. He'd seen the sunrise many times in his life, of course, but this was an entirely new experience. Laoni should be here beside him, he thought. The sudden strength of his longing for her startled him.

Bowls of steaming soup were set in front of them, and the smell of the eel broth made his mouth water. Beacon Veliender handed him a slender wooden spoon. "Considering your recent convalescence, let's not worry too much about propriety, my tyr."

She began to eat with gusto, and Tejohn did the same. There was very little actual eel in the soup, but the rice, onions, and carrots were very welcome. Still, he did his best to eat politely, only lifting the bowl to his lips and scraping the wooden bottom when it was nearly finished.

The old fellow had also received a bowl, but he ate sparingly.

As the servants—Tejohn noticed they wore white robes, not red like the priests or gray like his—brought apricots and rice, a young woman in red hurried into the room, a stack of wax tablets in her arms and a stylus tucked behind her ear. She had large, watery eyes and a weak chin. "I'm sorry, Beacon Veliender. I came as quickly as I could." She set the stack precariously on the edge of the table and sat.

"I think," Beacon Veliender said, turning toward Tejohn, "that it is time for us to have our conversation."

"You want news," Tejohn said.

"I do," the priest responded. "Everything."

He glanced at the young woman, her stylus suspended over the tablet. "And why is she here? To share everything I say?"

"Not to share," Veliender said. "To remember."

Tejohn shook his head. "What I have seen is not for Finstel ears."

"The King's soldiers are still searching the streets for you, although most assume you have already escaped the city. The only reason we dare to sit out on the terrace is because the temple and the attached buildings have already been searched. More than once. To take your story to the king now would be an admission of treason."

"Unless," Tejohn said, "the king arranged for all this."

"Ah!" Her surprise appeared genuine. "Of course! A daring midnight rescue from the king's own dungeon, and here we are, offering you food . . . You suspect this is a ruse of King Shunzik's, yes? To make you tell all your secrets willingly."

"I do. But I am still grateful that I have been permitted to look out over the city with new-found eyes, until they are put out forever."

"Is that what you think will happen to you? Torture and blindness?"

Yes. Tejohn did not look away from the glowing sunrise. "Grateful am I to be permitted to travel The Way."

They did not speak for a while. Tejohn no longer felt hungry, but he forced himself to finish his rice and drink the heavily diluted wine.

But the view! Maybe it was his close call with death or his certitude that he was going back to Shunzik's dungeons, but this view of the city, with its low flat roofs revealed by the rising sun in slow, specific details, and the thin clouds blowing toward the horizon, astonished him. He could never have expected a gift like this, and he savored it.

The whole world was being devoured, and he had failed to save it. Soon, he would be back in chains, screaming under the torturer's white-hot brand. Until then, he had this. *This.*

Veliender pushed her empty bowl away. "According to the stories circulating now, Banderfy Finstel is the one who broke through the Bendertuk shield wall at Toram Halmajil."

"What does that matter?"

"When we tell our children the story of our people, do we lie to them? Or do we tell them the truth, like people of honor? Do we heap false praise onto the lives of our forbearers simply because it benefits us today? I would hope not. The things we have done matter, even if the grunts hunt us to extinction. Did you follow Banderfy through the shield wall?"

Tejohn glanced at the weak-chinned woman sitting on the other side of him. Her stylus was poised above the tablet as though waiting for the command to begin.

"I won't hear Banderfy's reputation sullied," Tejohn said. The woman made tiny scratches into her tablet. Were those his words? "He was a good commander and an honorable man. It was a privilege to serve under him."

"We don't want to dishonor him," Veliender said. "Only tell the truth. Did you follow him through the shield wall or did he follow you?"

"He followed me," Tejohn said. It was an uncomfortable thing to say; boasting was something commanders did, and Tejohn had never been much of a commander. "I would have died if he hadn't, and we would have never gone on to liberate King Ellifer from Pinch Hall. The victory was his, no matter who split the wall first."

"That's what our history will record." Veliender nodded at Ulmasc, and the scribe finished making marks on her tablet and set it aside in favor of a fresh one. Again, she held the stylus over the wax and fell still. "But there are other questions we must record, such as what happened on the first day of Festival."

The day the grunts invaded. Tejohn closed his eyes, the memory of the initial attack suddenly overwhelming him. He'd been there and seen it, of course. He hadn't been close enough to see it in the same detail he could see now, but it was enough. The flames, the screaming, the violence, all were as vivid as that same day more than two months before.

Glancing back at the city below, he could see more and more detail as the day grew bright: chimneys, puddles on roofs, beggars skulking down streets, and much more. If his vision had been fixed before that day, would his memories of the attack be more vicious and explicit? Would he have seen Queen Amlian's expression at the moment she died?

He couldn't bring himself to talk about it, even if he wanted to. Veliender refilled his cup.

"There are a great many stories circulating through the population about that day. Some say the Evening People came through the portal with grunts on long leashes, like hounds. They say Ellifer cringed from them, and the Evening People showed their contempt by setting the creatures free." Tejohn snorted in disbelief but said nothing. The priest continued. "In other stories, he stabbed his wife in the leg so the grunts would feast on her while he fled in terror."

"Too clumsy," Tejohn snapped at her. "If you want to goad me, you'll need to be more subtle than that."

She bowed her head. "Still, this is the story the King's people have been spreading. I told you that people tell lies about the past to benefit their present. If no one corrects a false history, Ellifer Italga will be remembered as a coward and a fool."

"Song knows what he did."

"But no human will," the priest insisted. "Not unless the history can be corrected by someone who was there."

"Song knows," Tejohn insisted. "That's good enough for me."

"As a beacon," Veliender said, trying a new line of attack, "it is my duty to aid and guide the people of Kal-Maddum. All of them. I can't do that if I don't know what's really happening in the world."

Tejohn laughed slightly, but there was no life or enthusiasm behind it. "Everyone has a duty, from the most powerful king to the meanest servant, but only priests and soldiers declare theirs to the world like a badge of honor."

She sighed. "Very true."

They were quiet for a moment. Fire and Fury, could he really tell this story to people who were almost certainly enemies to him and to his king? The more he thought about it, the less sense it made to keep it secret. Even if he could not complete the mission Lar Italga had given him, perhaps someone else would.

"There were no leashes," he said. Immediately, the scribe began to scratch on her wax tablet. He assumed they would tell him if he needed to speak more slowly. "There were no Evening People, either. The courtyard was decorated for the start of Festival, and the king and queen stood on the dais. When the portal opened, there was a pause that seemed to take forever. Then The Blessing charged through. That's what the grunts call themselves. The Blessing."

Tejohn told the story just as he remembered it. He described the grunts, described the fight as well as he could, then the escape from the city, with the spears utterly overwhelmed and Peradain burning behind them. He told them about the stay at Fort Samsit, the plan to fly to Tempest Pass to revive a spell that could defeat the grunts, and how that mission failed.

He told them everything, leaving out one detail: that Lar Italga, King Ellifer's only heir, was bitten by a grunt and had become one himself. In this telling, Lar suspected treachery from one of his people and vanished during the night, determined to carry on his quest alone.

Tejohn was sure a single stack of wax tablets would not be enough for his entire story, but there were three left over when he was done. At a nod from Veliender, Ulmasc carefully gathered her things and withdrew.

"Monument sustain us all," Beacon Veliender said. "King Shunzik did not treat you well, did he?"

Tejohn said nothing. He'd expected her to demand that he swear to the accuracy of his story, but now that she hadn't, he didn't know what to say next. He noticed the old priest at the next table suddenly staring at him with a fierceness he would never have expected from such a frail figure. He looked slightly familiar, too.

"If you think it's not important," she continued, "then it is not. Still, I apologize for the way you've been treated in our city. Your city, yes? You grew up near here, didn't you?"

"On a farm. I visited the city, but . . . ."

"Now you will see that King Shunzik did not free you and you are in no danger of being sent back to his dungeons. He isn't clever enough to think up that sort of ruse, not when he thinks he can have his way through brute force. You've already seen how he treats his own people, taking everything from them, making slaves of them—we no longer have to obey the Peradaini ban on that word, do we? Let us be done with empty codes. He is making slaves of his own people and working them to death in quarries. And for what? A berm of broken stone?"

She gestured out toward the rising sun, which had broken through the horizon during his story. There, well beyond the city walls, he could see it. A broad, flat stone expanse with a low berm on the border. That was the parade ground where he had marched in formation so many years ago and had worked like a convict only a few days ago. Even at this distance, he could see the berm wasn't very high. How was it supposed to stop the grunts with that? And where would he find the spears to guard it? "Whose idea was that?"

"The king's himself," Veliender answered. Her voice and her expression were flat. "He expects his court scholars to break that stone expanse into fertile farmland, and for the city to sustain itself."

Tejohn glanced out at the city again, which was now teeming with ordinary people hurrying about their business. With his new eyes, he could see them all clearly enough to note their hair color, body shape, and clothing choices. What's more, the streets were busier than he'd ever seen in his life. Ussmajil was packed with refugees.

Even if he could break the parade ground into arable soil—and he couldn't—there would never be enough land to feed so many. One look at the priest's face showed she was thinking the same thing. "He's gone mad," Tejohn said simply.

"Despair has ruined him," Veliender said simply, as though she was talking about a worn-out water wheel. "He makes useless plans to keep the people busy while he feasts his friends every night. They live like condemned men. Alone of the cities and holdfasts of Peradain, Ussmajil has best chance of withstanding the grunts' assault, but not with Shunzik Finstel on the throne."

Tejohn nodded. Ussmajil was the city of his childhood, no matter that it was less than half the size of the Morning City. He was grateful for the chance to see it one more time.

The beacon wasn't finished. "That's why we were hoping you would kill him for us."

Chapter Six

THE LAST BUILDING LAY ON THE FAR SIDE OF THE SECOND TOWER at the end of another low corridor. It was only one story tall, and not only was the room square, the floors were covered with stinking tidal-flat mud. It was possible, Cazia thought, that there was no floor, just heavy stone walls set into the mud. There were no windows, cubbies, beds, or other structures, and the only break in the wall was an open arch that faced away from the ocean.

Cazia, Ivy, and Kinz sat hunched in the low corridor, their shoulders pressed against the stone roof. None of them wanted to step out into the reeking floor with its mosquitoes and tiny, swarming gnats. They could see that just beyond the arch, there was a small pool, ringed with a solid hoop of black stone, that rose and fell like a breathing creature.

"I will go," Ivy said, stepping suddenly into the squelching mud. Cazia immediately followed. She hadn't realized the others were waiting to see who would go first; she assumed that none of them would leave the clean, dry corridor stone.

Ivy and Cazia took cautious steps toward the arch. If there was anything interesting in this room, it was buried in the mud, and that's where it would stay. However, the little pool of water, which was only about ten feet wide, was another matter. Cazia cautiously approached. The way the surface moved suggested it was being pumped, but that didn't make any sense. "Why is it moving up and down like that?"

"I assume it is connected to the surf by an underground channel," Ivy answered, as though this wasn't an incredibly alarming thing to say.

Ivy hopped by her and crouched by the edge of the pool, which seemed foolhardy to Cazia. She hurried forward and caught hold of the girl's shoulder. "Come away." Cazia had promised to bring the princess home, not to bring her to the water's edge where she could be snatched away and devoured.

"What do you think this place is?" Ivy asked, making no move to retreat.

The stone hoop around the pool was itself ringed with stones, and she could not see the bottom through the murky green water. Just the thought of it made Cazia's skin crawl, but she supposed it was too narrow to let an eel or sea giant pass. On the far side of the pool was a stony beach, rockslides of jagged black stones much like the stones north of Fort Samsit, and then the black cliffs of the Northern Barrier.

How long ago had she and Ivy come across the destroyed Indregai camp? It seemed like such a long time, but she still remembered the sense of disarray, the bodies, the broken things. There was none of that here. Whoever—or whatever—built this place, they left it in an orderly way, leaving behind only a few things.

"An outpost?" Cazia ventured. "Maybe something came in from the ocean and built this . . . winter home?" The idea gave her goose bumps, but the building had been abandoned a very long time ago, possibly hundreds of years. The Tilkilit's patrons, whatever they were, would not return here today. Not today.

"Or perhaps they came out of the portal, made the way to the shore, and after a brief delay for some reason when they built this shelter, ventured into the sea?"

In that case, they were definitely not coming back; the oceans were filled with the deadliest kinds of creatures. Most sensible people didn't even trust fresh water, unless they were Redmudds or something.

Still, she had no idea how to explain that monstrous eel skeleton in the freshwater lake. Something had forced it upriver to die in waters where it could not survive, but what? Could it have had something to do with this structure?

An odd shape at the other side of the arch caught Cazia's eye. There was another right-angled white lever much like the one on the upper floor, except both ends of this one were nearly as long as Ivy was tall. Also, this one did not have a space to fit a Tilkilit stone. Instead, the horizontal end swelled into a sharp-edged cube. If the other end had an ornamentation, it wasn't visible. That end went straight down into the mud.

There was a small stone arch laid across the horizontal length like a weight to hold it down.

Once she noticed that, Cazia examined the place where the levers met.

Yes, it was another stone hinge. She scraped at the mud around it, trying to clean it out. When she lifted the weight away, she would be able to rotate the whole thing and dip that sharp-edged cube into the pool.

"What does this do?" Ivy asked at her shoulder.

"Let's find out." Cazia removed the weight.

"Wait!" Ivy said. "What if it has some sort of magic?"

Of course. Cazia stood and peered closely at the cube. It *was* enchanted. She could feel the magic on it like the tingle at the edge of a high cliff. Some scholars, she had once been taught, could identify spells just by being near them, but her own training had never gotten that far. "You're right. It is. I wonder what it does?"

"Maybe it collapses the building," Ivy said, laying her hand on Cazia's. "Maybe it will set us on fire. Maybe—"

"Little sister, would you put a lever in your home that would make the roof and walls fall on you? You might build one that would close a door or, if I'm right, purify the salt water in that pool, but one that would burn you to ashes or crush you?"

"It could be a trap."

"Without even a lock on the doors? You distrust magic too much." Cazia immediately thought that she might not distrust it enough, but Fire and Fury, she'd just had her magic taken away again by one of those Tilkilit stones, and she wanted something back. She wanted whatever this lever would do for reasons that had nothing to do with common sense. She flipped the lever up, and the long end swung down and splashed into the pool.

The water rose up, then receded again, but the cube went deep enough that it stayed submerged. Cazia and Ivy watched it rise and recede again, then again. If there was any effect, it was invisible. Cazia dipped her fingers into the very edge of the pool and raised them to her lips. It was still salty. The lever didn't purify the water after all.

Rise, recede. Rise, recede. What had they done? Nothing? Ivy turned a quizzical expression to Cazia, who could only shrug in return.

Then something leaped from the pool and struck Cazia full on her chest. She screamed in fright, falling into the chilly mud at Ivy's feet and pushing the slimy thing away. The creature that had struck her hit the wall with a wet smack.

It was a fish as long as her arm and as thick as her neck. Its scales were a gleaming greenish black and its teeth looked like needles. It flopped in the mud twice, then shuddered, gasping.

"Ugh!" Cazia wiped her hands on the front of her shirt. Was there blood?

No. Good. The thing hadn't bitten her. Ivy took her hand and tried to pull her to her feet, but the sucking mud held onto her. Kinz climbed out of the corridor and hurried forward. She took Cazia's other hand and practically yanked her upright.

"Stay clear of the arch," Kinz said, drawing them both away from the opening. The cube was still there, under the water, and they waited to see if another fish would appear.

Cazia was soaked to the skin with stinking mud, and the buzz of mosquitoes set her teeth on edge. Whatever excitement she'd felt at the chance to use a little magic, even if it was the magic of some other, long-forgotten people, had evaporated. There was no place for her to clean her clothes except in the filthy puddle upstairs and in this pool in front of her. The one with *fish* in it.

"We are going to eat tonight," Kinz said, and of course she was referring to more fish.

"But we are going to cook it this time," Ivy said, "right?"

Kinz had a determined look in her eye. "If we can get enough wood to make the drying rack and the fire, we will not have to."

Still, no second fish appeared. Kinz crossed to the lever, lifted it out of the water and lowered it in again. She stepped back with the other girls. In very little time at all, a second fish leaped from the water onto the mud. This one was golden and squashed like a piece of flatbread.

"It works like a distress call, I think," Ivy said. "Like a pit trap. We have those back home."

Cazia relaxed a little. This was a good thing, actually. A necessary thing. As gross as fish were, they were food. She could create water for their trip over the mountains, but not food. In diverting from their mission, they had stumbled onto a way to stock up on provisions.

"It is not making to flop around the way it should," Kinz said.

The flatbread fish was not flopping around, it was true. It had beaten the mud twice with its tail, then lay still, as if it had given up. Cazia wondered if fish could understand the hopelessness of their situation and feel despair.

Cazia and Kinz approached the fish, crouching around it. Kinz laid her hand on its side as though holding it down, although it wasn't necessary. "We catch these in the Shelterlands, at the eastern edge of the continent. They are called sun wheels. When they are healthy, they make to fight the long time before they die." She bent low. "Look at its eye."

Cazia did. There were red splotches in it, and more were forming with each moment. "Blood?"

Without answering, Kinz turned her attention to the first fish. "This one, too. What does it mean?"

Ivy stepped through the squelching mud and stood over them. "I do not think we should eat them until we know if they have been poisoned or not."

"We must make to do this right," Kinz said. She took the piece of flint from her pocket, then sat at the edge of the corridor and gently struck the flint with the iron crown, slowly flaking off pieces. In a little while, she had honed the sharp edge.

Once that was done, it was short work to slicing the head off the sun wheel and look inside. They had to crouch at the base of the arch—with the water perilously close—for enough light to see, but it still took a long while before the eldest girl found something she thought worth mentioning.

"Its skull is made cracked," she said finally. "It is bleeding through. See, its brain is made like a string of beads, and—" She pried the bones apart with her fingers. Cazia wasn't squeamish about meat, not at all, but she had to look away when she heard the tiny cracking sounds. She and Ivy looked at each other, and the little girl looked just as uncomfortable. "Well, this is not right. In the Shelterlands, we catch these by the dozen in our winter nets, and it is the children who make to clean them. Their brains are not supposed to look like this."

"Like what?" Cazia asked, stepping closer to see. The memory of Doctor Whitestalk pressing a sparrow's guts against her tongue back before the Scholars' Tower fell returned to her, as sudden and vivid as if it had just happened that morning.

Kinz turned the butchered fish toward her and pointed at something with her bloody fingers. Cazia couldn't tell one piece of flesh from another. "This part of the brain is mush," Kinz said. "Like it has been struck with a rock."

She found the same thing when she investigated the other fish. While she cut it open, Ivy took the sun wheel and Cazia's muddy jacket through the low corridor back into the tower. By the time Kinz had finished with both fish, Cazia had an idea what was happening. "The magic in the lever is damaging them," she said. "Spells can affect anything but a person's mind. You can't magic someone into falling in love with you, and you can't magic them into undying loyalty. You can't make them fight or flee in terror—"

"Right," Kinz said, "or your soldiers would make magic in every battle."

Again with the soldiers. "Sure. The point is that you can't change a person."

"Then how does the translation magic work?" Kinz said. There was something odd in her tone, as though she was trying to uncover a lie that had bothered her for some time.

"It's a good question," Cazia said. "Doctor Twofin—he was my teacher—said no one is quite sure where to draw the line between what's possible and what isn't. Some believe the words exist as a separate thing from the person, that it's part of the world."

"Not a physical part."

"No, of course." *I could be hanged for this conversation.* "Not physical, but outside us. It doesn't change us when we hear translated words. Then again, some people believe magic can do much more than we've been told. That we've been lied to all along."

Kinz's expression was stoic. "What do you think?"

"I think there's too much I don't know. Peradaini scholars have the thirteen Gifts, and we've altered them in small ways. You know about that."

It wasn't a question, but Kinz treated it like one. "The Evening People gave you a spell to heal illness and you changed it so it would make to heal battle wounds."

"Yes," Cazia said. Fire and Fury, she should not be saying this, but they were all alone out here, with the ocean just on the other side of the wall and a mountain range between them and the dubious safety of the Sweeps. Cazia suddenly realized that she wanted the older girl's friendship. They'd been through so much together, and yet the clan girl with her beautiful dark face and her oiled braids—fraying now; should she offer to re-braid them after all?—still regarded her with suspicion.

How could Cazia convince the girl to stock up on food and head southward immediately if they could barely share a civil word? Getting home alive, and getting the princess home alive as well, would be hard enough if they worked together. Bringing the Tilkilit stones back to whatever scholars were left in the world would be impossible alone.

"Yes," Cazia continued. "That's why those stones in the pouch at your hip are so important. With them, scholars could create instant fortifications to protect people, without fear of going mad. And they could even join in the fight—"

"With a fire-lighting spell that became a torrent of flame."

So, she wanted to talk about the way the scholars changed the Gifts. "And the spell to purify drinking water became a spell to create it out of nothing, and—"

"Does that not seem strange to you?"

"I'm not sure what you mean."

"The spells are related because they both involve water," Kinz said, "but one makes water safe and the other makes it out of nothing. Perhaps it brings the water to your hands, the way the portal brought the Tilkilit to this valley. Perhaps it makes to transmute one element into another. Still, one is cleansing and one is creation. It is as though the child who had learned to scrape mud from his sole suddenly knew how to make the boot with nothing more than force of will. How do you get from one to the next?"

"I hadn't thought about it," Cazia answered, surprised by the question. "When you put it that way, it doesn't make sense at all. What I can tell you is that the way the spells are cast—the gestures and thoughts—are very similar. The differences between them are pretty slight."

"So, you change the spells however you like?"

Yes. "No. That's incredibly dangerous." She remembered the spell that Doctor Warpoole had cast as they fled the Scholars' Tower; that one hadn't been derived from one of the thirteen Gifts. *Wizard.* Doctor Warpoole had not gone hollow, but where had she learned that spell? How many more wizard's spells were out there in the world? Cazia would never know. "Making a spell any way you please is a sign of madness. At least, that's what I was taught."

"You are holding something back," Kinz said.

"It's hard to talk about this," Cazia answered. "I've been trained to keep secrets and tell lies."

"And when you told me so many days ago," Kinz said, "that I would need the special 'knack' to learn magical spells, was that the lie as well?"

Yes. "Yes."

Kinz's eyes narrowed. "That is what I expected. I thought you might be different from the others of your people, but no. You lie and you take and care only for yourself."

"What? Have you forgotten the king's ransom in raw iron I've already given you?"

"That was scavenge from this camp! By right of discovery, it belonged to all of us and was not yours to give!"

Cazia could have pointed out she had relinquished her share for Kinz's sake, but her anger was rising and she wasn't about to start quibbling. She'd lived her whole life as a hostage in the king's court in Peradain; she knew better than to mince words when someone wanted to be her Enemy. "You have the *gall* to call me a liar!" Her voice echoed off the stone walls. Arguing with Kinz was awful, but letting her voice grow to a shout felt like righteousness. "You lied to me and to Ivy right from the first moment we met, so you and your brother could spy on us!"

"But you knew we were making to deceive you," Kinz countered, "because of your translation stone! So, *you* were just as dishonest with us from the first!"

"And here we see it!" Cazia said scornfully. "The so-called logic and reason of the herding people! Do they teach you to *think* at all, or is everything you do completely justified because you're such a victim?"

"YES!" Kinz screamed at her. "We are victims! Your people rob and murder us, and I will never apologize for anything I do to the Peradaini."

"I'M NOT PERADAINI!" Cazia shouted. Kinz rolled her eyes. "My father is Surgish! Fire and Fury, Peradain is an *empire!* My people were farmers and woodcutters four generations ago when the Italgas *conquered* them. The empire is full of all different kinds of people! Do you know why I lived my whole life in the Palace?" Hadn't Cazia said this already? Why did she have to keep saying it? "Because my father rebelled against the Italga family. That's why King Ellifer kept me and my brother as hostages."

For the first time, a hint of self-doubt appeared in Kinz's expression. To Cazia, it looked like first blood, so she bulled forward. "And you know what? All those different kinds of people are *dying* right now, and we ought to help them. Fire and Fury, I'm sorry if that's just too *complicated* for you, but that's the way the world is, and if you think everything you do to me is completely justified . . . "

Whatever Cazia planned to say next vanished from her thoughts before the words could come together. She was done. There was nothing more to say.

"If you were the hostage," Kinz said without a note of apology, "why were you trained to be the scholar? Why would they teach magic to the enemy?"

So I could be close to the prince and loyal to his family. So I would go hollow and be executed, creating trouble for the tyr my father. "Yep," Cazia said, squelching through the mud as she marched toward the low corridor. Great Way, but she wanted to be as far from Kinz as possible. "Yep, yep, yep. Too complicated for you. Sorry to hear you don't understand *anything at all.*" Without turning around, she dropped low and crawled through the low corridor into the second tower.

Fire take her, why had she said those things? At the far end of the corridor, she crouched in the darkness and peered at the older girl.

Kinz did not seem troubled by their confrontation at all. She stood with her back to Cazia, arms folded, and watched another fish leap through the arch into the mud.

Cazia's own hands were trembling. Why had she tried so hard to win Kinz over? Why had she spoken that way about her Fire-taken father?

Song knew, she had never heard anything good about her father her whole life, and King Ellifer, Queen Amlian, and Lar himself had always been incredibly kind to her. Yes, the palace had been filled with people who hated her because of the rebellion, the death of Ellifer's first wife among so many others, but the royal family themselves had looked out for her, and Lar was her friend. Her best friend after Pagesh Simblin, another traitor's daughter.

And yet, she had just talked about his family as though she approved of her father's rebellion. She'd never even met her father that she could remember. To talk about him as if he was a hero felt like a betrayal of her entire life. Still, in that moment, it had been the clever argument to make, and even worse, there was a tiny part of her that believed it.

The Italgas were dead. Lar himself had been bitten by a grunt; unless someone out there in the real world had devised a cure for him—which was extremely unlikely—he was either dead or a monster, which was practically the same thing.

However, her father was probably still alive in his tiny holdfast on the western frontier. It didn't seem possible that the grunts could have gotten that far already.

She felt an inexplicable pang of regret that she hadn't immediately set out to the west to join him. Maybe—probably—he would have thrown her in a dungeon or had her tortured for information, or . . . Or something. Something awful like in all the stories she'd grown up with.

But maybe he would have welcomed her. Maybe she would have been safe among people who didn't treat her like an enemy of everything decent and honorable in the world. Maybe she wouldn't have ended up here.

There was no hiding the fact that this daydreaming was a betrayal. Lar, his parents, and Doctor Twofin as well had been kind to her, and she had just denounced them to win a stupid argument with a girl from a herding clan. *I'm not Peradaini?* Did she really believe that?

It suddenly occurred to her that Ivy was nowhere in sight and hadn't been for a while. She had walked off with Cazia's jacket and that butchered fish before the big argument and . . .

And she hadn't come running toward them when the shouting had started. How could she not have heard them, unless she had left the tower?

Cazia raced up the stairs through the broad, open room full of beds, then through the other corridor into the stinking first tower. The sun wheel lay on the ground floor by the exit, but Ivy was not inside the buildings. Cazia crouched by the open tower door and peered out at the beach. The princess was nowhere to be seen, but there was a crude trail in the stones leading from the hill where they had first come in sight of the ocean to the tower. Someone else, maybe Kinz, would have been able to read the trail to know if there were three sets of footprints or if a fourth showed Ivy heading back out, but Cazia couldn't do it.

Of course, Kinz was behind her, at the far end of the buildings, and she had their only weapon, that pointed stick. Was Cazia going to run all the way back there to ask her help in searching the beach for the princess?

She certainly was not. Cazia picked up a hefty sharp-edged stone and stepped out onto the exposed beach. She remembered all too well the sight of those servants, so long ago, dragged screaming out to sea. Of course, she and Kinz would have heard Ivy if that had happened to her, wouldn't they? They would have heard over the sound of their stupid argument, right?

Every moment that passed convinced her even more that the girl had been killed and Cazia had let it happen. More, that venturing out in search of her was its own death sentence. She did it anyway, taking step after step away from the entrance.

First, she hurried to the left, checking behind the towers. Ivy wasn't there, and she wasn't on the oceanfront side, either. Cazia stalked up the beach, inwardly cringing at every crunch her footsteps made on the stony beach.

Before she was halfway up the hill, Ivy appeared over the crest. She was hunched over and walking backward as if dragging a body. "Ivy!" Cazia clamped her hand over her mouth and sprinted up the hill. The sun was low over the mountains in the west. Night would fall soon.

The little princess turned and waved briefly, then went back to what she was doing. As she came close, Cazia saw that she was trailing a tree branch behind her, obscuring her tracks. "Ivy," she said, when she was close enough to be heard at a hiss. "What are you doing out here alone?"

"I thought we could throw the Tilkilit off our tracks," she answered simply. "So I rubbed fish blood all over your jacket and left it near the lake shore. With luck—"

From the sea came the sound of a monstrous roar.

Chapter Seven

IVY DROPPED THE BRANCH AND SPRINTED TO THE TOWER BESIDE CAZIA.
The bellowing had come from somewhere out beyond the waves,
beyond the great black stones standing in the water. Cazia peered at the
ocean as she ran, barely looking at where they were going. Somewhere out
there was a creature that could make a sound like the end of the world, and
if it was going to drag her beneath the waves and devour her, she wanted to
see it first.

They reached the relative safety of the black stone tower before the thing
appeared above the water. Ivy, being faster, bolted through the doorway first,
nearly slipping on the stones inside. Cazia followed her up the tunnel stairs.
They met Kinz at the top, and the terrified look on her face must have mir-
rored their own.

"This way," Cazia said, even though she had no idea what to do. They
ran together out of the stinking room, through the low tunnel, to the room
with the flat beds. There, they crouched beside one of the windows and
peered at the waves.

There was nothing to see. A second bellow came, then a third. As near
as Cazia could tell, it was beyond the ridge of black stone that ran into the
sea. Water suddenly splashed high into the air, glittering in the rays of the
setting sun behind them. Churning white wakes washed into view, but the
creature or creatures that caused them stayed out of sight.

Chills ran down Cazia's back. Kinz and Ivy had both begun to sweat in
the chilly sea air, and Cazia wiped beads from her own forehead. As terrified
as she was that some great monster would come out of the sea, now that

she could hear it, she wanted to see it, too. She was desperate to see it. That sound, that bellowing, made her imagination run wild.

On impulse, she grasped the blue jewel in her pocket. She herself had cast the translation spell on it, and not only had it made the Tilkilit's odor-speech intelligible, it had translated the screaming of the giant eagles and the roaring of the grunts. The only thing grunts said was some form of the word "Blessing" over and over, but it was speech. She squeezed the little jewel in her fist while the beasts outside bellowed and roared.

There were no words, just animal noises.

The sun set over the mountain range and the shadow of falling night swept quickly across the tower and the ocean. Things seemed to settle down at sea, just a bit, while the darkness deepened.

Then they heard the noise of churning water, and it grew louder with each moment.

"It is coming," Kinz said, her voice tight.

"What do we do?" Ivy squeaked. "What can we do?"

Cazia's people came from the westernmost part of the empire, and although she had never been there herself, she had listened carefully when storytellers and singers told tales of sea giants.

"We hide. Sea giants only come out after the sun has set, because their eyes are sensitive to light. They'll be able to see us if we stand at the windows."

"Are you sure this is a sea giant?" Ivy asked.

"No. I've never seen one, but this matches the stories. I thought they were only in the west, but—" Another bellow echoed across the beach and through the tower. Cazia tried to make her voice calm, hoping the princess would be reassured. "This tower has stood here for a long time. Either they'll leave it alone or they won't be able to damage it."

It turned out to be the latter. None of the girls raised their heads to look through the window, but throughout the night, they heard gigantic forms splashing through the shallows and stomping on the beach. The bellowing was painful to hear, and the thunderous blows to the side of the tower were even louder. Cazia wasn't sure if they were punches or kicks, but the wet slaps against the black stone made the whole structure tremble.

For half the night, it continued. The bellowing, the keening, the massive impacts against the side of the tower raged on and on. Cazia began to have flashes of the grunt she'd killed at Fort Samsit. There was no reason for that particular memory to come back, but there it was, large in her mind. In her mind's eye, she saw the beast leap onto the prince—the king, Lar was king then—and bite him. She had used the Tenth Gift to strike it down. The moment was right there, vivid in her thoughts. It was only later that she'd realized the grunt had been her own brother, transformed.

As far as she could remember, the grunt had died without a sound, but with every boom came the image of the iron tip of her dart sliding between her brother's ribs, piercing his heart. The flinches. That's what Old Stoneface Treygar had called it.

Despite everything she had been taught, she withdrew from the others and allowed herself to weep in the darkness. She allowed tears to touch her cheeks.

Eventually, her fear began to ebb and the whole thing became annoying. The tower was going to hold, it seemed. The beasts outside—whether they were sea giants or not—seemed less like deadly monsters and more like the worst neighbors in the world.

Somewhere near midnight, the moon rose and the noise began to recede. If Cazia was ever going to see the creatures, it would have to be right this moment. She rolled to her knees and peered through the nearest window. Kinz hissed at her in disapproval, but Ivy joined her.

She saw it, but not well. The silver moonlight shone on the thing's back as it moved into deeper waters. It looked like a silvery mound or a glacier. It was rounded, and where it might have had shoulders, there was no head. It was like watching a mountain of dirty ice glide into deep water.

The girls immediately fell into a deep sleep right there on the stone floor, and when they woke late the next morning, they began a long debate over what they should do next.

Ivy wanted to leave immediately. She abjectly apologized for bringing Cazia and Kinz to the water for her pilgrimage and considered it complete. She also thought they still had a hope of reaching the Northern Barrier before the Tilkilit. Cazia bit back a few sharp remarks about the religious significance of their night of terror; the princess had an exhausted, hunted look, and Cazia thought she might have caught a bit of the flinches herself.

Kinz wanted to stay there for a long while. At least a full month, possibly longer, if they could manage it. They had found a safe place, one that no one knew about, and a source of food. They needed to rest here before they moved on.

"What about the Tilkilit?" Cazia asked. The grunts were her main concern, but it wasn't Kinz's.

"They think we drowned, yes?" Kinz looked from Ivy to Cazia, checking their expressions. "They were still able to make read of our minds, and I kept thinking about how I had fallen in and was drowning."

"Yes," Ivy said. "So did I. Is that not what—Oh, Cazia."

Her expression must have given her away. "I thought a message to the queen asking to be rescued from the riverbank on the north side because I *thought* we were swimming to the southern bank."

Kinz exhaled loudly. "Inzu's breath, if you had thought about dying in the water, they would not be searching for us at all."

"I don't believe that," Cazia countered, but she did believe that their idea had been better than hers. She folded her arms so she wouldn't be tempted to sulk.

"They would have searched for us," Ivy said. "The queen would have insisted. That is why I laid out Cazia's jacket on the lakeshore where they can not miss it. They will find it before they find this place, and since Cazia's the only one they really want, I think they will give up."

"Even so," Kinz said, "we can stay here the while to make provisions. All I need is wood for the drying rack and the fire. If we can collect that early in the day, we might have it smoked before tomorrow morning."

Of course, they did not rush out to gather it right away. They slunk into the first tower and peered carefully through the windows. Luckily, for once, there was little fog. The beach showed no evidence of any activity of the night before, not even footprints. The stony beach looked much the same as it had the previous day, except there were more clumps of tangled gray seaweed. Whatever had come out of the water had left little evidence of the incredible commotion it had created. More importantly, it was not in sight now.

All three girls left the tower together, hiking over the steepest part of the hill to the land beyond. What they found surprised them: whatever had come out of the sea had ventured farther inland than they thought. Three trees had been crushed beneath a terrible weight, and the girls eagerly rushed forward to collect the splintered wood.

It stank faintly of sour salt water and rotten fish, and some pieces had a nasty reddish jelly on it. Blood? None of them were quite sure, so they didn't touch those. Cazia and Kinz loaded their arms with so much wood, their shoulders ached, while Ivy swept a leafy branch over their footprints to obscure them.

It was a little after mid day, and everything was still except the endlessly rolling waves. Cazia had to admit that while she still hated and feared the ocean, after a full day living beside it, she'd learned it was alluring, too.

Instead of entering through the tower entrance, Kinz insisted they walk around the structure to the stone block building at the back. From the outside, the deep pool and the arch looked like a place to empty chamber pots. The ground was made of gray, sandy mud, and the hopping flies that were so awful inside the building were twice as thick out here. The pit made it impossible to enter through the arch, so they threw the wood inside piece by piece.

Once inside, while Ivy operated the stone handle, Kinz used several of the longer pieces to build a rack. Cazia organized the firewood and quietly, slowly, tried to access her magic.

The Third Gift was complicated. She knew how to shape that spell in any number of ways, sending streams of flame or bolts of intense heat from her hands. In fact, there were almost as many ways of altering this Gift as there was for shaping a stone block or creating water, and she now understood those alterations instinctively.

Unfortunately, the Tilkilit stone had made her own power remote from her. She could make the hand motions and bring out the mental state necessary to summon her magic, but it was as if the magic that fueled the spell had been struck numb.

It had been a little more than a day since she'd last touched one of the stones. All she needed was a little tongue of flame, no bigger than the light of a lantern. Surely she could manage that.

And she did. It exhausted her, but she did it.

Ivy used the lever to summon up two dozen fish and a pair of eels. Kinz split the fish open and hung them to dry over the fire. The eels she roasted right away. By the time night fell, they had let the fire die out, but the delicious smoke still lingered. And the buzzing flies had fled. In the darkness, terrible blows fell on the towers, but the building held.

Magic. Now that she thought about it, Cazia could sense extremely faint traces of magic inside the walls and floors all around them. She had no idea who could have built this, but the fabled sorcerer-kings of ancient times seemed like the most likely candidate. Hiding here was like being inside Monument itself.

The thought gave her chills. Could this have been created by the sorcerer-kings? If so, where had they gone? Maybe there was another Door in the Mountain somewhere, or maybe they went into the sea. But Cazia had never heard of a building like this anywhere in Kal-Maddum; who ever cast the spell that created it had to be long gone, but where?

What's more, what was the connection between the sorcerer-kings and the Tilkilit?

Eventually, the moon rose and drove the creatures below the waves. This time, Kinz and Ivy held tight to Cazia's arms, refusing to let her peek out the windows.

In the morning, they wrapped the dried fish in one of the round cloths and prepared to leave. The tower might have been proof against the beasts of the ocean, but they could never defend it against the Tilkilit, and Cazia did not doubt they were still looking for her. While Cazia sat in the top of the tower, trying to decide if she could chance a stone-breaking spell to free the enchanted cube from its lever without ruining the spell, she saw Kinz wrap her heavy iron crown in one of the circular cloths and start down the stairs.

After a few moments, Cazia trailed behind. Before she reached the bottom step, she heard a loud ringing of metal on stone. She hurried forward and came to the entrance to the corridor.

From her spot at the side of the tunnel, she saw Kinz standing beside the lever. She had the cloth in hand, wrapped around the crown. As Cazia watched, she swung the weight a second, then a third time.

That was all it took. The stone lever shattered and tumbled out through the arch. The enchanted cube—containing a spell that Cazia had never even thought possible—fell into the pool and sank out of sight.

While Kinz stood beneath the arch watching the moving water, Cazia darted up the stairs. That spell, if she'd learned how it could work, would have been a powerful weapon against the grunts. She might have commanded them to run into the ocean. She might have commanded them to attack each other. She might have . . .

It didn't matter. It was gone now, and there was no doubt why Kinz had destroyed it: to keep it out of Cazia's hands.

Kinz returned with a long, black fish she had cut open with her flint. Cazia kept stoic as she piled the odd wooden tools from the cubby and lit them with the Third Gift. Ivy and Kinz chatted amiably as they ate.

That finished, they slipped out into the growing fog. Their boots crunched on the stony beach, and while they could not see which direction led to the ocean, they could walk uphill.

The fog became so thick, they could not see more than ten feet ahead. The girls held hands and kept silent, with Cazia in the lead and Ivy just behind her. Cazia kept the sound of the waves on her left, trusting that to be compass enough to direct her southward. Kinz carried the bundle of dried fish and the Tilkilit stones, while Cazia held the pointed stick.

They moved through trees, stumbling over roots and ducking below low branches. In the wet air, every twig that snapped beneath their feet seemed as loud as a slamming door. It took very little time for Cazia to convince herself that the Tilkilit were just ahead, tracking them.

Finally, a change in the wind blew most of the fog out to sea, and the sun burned off the rest. The three girls found themselves facing a cliff of black rock.

Any momentary delight that they had already reached the Northern Barrier was quickly squelched once they realized they were facing the ridge of black rock that they'd seen by the ocean. Cazia had been leading them directly south rather than southwest, but no one seemed to mind. They turned due west to go around the spur.

Moving away from the ocean lightened Cazia's spirits quite a bit, and the other two seemed to feel the same. They smiled more and dared to whisper once the sun was shining again. The only tension that didn't ease was between Kinz and Cazia. Cazia resented the older girl because of that enchanted cube and because she felt she'd been maneuvered into denouncing the Italgas. Kinz kept her distance for her own reasons.

When the sun was near the western peaks, the giant eagles appeared overhead, gliding in slow circles as they searched for prey. Cazia couldn't believe they were still hunting inside the Qorr Valley when they had the whole continent laid out for them. Let the birds take a few of The Blessing out of the world, she thought, and immediately flinched at the memory of her brother's death. Her voice was sharper than she intended when she suggested they find a hiding spot among the rocks.

After they'd eaten their modest portion of dried fish, Kinz slipped away to dispose of the bones far from their camp. Cazia had expected to hate the food, but she didn't, and she could not bring herself to say so aloud.

"You and Kinz had words," Ivy said.

There was no avoiding this conversation. "Apparently, she thinks I'm the king of Peradain, and that every command Peradaini soldiers follow comes from me."

"Big sister, that is not fair."

"What about what's fair to me? Why is she blaming me for things I have no control over? I never ordered anyone to kill herders or collect taxes from them."

She half expected Ivy to say those taxes were really tributes, but she didn't join the argument that Cazia would have preferred. Instead, she said, "And yet you wear the clothes, and carried iron weapons, and eat cakes and compote, and you have learned magic. All of these things are either forbidden or impossible for her."

"And you."

"Yes. And me, too. You have never handed a spear to a soldier in your life, but you have enjoyed the wealth and comfort those spears have brought."

"What should I have done instead? Go naked through the wilderness, eating skewers of okshim?"

"Cazia Freewell," the girl said huffily, her fists on her hips like a disapproving schoolmaster. "You should know better than to try that sort of argument with me."

Freewell. Even her family name was Peradaini. She had no idea how it would have been pronounced in the original Surgish. Even when she was trying to learn her people's tongue, she had never had the nerve to ask. "So, where does that leave us? She has decided that we are enemies, so we are. I will work with her to get you safely back to your people. After that, we can go our own ways. Or fight to the death, I guess, if she's going to insist on it."

"Go our own ways will be good enough for me," Kinz said, slipping back into their hiding spot in the rocks. "I might make to change my mind if you keep talking about making the servant of me."

From far above, they heard an eagle's cry in the growing darkness. Cazia leaned out from under their protective outcropping to look at it, but the princess's tiny hand pulled her back. Fine. They slept like the dead all through the night.

The next day they started southward again. On this side of the spur, the fog was thinner. That let them navigate toward the mountain range looming ahead of them more easily, but it also left them exposed to the eagles. Cazia wished she had managed to get hold of her iron darts before she escaped. The others had already warned her not to cast a fire spell at the eagles because it would reveal their location to every living thing in Qorr Valley, and without darts, she would be reduced to casting rocks at their enemies, like a naughty child.

It was embarrassing.

For three days, they skulked and sneaked across the valley floor, keeping to the trees as much as possible and not moving at all during sunrise and sunset, when the eagles were most active.

When they finally reached the base of the Northern Barrier, they saw a twining shaft of that same noxious climbing weed they'd used to enter the valley. Kinz exclaimed quietly and lunged forward, but Cazia caught her arm.

They crouched together at the base of a twisted tree while Cazia peered into the distance.

"There," she said, pointing to a space below an overhang of rock. "A Tilkilit soldier, standing guard."

CHAPTER EIGHT

Ivy was sure there was no way around the sentry. She wanted to retreat into the valley and create weapons for each of them. Stone weapons, of course, since knapping flint was the best they could manage.

Cazia hated the idea. The Tilkilit's spear points might have been made of copper—which wasn't even as good as the bronze weapons the Indregai used—but they were metal. She did not want to face a trained Tilkilit warrior with a piece of stone in her hand.

"Stone can kill people," Kinz said, as though she was tempted to prove it on Cazia.

"So can diarrhea," Cazia snapped. "But I don't want to rely on it in a fight. Why not go around him?"

Ivy peered through the trees at the cliff face. The climbing weed formed a sort of twining tower among the rocks. They were certainly faster and more convenient than using magic to tunnel. "That is the only vine for as far as I can see in either direction. There might be more, but the longer we look . . ."

"The more likely we are to run into a full patrol."

Kinz sniffed. "I would rather make the risk with the one guard. There are three of us and we have faced them before. I am not afraid."

"We were armed before," Cazia pointed out. "And I don't mean with flint axe heads and sharp sticks. Have you forgotten how strong they are?"

Kinz flinched and touched the shoulder the Tilkilit had broken. "Even so—"

"Even so, we can try to sneak by them and fight if we have to. All we have to do is wait for nightfall and sneak over to the side of the mountain.

We can tunnel up to the ridge the same way we did on the other side of the mountain."

Ivy and Kinz shared a look that suggested they knew this was coming and they feared it. "We remember that well enough," Ivy said gently. "And we remember what it did to you. How it changed you."

This conversation was unavoidable. "It hollowed me out," she said. "It turned me into . . . into a wizard." Not that they would understand what that meant.

"It made you mad," Kinz said flatly. "You cared for nothing and no one, not even this girl you call *little sister*."

"It hollowed me out," Cazia said again. What did they think she was talking about? "But now we have the Tilkilit stones. If things begin to get bad for me again, you can touch one to me and return me to normal. You can lay the stone on me every three days."

"Every day," Kinz said. "You make the magic and, at the end, we *cure* you of it."

"I'd need a full day off to get my magic back. We don't have enough supplies for that. I did three days climbing the first time, so it should be enough."

Kinz was adamant. "Every day."

"Every two days," Ivy said. "Cazia is right about our supplies, Kinz. Also, Cazia, you tried to be careful on the way up the mountain, did you not? Knowing there is a cure nearby would make anyone reckless."

"Fine. Two days." Cazia half expected Kinz to argue but she didn't. "Maybe I ought to call you *little diplomat*. But going hollow isn't the only problem we face. The other side of the Northern Barrier is straight vertical— just about—and covered with fused rock. I knew what I was digging through as I went. On this side of the mountains, it's rock mixed with dirt, and you can't tell when you'll come out into a ledge or rift. What's more, we'll have to leave the bottom of the tunnel open to circulate air. I can partially block it, but if the Tilkilit find it—"

"They will have found us," Ivy said.

"Probably. The thing is, the stone I create to block the tunnel will be pink granite; it won't match the rock around it. I don't know how long it would take them to dig through—I'm sure they could, eventually—but they would have a hidden path to the top of the ridge. They wouldn't be able to get their worms out of the valley, but they could get troops out and, I don't know, capture a scholar from somewhere to dig their big tunnel."

"I would rather you made to collapse the tunnel behind us," Kinz said.

"I would rather breathe," Cazia said sharply. "On the other side of the mountain we had the Sweeps winds to stir the air in the tunnel. For this trip, we'll have to break through the wall more often."

Ivy glanced upward. Three of the giant eagles circled overhead. "But just small breaks, yes?"

"As small as we can get away with."

The Tilkilit sentry was about two hundred feet above the valley floor, wedged into a space below a broad overhang. The dark red of its shell was nearly perfect camouflage in the mountain of the rocky overhang, but its white sash had given it away. The spiral vines grew just below it; the warrior had a commanding view of the area. Worse, the ground was largely made of loose stone with few trees. The girls would have no cover and no way to move quickly or quietly across it.

There was nothing to do but wait for whatever protection darkness might provide.

Kinz spent an hour of the fading daylight searching for a second stick that they might sharpen. There was little flint available on the bed of the forest, but a long branch with a sharpened point would be better than nothing. While she searched, Cazia found a handful of slender sticks about the width and length of arrows. The Tilkilit had taken her iron darts, and she wondered if she could fashion wooden ones as a substitute.

They were not all completely straight, of course, and she had never studied arrow-making. Still, she sharpened one end and straightened them as best she could.

When they seemed as ready as she could make them, she slipped away from the others to try them out. The spell that shot darts was her favorite and had been since she and Lar made a game of it in the practice room; as absurd as it sounded, she missed it.

However, her wooden darts were a complete failure. They had no ribbon at their tail and no fletching, so they couldn't be made to fly true. She tried breaking them down to much smaller sizes, from the length of her hand to the length of her middle finger, but it was no use. No matter how she cast, the spell made the darts tumble after they left her hand.

Ivy might have had useful advice for her, but Cazia didn't ask.

She could still cast stones, of course. The Tilkilit themselves, having a shell where humans had soft skin, carried a small mace instead of daggers. Maybe a blunt stone would be a better choice than a sharp spike.

She also had her fire spells. Since going hollow, she could attack farther and hotter, either as streams or bolts. Before the Tilkilit had captured her, she'd killed one of those monstrous eagles with a single spell.

Still, she wasn't powerful enough to take on a whole army, and the others were right: a fire spell would burn like a beacon. *Here is the scholar you were hunting.* Every Tilkilit in the Qorr would converge on them. Cazia could fight—especially now that she'd gone hollow and then been cured—but spells were complex and slow to cast. Scholars were like archers: easily overwhelmed in close quarters.

There are three of us and we have faced them before. I am not afraid. Kinz had said. For all her bravado, Cazia was acutely aware that Kinz herself, the largest and strongest of the three of them, had not killed a single Tilkilit warrior. At least, not that she'd noticed. Little Ivy had shot at least two. The rest had fallen to Cazia's Gifts.

It was odd that her memory of the fights in the Qorr Valley were so vague while the escape from Peradain and the shot that killed her brother were so vivid. She shut her eyes—just for a moment—while the familiar flush of nervous anger—

Tap tap tap.

That was the Tilkilit click language, and it was coming from somewhere to the west. Cazia retreated to the little copse where she'd left the other girls. They stood in the gathering darkness, holding their pointed sticks like warriors readying for battle.

"Where were you?" Ivy whispered. "They're coming."

"Up," Cazia said. "There are too many to fight."

She boosted Cazia up into the lowest branches of an old—actually, she had no idea what kind of tree this was. Its bark was as yellow as a daisy and as smooth as ice. The bare branches were so thick, they didn't even rustle as she climbed, and the trunk bulged in places as though it was full of tumors. Once again, she was reminded that it wasn't only the creatures that were strange and alien inside the Qorr.

Ivy scampered into the place where the trunk split into a fan of thick branches, then kept climbing. Cazia knitted her fingers for Kinz to step into them, and after a moment's irritated hesitation, she did. Once she settled into the notch of the tree, Kinz lowered her long stick to pull Cazia up.

Cazia fought the impulse to turn and run, leaving the girls up in the tree. She wasn't sure if it was because she wanted to save or abandon them, but she knew it came from an absurd and immature desire to show them how much they needed her. Instead, she grabbed Kinz's stick and climbed, wishing she were the sort of person who went through life without ever suffering dishonorable impulses.

It took longer for the Tilkilit to come into view than expected. The sun had sunk below the highest peaks by then, and the glowing sky barely lit the forest floor.

The warriors moved carefully through the gloom. They carried their copper-tipped spears and parry sticks, of course, along with nets and some sort of lash Cazia hadn't seen before. Their heads did not come anywhere near the lowest branches of the tree, and as slowly as they moved, none of them thought to look up.

As they moved away, vanishing in the darkness, Cazia realized she was holding her breath. Good. She held it for a little while longer, letting the creatures get farther away before she made any sound at all. If they were going to be caught, it wouldn't be her fault.

"Hinge," Ivy whispered, so quietly that Cazia wasn't sure she was speaking at all. "That was a hinge sweep, where one end of the line barely moves at all and the other circles it. My uncle said it is used to drive your enemies toward a place where they can not retreat. That is why they were making so much noise."

The little princess had the most rigorous schooling of anyone Cazia had ever met. "I didn't notice," she admitted, although it made her a little ashamed to say so. "Which direction were they trying to drive us?"

"South."

That meant the warriors were heading for the Northern Barrier. Fire and Fury, it would almost have been better to be driven toward the mountainside. At least they would have been closer to home.

Unless there were more Tilkilit in hiding near the rocks.

It didn't matter now. The creatures were headed toward the cliff face. The girls wouldn't be able to make their escape until the way was clear.

They ate sparingly and slept in the unyielding branches of the strange tree.

Ivy woke Cazia before dawn. "You were snoring," she whispered. Cazia apologized and groaned. Her back and legs ached, and her belly was empty. She was hungry all the time now; if she ever returned to civilization, the first thing she planned to do was eat until she was stuffed.

Fire take her, she meant *when she returned to civilization. When.*

"It will be light soon."

Kinz was right. The eastern sky had faint traces of dawn. If they were going to move, it would have to be now, while the dark still hid them. Otherwise, they would be stuck in the forest for another day, hiding from enemy patrols.

The three of them crept from tree to tree, heading south toward the mountains. There were no signs of the Tilkilit, except for that single sentry. She could see firelight dimly flickering in the cleft behind him.

"He'll see us," Kinz said. They all looked eastward, where the ground became stony and the trees sparse. The moon had not yet gone down. "There isn't enough cover that way, and we're only going to find more sentries if we head westward."

"Back!" Ivy whispered, pulling them closer to the tree trunk. A shadow moved against the stars above them. One of the giant eagles was hunting this part of the valley. No, there were two. Maybe more.

"Inzu's breath," Kinz said. "We need a distraction to get across this open ground."

The Tilkilit's fire. The more Cazia thought about it, the more she thought there must be some way she could use it. It was small enough that the overhang hid it from the eagles above, but—

"I have an idea," she said, a little too loudly. She searched back in her memory for the opening to the Ninth Gift. Doctor Twofin had taught it to her when she was younger than Ivy, but she hadn't practiced it much.

It was a spell for fighting fires. Six months before the Ninth Festival, half of Peradain had burned to the ground, and the Evening People had given the Peradaini king a spell to put out fires at a distance. A great distance, in fact. No other Gift had a range like the Ninth.

According the Doctor Twofin, the king had been dismayed at first, until one of his commanders used it to extinguish the cook fires of the Paydl holdfast for forty-two days straight. The local tyrant eventually threw open his gates and broke his spear against the stony road.

Cazia herself had used it in the palace when the servants were especially cruel to her, at least until Doctor Twofin had ordered her to stop.

There it was in her memory: the opening mental image was an expanding cloud. She moved through the motions and visualizations of the spell, feeling her own magic reaching out to quench the fire.

But not all the way. She was careful to make the fire die down but not go all the way out. The sentry needed a few moments to notice, but once he did, he quickly set to tending it.

From where she crouched, Cazia couldn't see what the Tilkilit was doing, but she saw him move toward it and do something. With luck, he would not simply rearrange the fuel. He would add more.

She pressed harder, squeezing the fire down without killing it. Her conversation with Kinz about her water spells came back to her, but she tried to clear them out of her mind. No, it didn't make sense that she was squeezing fire, but that was what she did.

The sentry continued to tend the fire. When Cazia saw him draw back in what she imagined to be consternation, she broke the spell.

As she hoped, the Tilkilit had been adding fuel to his dying fire, and this new fuel caught and flared. It was brighter than she'd dared hope for. The light glowed against the vine tower and some of the stones of the cliff.

Immediately, from high above came the shriek of one of the giant eagles, then another and another. Cazia heard their beating wings before she saw their silhouettes hovering near the sentry's post. Their cries were piercing and full of rage. The temptation to grasp the translation stone in her pocket was strong, but Cazia resisted it.

Ivy had already sprinted out of cover.

Cazia ran close behind. The eagles swarmed above them and to the right, raising a terrible noise and panic around the sentry's position. One bird tore at the vine tower. Another touched down on the overhang as though trying to push it onto the warrior below.

Slipping her hand into her pocket, Cazia gripped the stone. Instantly, the shrieks of the monstrous birds became words.

"Make it touch the ground! Drive that weight away from here! Drive it to the ground and tear it apart!"

She stumbled, almost dropping her translation gem. Kinz caught her elbow and helped her upright, then they ran again. Cazia put the stone in her pocket and left it there. She didn't need to hear any more.

The spot Ivy ran toward was sheltered, but not well. Cazia already had the Eleventh Gift in her mind as she came up on it. Again, she began the spell so that the stone she crumbled would fall out of the wall onto the ground around them. Then she did it again and again. They climbed inside the open space; Song knew how much she hated the feeling of crawling across sharp, broken stone. She cast the spell again.

Stones tumbled down around her, filling the space behind. She heard Ivy and Kinz follow her into the tunnel but ignored them. She cast again and again, going deeper into the stone out of sheer panic, making the tunnel wider with every spell.

Despite everything she'd said earlier, she dug in a way that blocked the tunnel behind her with loose stone. The darkness around them was so complete that Cazia had to press her hands against her eyes to see spots, and the air was thick with dust. The stones above might collapse on them. The

Tilkilit might hear them through the rock and crawl in after them. The eagles might scrape them out. There were Enemies everywhere, and not the sort who would hide a wet mop head in your sheets. These Enemies would kill them all.

Calm. Calm. She cast the Eleventh Gift two more times, first to create a narrow vent for air no wider than her thumb, and another to create a small chamber for them to crouch in. She shoved the loose stone out the vent, knowing it might give away their position but trusting that her diversion was still going.

She heard the others coming close and chose a stone the size of her fist to turn into a lightstone.

Ivy and Kinz were both grinning at her, their eyes alive with excitement. Cazia realized they were right to be excited, and she barked out a little laugh.

They all clasped hands. "Together," Ivy said. "Together together together together."

Cazia squeezed their hands and felt a sudden flush of goodwill toward them both. She really hoped it would last.

CHAPTER NINE

TEJOHN WAS STARTLED. KILL THE MAN WHO HAD TORTURED HIM, WHO had ordered him stripped of his belongings and sentenced him to a year of hard labor for the crime of eating a heel of bread? Kill the man whose orders ensured the fall of Ussmajil and the deaths of Tejohn's own people?

"I won't do it," he said.

Beacon Veliender did not blink. "You've killed men before."

Tejohn realized the old fellow at the next table was staring at him even more intently. "I've killed men and women in battle. Some were so young, they were practically children. Some were so inept with their weapons, they might as well have been unarmed. But I've never been an assassin."

"That's not the only reason."

"No. Is this what it's like to have strong vision? To see every detail of a person's face and read their intent?"

She smiled and picked one last apricot from her bowl. "Am I so easy to read?" she asked before eating.

"Not at all," Tejohn said. "You're very controlled at the moment, and even if you weren't, I would have a hard time. It's not as though I've had a lifetime of practice. Still, no, it's not just that I would become an assassin. A few short months ago, the very idea would have driven me into a fury, but since then the world has been destroyed. I've been everything from a"—*regent of a ruined empire*—"king's shield bearer to the lowliest of servants to a prisoner in a dungeon. Someday, I'd like to return to my family to be a husband and father again. But . . . "

Everything he wanted to say sounded ridiculous, but he soldiered on. "Everyone I've ever killed has been someone's child, but Shunzik Finstel is the child of my tyr. My old tyr, when this city was still called Splashtown and I was a young man still raw with my grief. Samper."

"You fought for Tyr Samper Finstel."

"No. I fought for my own reasons, but he was our leader. Our tyr. He was a hard but honorable man and he deserved respect. My father thought so, anyway. He lost as much of his family in those battles as any of us, but when I asked him to let me follow the Italgas back to Peradain, to get away from the memories here, he was kind enough to let me go."

"And how you have returned. With Shunzik Finstel out of the way, there would be one true tyr left inside the city." Tejohn gasped in surprise. This was not what he'd expected to hear. "Someone who had been born here and had led our people to victory a generation ago when hope seemed so thin. Someone with experience against this new enemy. Someone who could make *proper* preparations for the upcoming fight."

Tejohn felt dizzy for a moment. Could the temple truly make him tyr over Splashtown and all her lands and people? Make him king?

The very idea made him want to walk away. It was impossible. Ludicrous. Someday, someone might write a song about him, but it would not be a tale about building a tower.

"A king with no spears but the one in his hand is not a king at all," he said. "But even if you could make me believe the soldiers of Ussmajil would rise up to support me, I won't kill the old tyr's son. I just won't do it. When I needed to get away, he let me go." *I have more important things to do.*

"I was afraid of you," the old man said. He pushed back from the table and shuffled over to sit beside Veliender. "You were so angry and so popular with the soldiers. More than you knew. You still are, I think."

Tejohn stared, astonished. Could this tall, lean man with the sullen brow and the clean-shaven jaw really be him? Tejohn put his hands on the table to push his chair back to stand, but the old man . . . Samper Finstel waved at him to be still.

"Don't stand up. I'm not a tyr any longer, just an old priest without even any duties. Sweeping. They let me sweep. Don't be surprised, my boy—Song knows, I shouldn't call you that—it's long been the tradition of my family for leaders to retire into religious service when they became too old to fight alongside warriors in battle. It goes back to the days before the empire, but it's not public knowledge anymore." Samper managed to lower himself into the chair, but it was obviously painful for him.

Tejohn lowered his voice. "Was this a test?"

"No."

"Do you *want* me to kill your son?"

"Yes," the old man answered. "But no. No, no, a thousand times no."

Tejohn turned his attention back to Veliender. Common sense suggested that seeing the king's father here would confirm that his escape from the dungeon and time on the sleepstone had been a trick, but he didn't believe it. Now more than ever, he knew he was free.

"I have another duty," he explained. "Even if I were willing to turn my steel against the Finstel family, I can not spare the time. The king—Lar Italga—gave me a task before we separated, and I intend to complete it."

Veliender waved her hand as though her previous offer was a wisp of smoke she could dissipate. "You still plan to go to Tempest Pass for that spell, even without your scholar-king."

"I am. Still." Tejohn turned his attention to his old tyr. "I'm sorry, Beacon, but this mission might save everyone, not just the people of Ussmajil."

"We will help you," Veliender said. "And provide you with a companion who has had scholar's training. He can learn your spell."

Tejohn nodded gratefully to her. "Thank you."

Samper's gaze was unyielding. "Return quickly. Your people need you."

The old man shifted in his seat to look out to the eastern sky. Tejohn had the feeling he had been dismissed, but he did not stand and back out of the room, not when the sun was still rising, showing him not only the city below, but the Southern Barrier and Great Falls as well.

Not that anyone would be using those Peradaini names anymore. Tejohn would have to learn the old ones again. Someday. For the moment, he sat on the terrace and watched the day begin. It was glorious.

The priests eventually got up and began their day, but Tejohn stayed. Movement, detail, spectacle: the strained expression of an old man lifting his barrow. The cracks in the black mud smeared between roof tiles. An orange-striped cat sauntering over a sill into someone's apartment. The world was finally revealing itself to him, and it was overwhelming. How could people live their whole lives with such extraordinary detail and think it mundane? Someday, it would be the same for him, he knew, assuming he lived long enough to get accustomed to his new vision.

Eventually, he became restless; he had a mission to complete, which had already been delayed for too long by his imprisonment and recuperation. He stood and noticed Javien sitting behind him.

Tejohn's first instinct was to begin issuing orders, but he quashed that. He wasn't a commander anymore, and Javien certainly wasn't a servant. Tejohn would never take another servant again if he could help it.

Servant or not, Javien nodded and immediately began gathering the supplies Tejohn would need for his journey. Food was scarce within the city, as Tejohn guessed, but water was never hard to come by. They would have to find most of their supplies in the lands outside the city.

Worst of all, they would be traveling without spear, shield, or armor. Only red priest's robes would allow them to pass unhindered out of the city. Any weapons or armor they would need would also have to be scavenged or traded for. At Tejohn's insistence, they packed gray robes so they could change once they were out of sight of the city walls. They would not be sneaking through the Southern Barrier wearing red if he could help it.

It was midday when everything was ready. Too late to start, but too early to sleep. He spent the afternoon working in the temple, splitting firewood in a basement room beside a furnace. It was vigorous work and he enjoyed it, but he was anxious to be on his way.

That evening, he had the real surprise. He could not wear red robes with his beard. It would have to be shaved off.

Fire and Fury, but he felt strange afterward. Looking at his reflection in a bucket of water, he thought he looked almost like an incredibly ugly woman. Laoni would have barred the door against him if she'd seen him like this. He rubbed his chin vigorously. "Fire and Fury."

Javien, standing beside him with the razor, said, "The Little Spinner never slows."

True. It would grow back. But Fire take the world if he was going to die beardless.

They gave him a priest's cot in a private stone chamber for the night. It wasn't luxurious, but it was a king's feather mattress compared to the boards he slept on in the servant's quarters. His face chilled by the cool night air, he slept heavily and did not dream.

He woke in the darkness. Glancing eastward, he saw once again the faintest glow of the beginning of the day.

He shook Javien, who did not exactly spring awake happily. They ate a large bowl of watery rice beside the kitchen fires, gathered their packs by candlelight, and headed to the door without anyone to bid them well. Tejohn felt like an escaping prisoner again.

The streets of Ussmajil were not as crowded as Tejohn had expected. When he'd been there twenty-three years before, he'd seen refugees sleeping in the gutters and alleys. He'd expected to see worse today, but of course the refugees had been treated just as he had: they'd been turned into servants.

Just the thought made Tejohn reconsider Veliender's assassination mission, but only for a moment. Laoni, Insel, Alina, and Teberr—his wife and three children—were on the far side of the Straim, the widest, deepest river in Kal-Maddum. At least, they were supposed to be. Grunts couldn't swim, but that wouldn't keep them out forever. He needed to turn this conflict with the grunts around before they were lost.

I can not bear to lose another family—

No, those thoughts would only drive him mad. He had to focus on something else.

"Javien," Tejohn said. "Have the grunts crossed the Shelsiccan River?" The priest's answer surprised him.

"Yes, my tyr, but not in force."

"Then Fort Caarilit did not hold?"

"They have. However, while the grunts have not crossed the water, men and women who have been bitten have. We don't have enough soldiers to patrol the entire riverbank, and some have slipped through. While there are none of the original grunts in Finstel lands, transformed humans have begun to run amok."

The answer made him feel a bit sick inside. Humans who had already been bitten but hadn't turned might cross the Straim easily under the cover of a moonless night.

Anxiety flooded through him. His children, murdered again, but this time, he would be on the other side of the continent. Memories of that first tragedy flooded back, and the pain made him stumble slightly.

"My tyr, are you well?"

"Don't call me that any more," Tejohn snapped, but he couldn't bring himself to look at Javien. His head was bowed but he could not see the muddy cobblestone street. All he could see was the body of his first child, distorted horribly by the spear thrust that had cut him open. It had been the first time Tejohn had ever seen a human being killed by a weapon of war, but it had not been his last. Not at all.

He let Javien lead him through the streets, barely aware of the people they passed, the decaying wooden buildings, or the smells of morning fires. Instead, he suffered an internal pageant of blood, grief, and terror of the sort he had not experienced in many years, knowing it could happen to him again.

At the little gate, Javien answered the guards' questions. Tejohn came back to himself after they'd received permission to leave the city and started across the westernmost bridge over the White Cap River. *This bridge should be destroyed,* he thought, momentarily confusing the bridge from East Ford that crossed the Straim with the one he was standing on, and then he snapped out of his trance.

"Are you well?" Javien asked. His expression and tone made it clear he was rethinking their expedition.

"I am," Tejohn answered. "I have not been haunted by my memories in that way for many years, but it has passed."

Javien glanced back at the gate as though about to return through it, but he didn't.

"Javien," Tejohn asked. "Did the temple spare you any coins to purchase food for our trip?"

"Not a speck," he answered. "There's no meatbread to be had, either, not for the prices we would have to pay. Supplies are scarce with so many refugees. We will have to work for our meals."

Or steal them, Tejohn thought. Their mission might stop human extinction; surely they were obligated to complete it without unnecessary delays. It was an unsavory thought—he was sure the priest would mutiny if he heard it—but Tejohn had done worse. "I'm sure the White Cap River isn't called that any more. What's the Finshto name?"

"Uls, my . . . " Javien stopped himself. "I'll have to be careful not to do that again."

"Say *friend* if you have to, but it's better if you don't have to. Priests don't call each other 'friend,' do they?"

They reached the other side of the bridge and started down the broad main square. The shops on either side of the street looked very like the shops inside the wall, but the early risers setting up for a day's custom were armed with knives and bludgeons. The looks they gave Tejohn and Javien were not particularly welcoming. "Not as a habit."

"So, that's settled. Have you chosen a route through the Southern Barrier?"

"I have. We'll be keeping to the main road through Finstel lands. This is the Sunset Way we're walking on now; it will be heavily patrolled by the king's spears, so we're unlikely to be waylaid. In the middle of the third day, we should come to a northwestern caravan track that will take us to the Salt Pass. The fort there is held by friends to the Finstel people, unless the Bendertuk have done what the Bendertuk like to do."

"And from there into the Sweeps," Tejohn said.

"Yes." He stopped himself from saying *my tyr*. Good. "I don't know those lands at all. No roads, I'm told."

"No, but we'll manage."

Javien wrung his hands. "There are bandits, I'm told, once you get off the Sunset Way."

Tejohn noted a group of young men gathered at the mouth of an alley. Crowds moved along the road, carrying baskets and sacks for the day's shopping, but those boys stared at Tejohn and Javien with an unwavering intensity.

"We will treat everyone as a bandit," he said, "including soldiers." Javien was about to protest, but Tejohn cut him off. "What do we have that would be valuable to thieves?"

"Our knives."

"Everyone has knives. Don't play games with me, priest."

Javien looked uncertainly around him. He didn't notice the crowd of young men that had stepped from the alley and now trailed the pair down the street, but he did notice the lingering looks people gave them. "Our robes. The gates of Ussmajil are closed to everyone but the tyr's inner circle, the king's soldiers, the wealthy, and priests."

"Fire and Fury," Tejohn spat. "You could have told me this before. We shouldn't be walking around—"

"I'm a priest of the temple," Javien insisted, his voice sounding thin. "I am not ashamed of my calling."

"You should be ashamed of your stupidity."

Tejohn whirled around. The group of young men—Great Way, they looked so young—had come close. Tejohn glanced at the tallest of them, thinking he might be the leader, but no, there was fear in his eyes. It was the shortest of them, built like a tree stump, with the authority.

"Which of you would like to donate your weapons to the holy temple?" Tejohn asked.

They laughed at him. The little boss let his cudgel rest on his shoulder and said, "We have had our fill of donating to you priests. Come into the alley with us. It's time for you to donate to our temple."

Javien tried to step around Tejohn. "Blasphemy!"

If the young priest expected them to be cowed, he was disappointed. One of the young men put his knife between his teeth and made a rude gesture. Two others with cudgels mimicked their leader's body language. Without turning his head, Tejohn placed his hand on Javien's chest and pushed him back. It was one thing to have another soldier at his shoulder, but this priest would only get in his way.

The cudgels didn't frighten him; in unskilled hands, a club was good for intimidation and killing enemies who have already surrendered. But those two knives—

"Boys! Boys!" The call was loud, shrill, and cut through the noise of the crowd like a knife through apricot pulp. "What are you doing to those priests?" The crowd of shoppers parted to let an old woman push through.

The young leader rolled his eyes and let his cudgel drop to his side. "Nothing, auntie. We were just talking."

The old woman charged up to the leader and jabbed her finger in his face. Her gray hair was a tangle of dreads, and her face was tanned so dark she could have been Cazia Freewell's Surgish grandmother. But no, her accent was pure Finshto. "Don't you lie to me, young man! Don't you ever! If your father could see what you've grown into, he would brain you where you stand! Trying to rob a priest right in the middle of the street, yet!"

Javien tried to push by Tejohn again. "And they blas—"

Tejohn elbowed him in the gut and he fell silent. "Grandmother, we were only talking. There's no need to be angry with them."

The old woman turned on Tejohn as though about to scold him, then she looked him over, appraising him as though he was a suspect piece of fish. "You're no priest. That one is, maybe, but not you."

"We're all taking roles we never expected to take, grandmother. Let me ask you, do you know the danger that is coming?"

She glanced around warily. "I've heard rumors." Her nephew edged closer.

Tejohn shook his head. "It's going to be terrible, worse than a generation ago. It will be like facing a raiding army of grass lions."

"You've seen them?" she said, squinting harder.

"From a distance. I've also seen brother turning against brother, wounded men executed, and general panic. The berms and walls of Ussmajil won't protect you. These boys need to be preparing for the fight that's heading toward you. Don't you have someone to teach them to handle a spear? Those sticks and kitchen knives will do them no good, and they've told me they're anxious to learn."

"I know someone, but the king's spears have forbidden it."

Tejohn's scowl demonstrated how he felt about that. "Song knows who will fight for their family and their lands, and who will not. Let the king's spears collect their tributes from the common folk. You have to look after yourselves."

"These boys," the old woman said carefully, "were going to rob you—don't bother to deny it; I know who they are. And they blaspheme, too, when they think I can't hear. Why are you lying for them?"

"Because a time is coming"—Tejohn glanced over at the leader, who stared defiantly at him—"when they will have to fight harder than they've ever fought in their lives. A time of terrible danger and great deeds. And you will need them. If they linger in alleys, they won't be ready. They'll be torn apart in front of your eyes, or flee in terror through the wilderness. But if they learn to fight, they—and the others who stand with them—will slay their enemies the way the Finshto always have."

The group of young men—Tejohn couldn't bring himself to think of them as boys, as the old woman had said, not when he'd seen younger men killed in squares—shifted uneasily. The old woman glanced back at them. "It hardly seems likely."

Tejohn bowed his head to her out of respect. "Grandmother, can you recommend a shop where we can purchase supplies? We have a long journey ahead of us."

She got a little gleam in her eye, then ordered the young men to wait for her in her courtyard. They shuffled through the crowd, looking from one to the other as though they'd been given a gift they didn't want, while her sharp words followed them. Then she took Tejohn by the elbow and dragged him off the Sunset Way down a narrow sidestreet into an empty bakery.

The man behind the counter had thinning hair and gray pouches under his eyes. His skin sagged as though he'd once been quite fat but had been starved since. Working behind him was a tall girl with frizzy hair bristling off her narrow skull. She was covered with flour and jam stains, and her work at a bench that was too low for her left her with a permanent stoop.

"Beacons!" he called with the delight of a man who sees too few customers. "How may I serve you today?"

"You're old enough," Tejohn said to him. He turned to the old woman and waved her off, driving her out of the shop. She took it as an insult, but she went. To the baker, Tejohn said, "You're old enough to remember the last time these lands were at war."

"I am," he said, wiping his hands on a dirty cloth. The stooped-over young woman edged toward the counter.

Tejohn looked sharply at her. "I don't like to be stared at."

The baker shooed her back toward her bench. "Don't mind my daughter, sir. She's an honest girl."

Daughter. Perfect. Tejohn began to haggle.

CHAPTER TEN

Javien was furious, of course. He was of the opinion that a beacon's robes were sacred, and that Tejohn had blasphemed by trading his away for mundane things like loaves of meatbread and other supplies. Tejohn let him rant for a long while about trusting in The Great Way and the special significance of red and the duty every Peradaini had to lead others along the right path and priests especially so and blah blah blah. It was insufferable, really.

Still, Tejohn let him exhaust himself all through the long walk to the end of the market, where the king's spears gave them a quick glance and dismissed them. If they were still looking for Tyr Tejohn Treygar, they were not much interested in a beardless man with a long, morose face being hectored by a shrill priest twenty years his junior.

However, the guards were very interested in a farming family heading toward the city in a hay cart. Every one of them, old woman to young child, stood in a circle of spearpoints, stripping down to their skins.

When they were well past the guard post and out into the farmlands, Tejohn laid his hand heavily on the young priest's shoulder. "That's enough."

"No, it is not enough! You don't seem to realize—"

"Be quiet or I'm going to cut off your ear." That caught his attention. "Beacon Javien, what role do you think you have on this mission?"

The young man seemed a little uncertain. "Beacon Veliender put me in charge."

"That's not correct. Young man, you are a convenient basket. I'm going on a long trip to retrieve something of value, and you are a convenient means for me to carry it back to civilization. If you become inconvenient, I will discard you and find some other means. Your whining and hectoring were invaluable in getting us past the guards, but I've had enough."

Javien wasn't satisfied. "Beacon Veliender ordered me to bring this spell of yours back to the temple so we can save the people of Ussmajil. And how will we bring it into the city without robes? Do you see how this hurts us? It's a simple task, but . . . She gave you your sight!"

"And it's a glorious gift," Tejohn said. "I plan to make good use of it while I try to save all our lives, but this mission came from Lar Italga, the last king of Peradain. That might not mean much out here in these splintered lands, but should mean quite a lot to his uncle, the scholar hermit we're traveling to see."

"But to trade away that robe!"

Apparently, Javien had already forgotten Tejohn's threat, or perhaps he thought it was a bluff. Tejohn considered cutting off one of his lobes—just a little bit—to make his point. But no. It would feel good, but no.

"That robe might save that girl's life. That's why the merchant bargained so dearly for it. His daughter—his only child—had been barred from even the dubious safety of Ussmajil, with war coming. I'm sure he hasn't forgotten how it felt the last time. Do you think I care about some red cloth? Do you think he cared about blasphemy? He wanted to protect his daughter, his only child, and I helped him do that. But what are you worried about? Clothes. Propriety."

That silenced him for a time. Tejohn took advantage of the quiet to become accustomed to his new vision. The road was lined with trees that, in the growing heat of the summer morning, bristled with leaves. What had once seemed to be clouds of color was now an intricate arrangement of discrete leaves and branches. He knew all these trees had names and he resolved to learn them soon so he could understand better what he was seeing.

What's more, it seemed as though he could hear better as well. When the wind rustled leaves, he could look up and see it happening. A different rustle came from a branch being shaken by a climbing squirrel. His senses were tied together now in a way he hadn't appreciated before.

It astonished him. Everything did.

The road had been built well; flat stones were joined close with pulverized rock and dried mud. The ditches on either side were deep, and beyond them, the farms sloped upward gently. To the north was the Southern Barrier, as misty and beautiful as Queen Amlian had described them so many months before. To the south, the land was uneven, but he knew it would eventually slope downward to Deep Stone Lake and the Waterlands to the southeast.

This was wheat country, and judging by the height of the stalks midsummer had not come quite yet. The smell of dung was quite strong at some fence lines, where the farmers had let too much fertilizer run down into the roadside ditches.

It wasn't an unpleasant smell for Tejohn—it reminded him of hours spent working with his father, not very far from here. It also brought back darker, less happy memories.

Midday came and went before they saw people. At a bend in the road, two old men with leathery skin stood at the bottom of the fence line, talking in low voices. Tejohn was startled to see that they looked like servants in better clothes. Was that how he and his father looked in their day?

"Good day, Beacon," the skinnier old man called. The hefty one turned and waved reluctantly at Tejohn and Javien.

"Good day to you both," Javien answered. "What news?"

"No news," the skinny one said. "But we have plenty of rumor. If we could collect rumors by the bushel, we could buy the whole northern side of the valley. What news from the east?"

"The city is still closed," the priest answered. "Have you seen refugees heading west?"

"A few, a few," the farmer said. "But they weren't Finshto. Our folk don't get a warm welcome in Bendertuk lands, even still. Lots of folks seem to have fled in the night." The old fellow cleared his throat, glanced at his companion, then glanced nervously into the hills. "Any word of . . . them?"

Javien turned his empty hands toward them. "Rumors. My pockets are full of them."

"And little else, I'll wager," the heavier farmer said.

"You'd win that one," Javien said kindly, "but the only prize would be another tall tale. Still, the walls of Ussmajil stand, and king's spears guard the roads."

"Aye," said the skinny farmer.

"That's a blessing," said the heavier one.

Tejohn took hold of the priest's sleeve. "It's time we moved on. We have a long journey ahead of us."

"Where are you folks heading?" the heavy farmer said. "If you don't mind me asking."

"Simblin lands," Tejohn answered immediately. "We're hoping to turn some rumors into actual news." Javien looked startled by that answer, and the two farmers noticed. Tejohn bulled on anyway. "We're hoping to go cross-country at some point ahead, roads being what they are. Do you think there's a friendly farmer in these parts who might give us passage across his land?"

Both farmers snorted. The skinny one said, "If you see a piece of land without a fence on it, you give it a try." There had been no breaks in the fences since they'd left the market.

Javien performed a brief prayer over them, for which they nodded their heads in thanks. The heavier farmer called, "May Fury bless you," as they walked away.

"Why did you do that?" Javien snapped. They were not quite out of earshot, and Tejohn clenched his fist to urge him to silence. Unfortunately, the priest was not so easily cowed. He spoke again, his voice quieter but just as urgent. "Farmers will usually make donations to traveling beacons. If you'd given me more time, I might have gotten some eggs or flatbread out of them."

"The Blessing says its name," Tejohn whispered. "Didn't you hear me explain it to Beacon Veliender? It's not simple grunting noises that the grunts make; they're calling out their name in their own language. When cursed humans begin to transform, they start to say it, too. 'Bless this bless that I don't bless what you're blessing.'"

"Do you think he might be . . . Could the curse be so close?"

"We need to get off the road." Tejohn started walking faster, then glanced over his shoulder. "Soon. And you need to stop giving away my lies. Cultivate some control over your expression."

They kept going, striding down the empty road all through the middle of the day. Tejohn broke a heel of meatbread and they ate it on the move.

There were no people. A road like this so close to the city, even during the summer when there would be few crops to sell, should never be this desolate. Were there no vagabond musicians, no tinworkers, no young fellows crossing the valley to spy on some farmer's daughters?

No refugees?

Tejohn heard the clack of crockery tapping together from up ahead. Javien started toward the nearest fence, but Tejohn grabbed hold of him and kept him close.

An okshim came plodding around the bend of the road. Its short fur was mostly gray with a few scattered patches of brown, and the curving horns above its eyes were thick and heavily ridged. It was an old beast, slow-moving and tired. The leather yoke around its neck was worn and split.

Behind it was a wooden cart loaded with everything a farm family might want to save from their home: folded cloths, a box of tools, a coil of rope, leather straps, cooking utensils, and more. They were common goods, but that was what they had.

A short, curly-haired woman sat at the front of the cart, holding the okshim's reins. A pair of young children with pale eastern complexions sat on the back of the cart, and their father, a big, yellow-haired man who must have come all the way from Indrega, followed behind, singing quietly to them.

Tejohn hailed them, then moved almost into the ditch to let them pass. It was the okshim's horny soles making the crockery noise against the stones of the road, and he'd seen the beasts lash out to the side with those big, flat feet. No okshim was ever so domesticated that you didn't have to worry about a sudden kick.

The curly-haired woman was older than he'd first thought, just a few years younger than himself. The blond man was at least ten years her junior. "It's a fine afternoon to be out, Beacon," she said, ignoring Tejohn all together.

"Indeed it is. We're so close to midsummer, I would have expected more heat."

"Once the rains stop blowing through, we'll have enough heat to frizz your hair worse than mine. Safe travels to you."

With that, she turned her attention to the road. She wasn't interested in any further conversation. "The roads seem unusually empty," Tejohn said.

"Think so?" She glanced at him but did not slow the okshim's slow steady pace.

Javien had stepped toward the woman when she spoke, but Tejohn pulled him back. "Are you heading to Ussmajil?"

"We are. And you should be, too."

"It's dangerous there."

The young husband moved toward the back of the cart and laid his hand on a billhook.

"Points high," Tejohn said, showing his empty hands. "There are king's spears at the edge of the market who examine everyone who comes down the road. If you have any bite marks on you or patches of blue fur, you're better off turning back."

"If we had bites on us, there would be nowhere we could turn, but I thank you for the warning."

"What's happening here?" Tejohn insisted. The cart had come even with him and he walked backward to stay within the woman's sight. "This priest and I have a long way to travel yet, but I can't protect him if I don't know—"

"Many of these farms are empty." Her voice sounded flat. "Many of my neighbors have been carried away. If I were traveling westward through the Whiswal Vale, I would stay off the road, seek out no human company, cook nothing, and do no hunting. You never know what you'll find in the heavy brush at the edge of a stream."

"And the people?"

"The people are gone," she said, then clicked her tongue to make the beast pick up its pace. Her pale-skinned, pale-eyed companion watched them suspiciously as he passed.

"The Little Spinner never slows," Javien said. "Fire pass you by, and peaceful be your journey on The Way."

The man from Indrega said, "Grateful am I to be permitted to travel The Way." There was an ironic note in his voice, as though he was pledging an oath he knew he would break.

Tejohn and Javien watched them go, then started westward on the road again. "I had hoped to avoid this," Javien muttered. "I had hoped the danger would not have reached here already."

"Misplaced hope has killed more people than spear and sword combined," Tejohn said. "Let's move quickly."

They did not leave the road immediately. They followed it along the base of the valley as it wound around gullies and tumbles of rock. Finally, toward the middle of the day, Tejohn saw what he was looking for.

It was an orchard, planted on a slightly steeper part of the northern side of the road. Tejohn led Javien over the fence of the adjoining property—they were growing hops, and the smell of it kindled many happy childhood memories—then climbed the wooden rail fence that separated the farms. Tejohn showed the priest how to jump from the top of the rail to the other side of the netting at the base of the orchard, something he hadn't done since he was a boy, then they moved quietly up the hill.

"Time for you to change out of your red robe," Tejohn said.

"What if the farmer objects? A beacon's colors can still smooth over—"

"I think this property is abandoned. Did you notice the rents in the netting at the base of the hill? We're going to approach the farmhouse cautiously. If there's firelight inside, you can change again."

"It will be some time before the end of the day," the priest answered.

True enough. They climbed the hill as quietly as they could. When they finally reached the crest, they came to a bare meadow with a modest house at the far side. It was larger than Tejohn expected, with mortared stone walls on the western side and a wooden tile roof. Someone had done quite well for themselves.

They crouched just out of view of the house and waited for darkness to come. Tejohn had to stop the priest from making a fire, which clearly annoyed him. Javien insisted that a campfire at night would keep wild animals away, and Tejohn spent a long time explaining that would not work on grunts.

They ate sparingly from the packs, watching for signs of life inside the house. There were none. Finally, early in the evening, Tejohn ordered Javien to stay where he was and ran to look into the house.

All but one of the shutters were closed, and the back door had been broken off its hinges. Knife in hand, Tejohn crouched in the doorway, utterly unable to see into the pitch black of the room. There was no stink of blood or rotting corpses, for which he was grateful, but he would not be able to truly investigate the house until it was lit by daylight.

He withdrew and circled back to break the news that Javien would be spending the night on tree roots without a fire. Tejohn took first watch. It was well past midnight when they switched.

A gentle hand shook him awake. His eyes snapped open to see pre-dawn light shining through gentle drizzling storm clouds. Javien's face was close to his. "Fire has come to take us both."

Tejohn rolled over quietly and lifted his head high enough to see the house. Someone or something was crashing around inside, and it was only a few moments before a pair of shutters burst open and a grunt began to climb through.

It was one of the blue ones, Tejohn saw, what King Lar had called a "little brother." The original grunts who had come through the portal in Peradain were huge creatures and had a faint purple coloring to their fur. This was a transformed human, turned into a monster with a bite.

It was covered with dark blue fur with red stripes running across its head and torso. The skull was shaped like a melding between a human and a bear, but the eyes were quite close together and the sloping forehead was covered with a thick bony plate.

Its thickly muscled arms ended in humanlike hands, but they were longer than they should have been. It tumbled onto the grass, and Tejohn could see that its legs ended in a second pair of hands. All four limbs sported long claws that were as curved as a hawk's talons. There were sharp little spurs at its elbows and knees. On its back, protruding from swirls of red and blue fur, were bony protective ridges.

This was his first good look at a blue one while it was alive. While the big brothers had tremendous, irresistible power, this one had a deadly quickness about it.

Javien gasped slightly when he saw the grunt, but the light rain muffled the sound. The beast lifted its bearish head and displayed its long fangs. It appeared frustrated, as though it knew prey was close but could not locate it. The beast lifted its leg and urinated against the side of the house.

Tejohn laid his hand on his knife. As weapons went, it would not be enough to defeat a grunt but, with luck, the creature would lose its life taking his.

The pointed ears on the top of its head twitched, and it turned to the east, rising up on its hind legs to stare off into the distance. It huffed loudly and growled, then sprinted across the meadow toward the next farm. Fire and Fury, it was fast and graceful.

"Monument sustain me," Javien said. "Was that the thing that tore down the Peradaini empire?"

"No," Tejohn whispered. "That was its little brother. Follow me."

The priest objected in a low, harsh voice, but he followed all the same. Tejohn led him along the edge of the meadow to the path the grunt had taken. It was a trail wide enough for an okshim, and the grunt had already sprinted down the long slope almost to the rail fence.

On the far side of the fence was a piece of pastureland. Sheep fled uphill, bleating in terror. Standing partway up the hill, maybe twenty paces from the rail, was a line of five soldiers.

CHAPTER ELEVEN

CAZIA KNEW IT WOULD BE MORE DIFFICULT TO CLIMB THIS SIDE OF the Northern Barrier, but she had underestimated it. The far side of the range was made of rock that had been melted into a uniform solid. This side was a mix of dirt and stone that crumbled and shifted as she dug. That first antechamber had been a little too wide and the roof began to shift. Ivy squealed in terror; Cazia created a narrow block of pink granite to shore it up.

"Mining," Cazia said weakly. "Amateur mining." None of them wanted to linger in that space.

They climbed higher, carefully clearing small ventilation holes with their hands so that the stones wouldn't tumble down the side of the cliff and draw attention to them, then stopped for a short while, sleeping in a line in the narrow tunnel.

When they woke, they could see daylight through their narrow air shaft. It was barely past noon. They ate lightly and Cazia began to cast her spell, breaking the stone above them to the east, then pushing it behind her.

Had it been such slow going the first time? It must have, but it hadn't seemed so.

At the end of that day, she created a narrow space for them all and announced it was time to rest. Kinz immediately pressed a Tilkilit stone against her leg. Cazia gasped as her magic was torn away from her, but she had gotten used to the effect and recovered quickly.

"That was dumb," she said.

"Every two days," Kinz said, as though she knew all along that Cazia would protest. "That was our agreement we made. Two days of spells: dart-shooting and stone-breaking. One day becoming the normal person again."

"I know. But you could have at least waited for me to create enough water for my recovery day."

Kinz seemed genuinely abashed at that. At least their lightstone was new enough to last a few days. Cazia covered it and they did their best to sleep on the stony floor.

When she woke, Cazia had no idea what time it was or how long she'd been sleeping.

Kinz murmured, then spoke. She was talking in her sleep, pleading someone precious to her that they should "leave the others." She sounded terribly upset.

Cazia laid her hand on the older girl's shoulder and said gently, "It's just a dream. It's just a—"

Kinz suddenly thrashed awake. "OFF," she said, her voice a harsh whisper. "Never make to touch me! Never!"

Cazia couldn't believe the girl's nerve. "You were talking in your sleep and I—"

But Kinz wasn't interested in an explanation. She wanted to hold on to her outrage. "Never!"

"What is it with you two, anyway?" Ivy said, obviously annoyed. "If we are going to be trapped in these awful, filthy tunnels again, can we not be decent to each other?"

"Tell her that," Cazia snapped.

"I am telling both of you! I hate the digging. I hate the cramped space. I hate the way my knees get all scraped up. Do you understand? This is hard enough without you two doing *this thing*. I wish you were Ergoll so I could order you to behave."

"We will behave," Kinz said. "I have made polite in less agreeable company."

Cazia sighed. "I'm not very good at polite, little sister."

Ivy grinned and hugged her. "But you will try for me, yes?"

The girl was adorable when she smiled. "Absolutely not," Cazia said. Ivy laughed. Cazia loved to hear her laugh. "We're going to be stuck here a while. Why don't you tell us something about your people? Tell us about the way you grew up."

They spent the day talking about themselves, sharing more of their personal histories than they ever had before. The princess started first, and everything she said surprised them. Her family didn't have a palace and she didn't live separate from her people. They had a series of high-peaked houses where they spent the year, migrating from one part of the peninsula to another. Only the villa atop Goldgrass Hill had a sort of wall around it. Ivy lived among her people, being scolded by baker's wives when she misbehaved and generally running wild in the mornings. Her afternoons were spent with tutors, and her evenings were spent with her parents, working with them by the fire on their weaving or leatherwork.

"It's stories all the time with us," she said. "There never seems to be an end of the stories my father or uncles had to tell me. Usually it was absurd tales that made no sense. My uncle Nezzeriskos had only recently begun to tell me grownup stories. You know, histories and things."

Cazia knew Ivy's uncle had been living with her in Peradain when The Blessing overran the city. "What was your uncle like?"

"Funny! He had a very sharp wit and knew just how to make me laugh. It was wordplay with him all the time. He could be melancholy, too. Once, when I found him sitting alone by the fire late at night, I asked him why he was sad. He promised to tell me someday when he was older. Now I'll never know."

Kinz took Ivy's hand and squeezed it.

Cazia took a deep, calming breath to prevent her from saying her next thoughts aloud. Any of them might die without their stories being heard. All the things she had seen in the Qorr Valley would be lost if the tunnel collapsed or the Great Terror swooped down on them from above.

After she had gone hollow, she had wanted to return to human civilization for . . . what? The memory was a bit fuzzy. She remembered *having* the feeling, and that the feeling had been strong, but she had been a different person. She'd wanted to return to the world and be famous for what she had seen and done. She wanted to tell her story.

To say that was an unexpected side effect of going hollow would be to understate things quite a bit. Cazia herself had never sought fame for its own sake; everyone in the Palace already knew who she was (and most hated her). Fame had always seemed more burden than anything else. Her hollowed self had also been powerfully curious.

She looked around at the tunnel and the situation she was in; obviously, curiosity was her own trait as well. But why—

Kinz broke her reverie by talking about her life following an okshim herd. She described the long treks, the travel through the Sweeps, the time and effort they spent fending off attacks by mountain lions and lakeboys. She described the Shelterlands where they spent their winters, so close to the ocean, but which was, she insisted, perfectly safe.

Her people too, told stories, but they told the same stories to young and old. Fantastical tales, tales of virtue rewarded, tales of heartbreak and lost love.

The last kind had been her favorite. She admitted, with a little flush of her sun-darkened cheeks, that she had sometimes imagined herself in the center of one of those stories.

Well, duh, Cazia wanted to say. Of course she could be in a story about heartbreak. She was the most beautiful girl Cazia had ever seen, no matter how dirty she got.

Before she could say anything, Ivy asked, "Were you chased by boys?" with unashamed glee.

At this, Kinz became uncomfortable. "Boys, yes. And men, too. It was not like in the stories. It was not always very nice. The women in our clan made to protect me sometimes. Too many times. Of course, all of those people are dead now."

Kinz glanced at Cazia as though expecting her to say something hateful or horrible, although of course she would never. But Cazia felt she ought to say something kind or comforting. Her mind was blank.

Ivy took hold of the older girl's hand and held it tightly. "Tell us about them."

She did. She spoke for many long hours, and she shed many tears.

Eventually, it was Cazia's turn. She did not think at all about what she might say, and let the truth spill out. She told them about living as a hostage in the king's court, about the father she never saw and the friends she was never parted from. She talked about the kindness of the royal family and the petty cruelties from everyone else. She did her best to minimize the frustration and loneliness and talked more than she'd intended about the first Italga queen, the one her father had killed. It was supposed to have been an accident, but no one cared. She'd died before Cazia had been born, obviously, but it seemed that nothing rekindled the palace folk's love for her more readily than the sight of Cazia there within the walls. Then she changed the subject so she could talk about the food she stole from the kitchens.

It seemed that she had gone on longer than the others, until she suddenly ran out of words. She was describing the old scholars who toiled endlessly in the Scholars' Tower, and then there was nothing else to say. Darkness had fallen outside and her throat was dry. If only she'd had a chance to create some water for them.

But her magic was still barely a tingle. There was nothing to do but sleep. The other girls looked at her; she looked back, uncertain what to say. *I murdered my brother.* She wasn't the only one enduring grief.

On the morning Peradain had fallen to the grunts, one of the people she'd fled with—the Scholar Administrator, Doctor Warpoole—had looked back at the city and lamented at the loss of music, theater . . . Great Way, the *writing* that was lost. Such a rare, precious skill. The tower was full of maps. Had they been lost when the city burned?

It made her sad and sick to realize that so much had been wasted. On the same day, everyone that had come to live in the city with Ivy had been lost. The members of her royal family that tutored her and cared for her, plus all their servants and relations.

And shortly after, Kinz and her brother had lost everyone they knew, leaving them to wander alone in the Sweeps.

All lost. All orphans. They stared at her so strangely, and she knew she was staring back. She'd been so self-righteous with Kinz back in the tower on the beach, and it had felt so good. It had felt like strength.

Cazia felt tears welling up and so she lay down on the stony floor and covered the lightstone with the edge of her skirt. Yes, it would prevent the light from shining out of their ventilation hole, but it would also hide her tears. Scholars should not weep.

They woke hungry and parched. Cazia's magic had mostly returned; she created a depression in an empty part of their chamber and filled it with water. They took turns easing their thirst, lapping at it like cats. She encouraged them to drink as much as they could, because their smoked fish was already half gone.

Then the tunneling. The higher they went, the more loose the material they moved through. The tunnel seemed slightly less stable with every few feet. Finally, about midday, the thing Cazia had feared finally happened. As she finished a spell, the mountain around her collapsed suddenly. They fell outward, thankfully, exposing all three girls to a blinding shaft of daylight, but it was the noise that was most alarming. The minor avalanche made the entire tunnel vibrate. She'd come out into a rift in the mountainside.

There was an immediate shriek from just out of sight, and Cazia scrambled backward as the shadow of one of the huge birds passed over the end of the tunnel. "Move! Move!" she whispered, driving the other girls deeper into the tunnel with her heels.

Something heavy struck the tunnel ahead, collapsing it further. A wedge-shaped rock broke free of the tunnel roof, and Cazia had to curl herself very small to avoid it. She scraped her forehead on the tunnel floor and thanked Fire for passing her by.

Crouching in the darkness, Cazia peered over the stone that had nearly crushed her skull at the daylight visible ahead. A plume of dust obscured her view, but she quickly realized she didn't need to see. The dust swirled as the eagles beat their wings near the opening, screeching and swooping toward the rift.

Had they seen her? If they dropped a stone or one of those gigantic tree trunks, the tunnel might collapse, crushing or suffocating all three of them. Gooseflesh prickled on Cazia's back as she realized the sight of motes churning through the air might be the very last thing she saw in her life.

It didn't happen. The eagles moved away, taking their noise and commotion with them. Something had them agitated, but Cazia couldn't imagine what it could be . . . Unless they assumed her tunneling was one of the gigantic Tilkilit worms trying to catch them by surprise.

Of course, if she had taken hold of the translation stone in her pocket, she would have known what they were saying, but to do that she would have had to shift the piles of dirt and small stones on her, creating another small dust cloud. She was curious, yes, but not so curious she was willing to risk catching their attention again.

It took some time, but the eagles eventually moved far enough away that their cries were barely audible. Cazia counted to a thousand, then shook the dirt and stone from her hair and clothes. They retreated to the little chamber where they'd passed the night, and Ivy took the lightstone from her pocket.

"I'm sorry," Cazia said. She hadn't planned to apologize, but it came out of her anyway. "I couldn't feel that rift in the mountain."

Kinz tried to wipe dirt from her forehead with her dirty hand. Cazia realized she was drenched with fear sweat. "They seemed mildly annoyed." Her deadpan tone made Cazia and Ivy laugh a little despite themselves.

"It might happen again," Cazia said. "I can't always tell how much rock there is when I cast a spell. And that collapse might bring more eagles."

"Or the Tilkilit," Ivy said.

None of them liked the thought of that, but if their enemies met, they might occupy each other long enough for Cazia to . . . what? What could she do against three giant eagles or a full squad of warriors? Even now that she had become a wizard—the first sane wizard in history, as far as she knew—she didn't have enough control of her magic to defeat that many enemies at once.

"Can we double back?" Ivy asked. "Can we head westward up the cliff face, away from the rift?"

They had to. Cazia led them back up the tunnel, and, near the top, she cast her spell directly to the south. They couldn't do a switchback like a mountain trail, because the tunnel floor might collapse, but she could cut deeper into the rock and slowly angle back toward the cliff face and the fresh air it allowed them.

Cazia had learned the spell miners use to break rocks, but she had not learned the skills they needed to break rocks safely.

She led them in a curving section of tunnel, making it very steep, until she came once again to the cliff face. The air shaft she dug and the daylight it showed her were more than welcome, but the sound of beating wings that came directly after made her blood run cold.

She began to make the air vents on an upward angle, and that pleased them all. Cool, fresh air flowed down the hole toward them, and the girls paused at each new one to take a break from the dust-choked air.

One good thing about digging the tunnel so steep was that gravity helped tumble the broken rock from the path ahead. The down side was that Cazia had pebbles and grit in her hair and down her neck. Ivy was right. Tunneling up the mountainside was awful.

Finally, in the late afternoon she reached the peak.

"It can not be," Kinz said from behind her. "We could not have made to reached the top so soon."

"But it is," Cazia insisted. "I can feel the edge of the stone above us, and on all sides, too."

They glanced back down the steep slope, lit only by the dim daylight entering through the air holes. Could they have reached the top after only two slow days of digging?

"Maybe the ground is higher on this side of the mountains," Ivy said. "The peaks are the same, obviously, but—"

"The ground *is* higher," Kinz said. "And the peaks are a little lower in the east as we make near the sea—"

Cazia felt a sudden clutch of fear when she realized she had been moving eastward. What if she caused an avalanche that swept them all into the ocean?

"But still, I do not think we are there. Not yet."

"I would be surprised, too," Ivy said. "But why not break open the southern face so we can see?"

Cazia took a deep breath and began the spell, taking care to break only a small portion of the stone. It fell away, revealing a little space of air, and then another sheer stone cliff.

Of course. She had led them up one of the false peaks that stood beside the cliff. "Monument sustain me." She cleared a slightly larger gap so she could get a better view, and leaned forward. The gap was only about six feet across, but it was about thirty five feet straight down to where the two stone walls met.

The cliff face opposite her rose straight up. That couldn't be the top of the Northern Barrier, could it? To the east, partly hidden by fog, was another peak, even steeper and higher than the one she'd climbed. To the west was a jutting rock that blocked her view of everything beyond.

Kinz and Ivy squeezed into the space beside her. "We will have to backtrack," Ivy said, sighing.

"Song knows I'm in not mood to cover the same ground yet again. I have a better idea." Cazia cast the Eleventh Gift twice more, first widening the space where they were all crowded together, then to open a space in the stone opposite. She didn't like the noise and dust the falling stone made, but there was no other choice.

After that, she was quiet a moment, considering the changes she would have to make to the Sixth Gift to make it do what she wanted. Yes, that should work. She cast it.

A broad flat pink stone appeared, bridging the gap. Cazia leaned out and put her weight on it. It wobbled a bit, but it wasn't too bad. Not too bad at all. She started across.

"I should go first," Ivy said. "I'm lightest, and . . . Without you, none of us can get away."

A bank of fog blew through the gap, and Cazia was almost glad to see it. More stones fell from somewhere; she could hear the sound of them striking bottom echoing in the cleft.

"I have to cross to continue the tunnel. I'll be fine, if you'll watch the sky for me."

Cazia started across, a little unnerved to hear stones still bouncing down the mountainside. The fog would hide her from the eagles above, she was sure, but she could tell those sounds were coming from too far away to be caused by her tunnels. Were the eagles perched just above, ready to swoop down on her as soon as the thin fog cleared?

More noises from falling stones, but this time, they made Cazia's hair stand on end. Before she even realized she was in trouble, she slipped her hand into her pocket and touched the translation stones.

"Advance!" she heard, in that distinctive high Tilkilit voice. "Hunt! Capture! Ward!"

She glanced westward toward the top of the overhanging rock. Perched high above, barely visible in the blowing fog, was a Tilkilit warrior. It pointed its spear at her.

CHAPTER TWELVE

Instinctively, Cazia began the Tenth Gift, but of course she had no iron darts, not anymore. She broke that spell and began the Eleventh as soon as she realized her mistake.

Too slow. There was no way she could get the spell off quickly enough. Maybe it would miss.

The Tilkilit warrior above reached into the pouch at its belt, drew back its arm, and then threw. There was no place to dodge. Cazia flinched, but kept her spell going. *Too late.*

Kinz stepped onto the bridge, her pointed stick held above her head. She swung, and was rewarded with the sharp crack of wood on stone. "I hit it!" she exclaimed, her eyes wide with surprise.

The Tilkilit on the rock above stood in apparent confusion for a moment, then reached into its pouch again. Two more appeared above the crest of the overhang.

The Eleventh Gift finished. Cazia directed it toward the base of the overhanging rock. It was some twenty or twenty five away—farther than she had ever attempted before, but she had stretched her will to the limits.

It worked. The stone crumbled and fell away, causing the overhanging boulder to shift. The movement seemed so small, but all three Tilkilit warriors lost their balance. The first one, another stone in hand, clicked loudly. She didn't need a translation stone to recognize its fear.

The stone continued to shift. It slowly rolled outward and, alarmingly, toward the makeshift bridge Cazia had created. The Tilkilit warriors were unable to cling to the rock, and they slid down its face. Cazia and Kinz could see them, coming closer and closer, as they slipped and tumbled down the side of the rock, then under it.

It's going to crush us, Cazia thought, her throat going tight. She seemed frozen in place.

But no. It shifted to the side and wedged against the spire they'd just climbed. It was only when the boulder became still again that she realized how loud it had been when it fell.

"Maybe they were alone," Kinz said, her eyes still wide.

"They shouted *Advance* before they fell," Cazia said, "so there are more close by. We have to . . . " She looked around. They had to what? What could she do? Continue her tunnel? The Tilkilit were born in tunnels. She did not want to face them underground.

Kinz searched the sky above them. As the fog blew around the rocks, they caught glimpses of blue sky. There were no predators in sight, but they could only see a sliver of what was above them.

Ivy crawled out onto the little bridge. "That was quite a swing."

"Thank you," Kinz answered. "On long treks, the only fun kids could make was to swat spitflies with our little spears." She looked guiltily at Cazia. "I was not very good at that game."

It was amazing how different things could be when their lives were in danger. "Today, you were. Now we need to figure out how we're going to—"

Ivy leaped from the little stone bridge onto the side of the tumbled boulder. Cazia would have cried out if she'd had the chance to catch her breath.

But the little princess did not fall the way the Tilkilit had. She landed in the narrow wedge where the boulder met the spire behind them, and she began to climb. The overturned rock was nearly vertical there, but the spire had enough crevices that the girl could climb the gap between them. Actually, she made it look almost easy.

Kinz sighed in resignation and jumped after her, the older girl's weight making the stone bridge slide back slightly at the force of her leap. Cazia let out a tiny *meep* of fear, but Kinz also landed neatly in the space Ivy had just climbed out of. In fact, there was an odd little stone shelf out there, not even four feet away.

Cazia stood, feeling suddenly very wobbly. It was one thing to dig through the rock, but jumping across an open gap with nothing but stone and corpses and the weapons those corpses carried below her . . .

Of course, she had to try the leap herself. Ivy and Kinz had both done it, and if she was too afraid, she would have had to call them both back down.

Cazia was not brave; she just didn't want to feel humiliated. After Kinz had climbed well above the little shelf, Cazia leaped for it.

Her foot landed perfectly but her chest hit the rock much too hard, and she almost bounced right back out of the wedge. Only her panicked grip on the stones saved her life.

She'd jumped too hard, put too much effort into it. Did the Evening People have a spell for people who overdo everything? She needed one. She needed something to teach her restraint.

A few loose rocks tumbled onto her head, getting tangled in her hair. "Sorry," Kinz whispered from above, but Cazia didn't care. She'd already spent days in the tunnel; her head was practically caked with dirt and tiny stones. What bothered her was that Kinz was struggling, just a bit, to keep up with Ivy.

Cazia began to climb after them. Ivy had managed it readily, but she was still a child. Kinz, who had worked out of doors her whole life, had to struggle to make the climb.

But Cazia had grown up studying in the tower, learning the hand motions and mental images needed to cast a spell, learning to read and write, learning all sorts of things, really. Yes, she had spent the last few months outside, climbing and walking and running, too, when she had to. And she'd eaten almost the whole time.

But she still had a bit of a belly. She had muscles now, more than ever before, but she also had a fair bit of flesh over them. She climbed, stepping from one knobby piece of stone to the next, praying for Monument to give her arms and legs the strength she needed.

She never felt so close to death in her life, not even when she'd found an arrow sticking out of a canteen in her backpack.

When she finally reached the top of the stone, she saw that the other girls were lying flat on their bellies. She crawled toward them, staying as low as possible. Where were the eagles? Surely they could see the white and gray of the girls' hiking skirts against the dark rock. They must have been as alluring as a piece of sweetcake on an untended windowsill.

She craned her neck looking around but couldn't see anything but fog and stone. She did hear the cry of one of the eagles. They were still to the west, flapping near the cliff face. Surely they weren't still harassing that Tilkilit lookout beneath the overhang, not after three days.

"Down!" Ivy whispered, and they all heard the clicking of approaching Tilkilit troops. "There is a column of vines there," the girl said, nodding toward the far side of the rock, "and they are climbing up."

"We could make to climb that little ridge," Kinz said. She pointed to a ledge that ran upward for quite a distance. Cazia liked the look of it immediately. It wasn't even as steep as the tunnel she'd been digging. They could practically run up it. "But we would be in sight of the bugs."

Fire and Fury, Cazia realized she was right. "I need to see," she said, and crept forward.

The vine column was there: two curving trunks twined around each other, both supported by other woody vines like a spider's web. She dared lean farther out, looking down the column. It was bigger than any of the others she'd seen. The vines were so far apart that she doubted she could climb it. The bottom was hidden by fog, but it could have been impossibly tall.

There was a flash of dark red, and she rolled back out of sight. The Tilkilit were climbing, making small leaps from one vine to the next, testing them. If they'd seen her, they could have bounded up to her in moments.

Cazia cleared her mind and began a spell.

"Big sister, you can not use your fire here. You will be too exposed."

She ignored Ivy to finish the spell. It was the Sixth Gift, the same one she'd used to make her little bridge, except this time she a stone as broad and as thick as she could. And she cast it high in the air.

The pink granite began to plummet a moment after it came into being, *whooshing* by them louder than the Sweeps wind as it fell. Then it struck the side of their stone and the column of vines—Cazia should have cast it farther out.

The noise was horrendous. Clashing rocks, snapping wood, and the terribly sharp drumming of the Tilkilit click language all joined together to make a terrible sound. Cazia jumped to her feet and ran to the sloping ridge Kinz had pointed out, determined to get as far as she could while the warriors below were occupied.

Ivy cried out behind her. Cazia spun and caught the girl's wrist. The stone beneath them trembled, and Cazia couldn't help but remember the way those three warriors had fallen to their deaths. She steadied the girl as they hurried toward the ledge. Kinz had Ivy's other hand. Their eyes met; if they couldn't agree on much else, they could look after the princess.

Kinz ended up getting onto the ledge first, then Ivy, with Cazia once again trailing behind. The ledge wasn't as wide as Cazia had first thought, but she could walk on it. Not run, but walk, and quickly.

A tiny stone suddenly struck the wall beside her, and she knew immediately that it had come from below. The Tilkilit were moving up out of the fog, leaping from stone ledge to ledge. She had no way to know how many she had taken out when she had collapsed the column of vines, but it hadn't been enough. They came in a swarm.

Fine. She began moving her hands, calling up the familiar images that would call out her fire. If the Tilkilit queen wanted to send her children to their deaths, Cazia would accommodate her.

"No!" Ivy said, grabbing at her hands and disrupting the spell.

"Fire and Fury, what are you doing?"

"They probably can not see us at this distance," the girl said. "If you blast fire at some, the others will know just where to throw their anti-magic stones."

Cazia's anger evaporated. That was entirely sensible. Together, they hurried up the slope, Kinz leading the way with her stick. Another stone struck nearby, then another. She glanced back and saw Tilkilit swarming. Worse, they were getting closer. Whether it made her a target or not, she was going to have to start burning them soon.

When she turned back, she nearly stepped on Ivy's heel. Fire and Fury, the girl might have tumbled off the ledge.

In the lead, Kinz was moving as quickly as she could, but the way ahead was not smooth. Their little path up the side of the cliff was not actually a path; it had gaps, choke points, and it was covered with treacherous loose stones. Cazia really, really wanted to run, because it was the only way to outdistance the Tilkilit, but did not have a clear stretch of solid earth to run on.

Kinz led them between a spire and the face of a cliff. Cazia crouched at the narrowest part, wondering if this was a good place to make a stand.

Not that she knew anything about picking a battleground. Tactics were for soldiers.

The Tilkilit could jump, clinging to the cliff above or below her. They could approach from different angles, and . . .

The other girls were already making their way under a bulge in the cliff face, and Cazia hurried after them, letting treacherous stones slide out from under her feet and tumble down the mountainside.

A strong gust of wind suddenly cleared the fog from the cliff below and they all had a clear view of the landscape around them. The forest was so far below them that it didn't look real, as though they had uncovered a huge, ornate painting. The wind rushed straight up the rock into their faces, and Cazia endured one absurd moment when she thought it might lift them all up and float them into the Sweeps.

It was a long drop. If she slipped, her shattered body would lay wedged between the stones until one of the eagles swooped down, scraped her out, and ate her.

"Oh!" Ivy called, as though she could read Cazia's thoughts. But no, she had simply suffered a moment of vertigo and turned to face the cliff.

"They're coming," Cazia said, urging her onward.

"I think I see a path," Kinz added, taking Ivy's hand as they picked their way across the tops of a small jumble of sharp-edged rocks.

Something struck the cliff beside them, hard. The sound was as harsh as if someone had shouted into their ears, and Cazia saw the faint white scratch the impact made on the stone beside her hand. Too late. They were close. Very close.

She was already beginning the Third Gift when she turned around. Her target was there, a reddish-black Tilkilit in a blue sash. Had she even seen a blue sash before? Absurdly, she felt a strong pang of envy. Where did it get the dye?

It stepped forward, advancing partway through the narrow gap between the cliff and the spire so it would have room to throw again, more accurately this time. It plunged its hand into the pouch at its waist, then drew back its broomstick arm to throw, but it was too late.

Bright fire rushed from the space between Cazia's hands, shooting forward in a tightly focused bolt. Before the warrior had a chance to react, the flames struck him directly on the bare shell of his chest. He burst open like a melon struck by a mallet and tumbled down the side of the cliff.

A sudden rush of clicking and tapping began, as the other warriors called out to each other. "Hurry!" Kinz shouted, and they all struggled up the uneven ledge.

It widened suddenly, offering room enough to sit down. To the right, the ledge turned into a broad, flat space that was littered with an alarming number of bones.

To the left, the ledge turned outward, forming a little flat platform some six feet out from the cliff face. The platform was covered with a tangle of grass and trees limbs, reminding Cazia of the gigantic lidded pots she'd grown up with in the Palace of Song and Morning.

"See?" Kinz called while she dragged Ivy by the hand. "There is a gap between the peaks here. If the ledge continues all the way across, we might make to reach the other side."

If . . . But she said nothing.

On an impulse, Cazia risked stepping out onto the platform and then swept the dried grass from the top of the tangle of plant matter.

Eggs. She'd revealed a clutch of three of the biggest eggs she'd ever seen. Each was pale pink with dark red speckles, and they were larger than her head. That's was why the eagles were still harassing the Tilkilit lookout to the west; it was too near their nests. The eagles were trying to turn back an invasion of their homes.

What's more, they were so busy harassing the first invader they saw that they didn't realize an entire square of Tilkilit soldiers was swarming in the east. There they were, creeping carefully along the ledge and clinging to the side of the cliff. They'd be here momentarily.

Cazia glanced at the eggs and her empty stomach rumbled, but the thought disgusted her. She could never have eaten one, no matter how hungry she was. The eagles *talked to each other.*

She turned her back and started after the other two girls. Let the Tilkilit come. She may not have been willing to eat the raptors' young, but that didn't mean she wanted to be their nanny, either. Destroying the nest would be an opportunity the Tilkilit couldn't pass up, and maybe it would give Cazia, Ivy, and Kinz the chance to slip away.

Let them destroy each other. Besides, she was getting a case of the jitters, and it felt as though she had an iron ball in her stomach. She would have a wizard's nightmares tonight, unless Kinz used the anti-magic stone on her. They had to get well away and out of danger before she went mad.

I thought you might be different from the others of your people, but no. You lie and you take and care only for yourself.

As awful as the eagles were, could she really leave their helpless children to be slaughtered by the Tilkilit? After what she'd said to Kinz?

Before she even had a chance to consider it, Cazia turned back, her mind and hands already preparing her spell. She came out to the edge of the platform and was startled to see the Tilkilit much closer than expected.

Flame blasted out from her. Fire and Fury, but it felt so good to channel this power. She pointed it at the nearest warrior and lit him like an oily wick. Then she played the flames along the cliff below and against the jagged rocks above. Fire splashed against the mountainside like a waterfall and, Great Way, it was glorious.

Then the energy she was channeling began to grow thin. It felt raw against her insides as the spell ran out of power, and Cazia immediately began another. The Tilkilit had been taken by surprise, but her advantage wouldn't last long.

Her pink granite block appeared in front of her, falling first against the slope of the cliff, then slamming down hard against the ledge. She knew it wouldn't block the warriors, but it would give her some cover from their anti-magic stones.

Cazia began another fire spell, this time widening the flames rather than shooting them like a jet of water. *I'm a wizard*, she thought, and a thrill ran through her. Wizards were monstrous villains from children's stories—and worse—but they were powerful. *I am a wizard.*

The fire left her hands in a sheet, moving away from her no faster than a person could walk but still deadly and inexorable. The Tilkilit clicked and tapped in terrible panic. If she could have gotten her hands free, Cazia would have taken hold of her translation stone to hear what they had to say. She wanted them to panic. She wanted them to flee. She wanted them to put her in their histories.

Great Way, were those her thoughts or were they coming from the hollow space she was recreating inside her?

Next, she created another long stream of flame and began pouring it against the rocks above and below her. It was time to withdraw. Her spells were powerful, but there were just too many warriors and the cliff face gave them too many ways to approach her. How many more spells did she think she could cast before one of them struck her with a stone?

But she could not leave these eggs unprotected. These huge, horrible eggs. The thought of a Tilkilit spear breaking through the shell and plunging into the unfinished baby birds—

Something huge passed above her with terrible sudden speed. It came from behind, and the pressure of it knocked her onto the granite block. She cried out in fear and surprise, and lost the concentration she needed for her spell. The fire sputtered out just as a second bird passed overhead, swooping down onto the insect warriors below.

The giant eagles shrieked, their harsh voices echoing off the side of the mountain. Great Way, they were *huge*. If one of those creatures plucked her off the rock and tore her apart while she was trying to defend their nests, Cazia was going to feel very foolish as she died.

She turned and ran after Ivy and Kinz, who were crouching between two boulders. She hissed at them and they bolted out of their hiding spot, running along their narrow ledge. Cazia followed them around a colossal rock, and they suddenly found themselves looking up at a notch in the mountains. It was hard to be certain that their little ledge went all the way through the gap, but it looked good enough to give them hope.

They hurried as best they could, but it was not fast enough. The sun was no longer overhead, and while they could see the daylight shining brightly in the flattish lands on either side of the mountains, they themselves were in shadow.

Cazia was hungry and thirsty, but she kept silent and kept moving. They were all hungry and thirsty—of course they were—but she wasn't going to be the one who—

"We should make to rest and eat," Kinz said, settling onto her haunches against the mountainside. She had chosen a small wide place in the ledge, and they all crouched together and ate morsels of fish and guzzled the water Cazia summoned.

"That is better," Ivy said. She turned to Cazia. "How are you holding up?"

There was no doubt what she meant, and Cazia had no intention of playing games. "I can feel the very early effects of the magic," she said simply. "I feel jittery and like I have a lump in my stomach. If I were to lie down right here, I'd have terrible nightmares."

"Should I make to touch the stone to you?" Kinz asked. It was nice to be consulted this time.

A small pebble tumbled from someplace far above them. "Not right away. I don't want to be stuck here. Even if we dug into the side of the mountain, I wouldn't want to be stuck here for a whole day, not after everything that just happened back there."

"What did happen?" Ivy asked. "What were you doing?"

They heard the cry of an eagle and immediately got to their feet. Cazia was glad that she didn't have to respond. What had she been doing? She wasn't entirely sure herself.

In the end, she only needed to tunnel into the mountain in two places where an avalanche had broken away their ledge. They came around a large stone and she suddenly felt a wind in her face. It was slightly sour with the smell of vinegar.

The Sweeps. They were so close.

"I swear," Ivy said, "these narrow mountain ranges barely deserve the name."

She began talking about the mountains in the Peninsula where she spent her earliest years. The sound of Ivy's voice was deeply reassuring, even if the wind carried away too many of her words to actually follow what she was saying. Cazia suppressed the urge to grab the girl and give her a fierce hug.

The sun was low in the west when they came out into the direct light. The Sweeps lay spread out below them, seeming much farther down than the floor of the Qorr Valley, and that awful smell was in her nose.

They were standing on a wide, flat place that sloped down toward the south at a relatively gentle slope. It would have been comfortable to camp there if it hadn't been so exposed. Cazia moved across the top of a flattish rock so she could get as close to the edge as possible. She knew the nearly impenetrable—by physical means—fused stone shielded this part of the Northern Barrier, but she wanted to be sure.

"Too close!" Ivy called. She was waving her hands nervously. "Come back!"

Cazia did, but before they could even begin talking, two huge eagles glided through the notch in the mountains and flapped just off the edge of the cliff, hovering there. Their dark predator's eyes were fixed on Cazia.

CHAPTER THIRTEEN

THE EAGLES DID NOT ATTACK. THAT WASN'T A SURE THING, BUT CAZIA had hoped they had sense enough to understand what she'd done. If only wizards could cast spells as quickly as they could raise their hands.

Kinz appeared at her shoulder, waving her pointed stick. "HAH! HAH!" she shouted.

"No!" Cazia snapped at her. She took hold of the useless stick and tried to push the point down. Great Way, the older girl was strong. Cazia didn't have the strength to force her, but Kinz backed down anyway. "Stay with the princess."

The giant birds were trilling to each other, sounding almost like cooing doves. Cazia took the translation gem from her pocket.

"—wants you to take it in as a pet, I wager it."

"I will not wager over this," the other responded. They seemed to be talking over each other, and Cazia had a hard time telling which words came from which creature. "I will not wager over the lives in my nest. Why did it defend me?"

"Food," was the response. "It wanted to devour you for its supper."

"That idea is burdened. If it wanted to devour me, it could have grabbed an egg and run for its tunnel. That's what the hairbacks do at home."

"It is greedy. It is stupid."

Enough. Cazia held up the little gem for them to see. The bird on the left shrieked. "It will burn us!"

Cazia turned to the one on the right. That must have been the mother. In fact, she intended to call it Mother. The other one would have to be Auntie.

She held up the gem to Mother, trying to make her body language as clear as possible. *I am offering this to you.*

Would birds even understand human body language? She moved forward, ignoring the warning call from Ivy, holding the gem so Mother could see it. Those birds hunted from incredibly high up, so their eyesight had to be good enough to see it.

"It wants to burn you!" Auntie shrieked. "Drop it from the ledge so we can feast on it together."

Cazia jolted back at that, suddenly feeling very foolish. If it killed her, Ivy and Kinz would die up here, too, and the Tilkilit stones would never make it back to civilization. Fire take them all, maybe she should start a spell anyway.

"Look at that!" Mother said. "It reacts as though it understands you."

Cazia pointed at Mother, then pointed at the gem.

"It wants you to take the gem as a gift," Auntie said. Cazia shook her head, but the birds wouldn't understand that gesture. She pointed at the rocks nearest Auntie's feet.

"No," Mother said. "It's saying that it can understand us because of the gem."

Cazia pointed at her. Then she set the gem atop a flat rock and backed up the slope, nearly losing her footing on the rough stone. The birds didn't come closer, spreading their wings in the updraft at the edge of the cliff and occasionally flapping to steady themselves.

Mother kept glancing at the little gem, then at the girls. Cazia made a fist, then laid her hand flat over it to show what the bird needed to do.

Finally, she had backed off far enough that the big creature felt safe enough to approach. It flapped forward and settled onto the rock, covering the translation stone with its huge foot.

Cazia knew she was only going to get one chance at this. "If either of you two weights tries to eat me, I will make you both touch the ground."

Mother shrieked in alarm and leaped from the rock, soaring out over the cliff. Auntie called after her and followed, both of them so loud that Cazia felt a sudden clutch of irrational fear in addition to her perfectly rational one. It seemed as though her legs had a mind of their own, urging her to *flee! Flee!*

But of course, there was no where to flee to. Instead, she ran toward the flat rock and saw that Mother, in her blind panic and surprise, had knocked the translation stone off it.

Now Cazia felt herself panic. She checked the top of the stone one more time to make sure the tiny gem hadn't fallen into a crack, then went to the far side.

Mother's foot had swept backward when she leaped into the air, so Cazia searched there, first. The real question was whether the gigantic stupid annoying bird had barely touched the gem and left it right beside the flat stone or had flung it hard enough to pitch it over the edge of the cliff, some thirty feet away.

The ground was still flattish but it was covered with loose stone and dirt. Cazia couldn't see the blue glint of the gem right on the surface, so she began to search near her feet, looking into the crevices all around each stone before moving on to the next. It was the same method she'd used to search for her brother's body in the field north of Fort Samsit a lifetime ago, and it diluted her panic with despair when she remembered how that had turned out.

Worse, if she lost the stone, she would have no way to make a new one. The spell didn't require an expensive gem, but it did need a gem or crystal of some kind. What were the odds of finding one up here?

If only Mother hadn't been so—

No, wait. She stopped searching and let herself go calm. The eagles were out over the Sweeps, flying in circles and crying out to each other. Cazia should have expected Mother to lose her composure. She should have planned for it. If she was going to get Ivy safely home, she was going to have to think things through more.

Starting with this search for the gem. Why was she searching with her eyes when she could calm herself and sense the magic directly? She closed her eyes and tried to settle her thoughts. There. She moved toward a spot just an arm's length from the flat stone and began to toss aside rocks.

She found it actually buried beneath two smaller pebbles. As soon as she picked it up she understood what the birds were saying to each other. Apparently, Auntie was convinced that Cazia's warning to them was a hallucination.

Cazia shouted at them to catch their attention. The birds tilted their wings and glided back toward her. It occurred to her that she couldn't tell them apart. Mother was the one she wanted to talk to, but Auntie was more likely to attack.

She held up the stone again, remaining still until she was sure they had seen it. Then she placed it on the flat stone again and retreated to the place where she'd been when Mother had felt safe enough to touch the gem.

The two birds seemed to contend with each other as they approached the flat stone. Cazia tried to pick out a difference between them—a few lighter feathers among the muddy brown, a less-curved beak, even a scar—but she couldn't. They looked identical to her, and not very pleasing, either.

One of the birds seemed to win out and swooped toward the rock. It landed, but it hesitated to put its foot down onto the translation stone. It had to be Auntie, and Fire and Fury, was she huge. Cazia waited patiently for the bird to work up its courage. When it finally set its foot down, it looked directly at her.

"Try to be more careful with my gem," she said. "If you lose it or break it, I can't make another one."

The birds began to squawk at each other. The sound echoed against the rocks behind her, but Cazia was completely still.

"Be quiet!" she shouted at them. "Be quiet! I can't understand you while you hold the stone! Don't you see how this works? The one with the stone can understand the one without it. All I hear right now are screeching sounds!"

But the birds were not panicking over her this time. They looked to be arguing with each other. There was no way to tell how serious their disagreement was, but their voices were loud and harsh. If they'd been humans, Cazia would have suspected a vicious fight to break out any moment.

It didn't happen. The one on the stone hopped off and moved toward the cliff, gliding out into the updraft. The other took up position on the stone and set its foot confidently onto the gem.

"First of all," Cazia said, "I don't know if the other one told you, but be careful with that little gem. I only have the one and I can't make more right now. Second, which are you? Was it your nest that I saved, or are you the one who wants to eat us?"

The bird leaped off the stone and moved away. Cazia took the hint and crossed down the slope to put her hand on the gem.

"Yes, it was my nest you protected," the bird said. "What are you? How does that gem allow you to use language?"

Cazia sighed. They still didn't understand. She moved back up the slope and let the bird touch the gem. "The gem doesn't *allow us to use language,*" she said, a little testily. "We talk to our kind just as you talk to yours. The only thing the gem does is allow us to understand each other. As for what we are, we're people."

The bird, seeing she had finished, glided away from the gem and let Cazia touch it. "It's funny you should call yourselves that. We call ourselves 'people,' too. You still didn't answer the most important question: why did you protect me in that nest when the bugs approached?"

They switched places again. "I protected your eggs for two reasons. First, I hate the Tilkilit enough to deny them the pleasure and modest tactical advantage they would have gotten for killing your children. Before you ask, yes, the 'bugs,' as you call them, speak to each other in their own language and are intelligent, too. Second, as much as I wanted to pay you back for the crimes you've committed, I didn't want to visit that punishment on your innocent unborn."

The birds began to squawk at each other, and she could see that her answer had riled them up, just as she hoped it would. Mother retreated again, but not so far this time. Cazia went down the slope and laid her hand on the gem.

"What nonsense is this? The bugs crawling in the valley have no language or culture! And only a weight and a burden would accuse my clan of being criminals! We are an honorable people!"

Cazia snatched her hand away from the gem to make her stop talking, then hurried up the slope.

"Cazia," Ivy said, "what are they saying?"

The two girls looked very small and nervous. Cazia knew she looked angry—Fire and Fury, she felt angry—but she hoped they could tell it wasn't directed at them. "The usual clatter about being honorable." She spun around to see Mother had taken her place on the flat stone. "Do you see the tall girl behind me? The one with the dark hair and skin? Huge birds just like you—part of your family, I assume—murdered her whole clan. They killed the elders, the adults, and they murdered children, too. Only she and her brother survived. I don't know if you understand the word 'brother,' but she has lost everyone in this whole world who loved her, but one. So—

Mother lifted her foot off the gem. This time she flapped directly upward. Cazia stormed down the slope to the gem. Fire and Fury, her anger had come upon her so suddenly and it was so difficult to deny. A small voice inside her urged caution, but her sudden rage was almost grateful to have a justifiable target. Well, another one, after the Tilkilit.

Cazia laid her hand on the gem. From above, Mother shrieked, "How could we have guessed you could think and speak? *You can't even fly!*"

That was all she wanted to say. Cazia took three steps back and waved Mother down toward the gem. The huge bird landed. Mother was big enough to snap her up in its beak and swallow her whole, but her anger helped her mask the fear she didn't dare to show.

"How would anyone know you are a thinking creature, when you can't even shoot flames from between your hands?" Mother squawked in protest but she didn't let go of the gem. "Look at us. We wear clothing. We carry weapons. We use tools. We build fortresses, houses, and wagons. We think! Don't try to pretend that we do not mourn for the people you kill, and the next time you want to talk to me about your honor, remember this: I protected your defenseless children while you have murdered ours!"

Mother leaped off the rock and glided out over the Sweeps. Auntie followed. They squawked at each other briefly but stopped when Cazia picked up the translation stone.

She carried the little gem up the slope toward Ivy and Kinz. The sun was well below the mountain peaks now, and a chill was setting in. Even though it was the height of summer, the wind in the Sweeps carried a chill.

"Was it wise to scold them like that?" Kinz asked.

"Who ever said I was wise?" Cazia countered. "Besides, I wanted to test them a little. If they're as honorable as they claim, we might make allies of them. If they're not, I'll set them on fire."

Kinz nodded. "That would be a fine start."

The two birds flew toward them, occasionally banking in the crosswind. One of them landed on the flat stone and regarded the three girls solemnly. It was only when it spoke that Cazia recognized Mother's voice.

"Person, please give the gem to the dark one."

Cazia turned to Kinz and held out the translation stone. "She wants to talk to you." Kinz hesitated, then accepted the gem.

Mother spoke. Of course, the only thing that Cazia heard was cooing and the occasional squawk, but Kinz's expression became intensely serious. After a short while, Kinz returned the gem to Cazia and, without saying a word, walked away to sit beside a massive black rock.

"I have offered apologies," Mother said, "and opened myself to challenge if the dark one would seek redress. I do not know if your people understand the concept of a duel, but it is very rare for an apex of a clan, such as I am, to open herself to challenge. Normally, it is a weight I would not bear, but the crime you describe is a great burden and I will risk burning for it. For her part, I do not know if she intends to offer challenge or leave me with my burden."

Cazia held up the jewel and moved down to the flat stone. Of course, Mother thought Kinz could cast spells, too, and for the moment, there was no reason to disabuse her of the notion. Mother glided out into the Sweeps, where Auntie tacked against the wind. Cazia set the gem back in its place and retreated. Mother returned and gently laid her foot on it.

"I don't think she knows what she wants to do, either. It's a new situation for all of us. You are recent arrivals to the land of Kal-Maddum, aren't you? Let us form a truce—just between us five—so we can pass the gem between us without fear of reprisal."

Mother hopped off the stone and let Cazia approach. When she laid her hand on the gem, the bird said, "I agree. Fair parley between us. I will call you 'The Gorilla People,' because your forelimbs resemble theirs and your eyes face front."

Switch. "I don't know what a 'gyurilla' is. Would you describe it?"

Switch. "We have seen similar creatures hunting in the wilderness, but these creatures were blue or purple, like flowers, while gorillas have black or silver hair. Also, gorillas do not have hind legs like lions—do you know what they are? Bow your head if you do. Good, I am glad I do not have to describe them, too. Also, real gorillas do not have the shoulders and necks of bears. Do you know—Good, I am glad you do. In truth, gorillas are peaceful creatures who eat plants, unlike the beasts here. But— You appear agitated. Do you wish to speak?"

They switched. "The blue and purple creatures call themselves The Blessing." Cazia tried to describe the grunts concisely, but she remembered her brother, and the flinches came on her so powerfully that she stammered.

Mother, looming above her, began to flutter her wings. Cazia lost her train of thought. The huge bird removed her talon from the stone. Cazia realized she could not have covered one of those long talons with both of her hands. They were as long as spear points, if spears were made like hooks. The girl put her hand on the gem.

"You are their prey animal," was all Mother said.

There was something dangerous in that voice. Where before Mother had been bold and then contrite, now the translation spell made her sound disapproving.

Cazia had heard that tone many times before. When she lived in the Palace of Song and Morning, she would sometimes greet and chat politely with new visitors or tutors brought in to try to rein in the prince. Everyone was so delightful and accommodating, until they asked her name and she told them. Suddenly, they acted like they'd discovered a turd in their sourcake.

However, Mother could not be allowed to condescend to her. Yes, she could slash Cazia open in the blink of an eye, but if they decided she was inferior, they would have to fight.

She pointed at the gem. Mother laid her huge taloned foot upon it. "We are at war with them," Cazia said. There was another flutter of wings. "Do you know what 'war' means? Bow your head if you do." Mother raised her face to the sky. She didn't know the word. "Huh. Welcome to Kal-Maddum. You'll have good reason to learn it soon enough. A war is like a duel, except it isn't fought between two warriors. Every able fighter among a nation or a clan girds for battle, and they slaughter each other in great numbers until one side yields. The losers give up land, money, and control of their lives. Sometimes, innocent people who do not fight are also killed. Sometimes, the fighting last for years. Homes are burned. Crops are destroyed. Starvation. Cruelty. Do you understand?"

Mother did not bow her head or raise it up. She did flutter her wings. Cazia figured that meant that the giant bird understood her but didn't approve. Well, her approval wasn't necessary. "They—"

Suddenly, she had no idea what to say. "Cazia," Ivy called, "she doesn't understand how close this has come to you. She doesn't understand about your brother. She—" Ivy addressed Mother directly. "May I speak? What she could not find the words to say is that the blue creatures used to be human beings like us, but they have been transformed by magic into bloodthirsty beasts. Her own brother was changed, body and mind, and she was forced to kill him."

Mother stared down at her without moving. Cazia had no idea what that look meant, but she stared right back up at her. It occurred to her that Mother was so alien that it was impossible to recognize her intent from her body language. The taloned foot moved away from the gem, but Cazia pointed at it, and Mother touched it again.

"I didn't know," Cazia said. "That was before we realized that the bite of a grunt would curse us. I didn't know it was my brother. I just thought it was another enemy."

Cazia's next words would have sounded like an apology or making excuses, so she shut her mouth. When Mother removed her foot from the gem, Cazia put her hand on it. "To kill one who came from the same nest," she said, "is a terrible crime among my people."

Cazia lifted her hand and Mother laid her foot down. "Among mine, too," Cazia told her. "Be sure your people know they mustn't let the grunts bite them, or they might find themselves in the same situation."

Mother fluttered her wings again. She shrieked to Auntie, but the other bird didn't respond. Finally, she lifted her huge foot. Cazia touched the gem. "Curse it," the bird said. "We have been tricked. We should never have let the gods convince us to try to take this continent."

CHAPTER FOURTEEN

CAZIA FELT A CHILL RUN THROUGH HER. THE "GODS" CONVINCED Mother and her people to come here? Had they sent The Blessing as well?

She tried to imagine what the people of Peradain could have done to displease the gods so much. There were temples in every city and holdfast in the empire, and new ones were being built in every newly conquered territory. Priests wore fine robes of many colors. The faithful kept sacred spaces sacred. As far as Cazia knew, they had been doing everything right.

So, why would the gods open portals into Kal-Maddum to let strange creatures invade them?

Cazia didn't turn around, but she could feel Kinz standing somewhere behind her, and Ivy, too. Both of their peoples had faced the spears and arrows of the Peradaini troops. Perhaps the gods had become angry because of the blood imperial troops spilled.

Except that was the way it had always been. For generations, clan fought clan. One people conquered another. Why would the gods punish the Peradaini now?

Not that the Peradaini alone had been targeted. Perhaps it wasn't the Peradaini empire that the gods wished to end. Perhaps it was the whole of the human race.

"You quaver," Mother said, "like prey. Why?"

Switch. "What gods set you against us?"

Switch. "The gods of our land. The Storm. The Bounty In The Grass. The Wave. The Shadow That Passes Above."

Relief flooded through Cazia. Mother was talking about the same kind of nature spirits that Ivy's and Kinz's people worshipped, which were as like the true gods of the universe as an unkind look was to genocidal war. Actually, no, because an unkind look could be a real thing, but nature spirits were a figment of ritual and imagination. Cazia had let herself get carried away. Of course the gods—the real gods—were not trying to destroy humanity.

Still, whatever the truth about their religion, it was not impossible that they had been tricked into an invasion. The only question was, if it was not their make-believe gods, who had fooled them?

Switch. "How did they trick you?" Cazia asked. "What happened?"

Switch. "Voices from nothing," Mother said. "Voices from the deep above and below. Does it matter? The gods play their games. We are the stones they drop and the targets they aim for." Mother changed the subject. "My people will be fascinated by you when I tell them. They will want to know about your world-breaking." Cazia lifted her face to the sky. "Are you refusing to answer?"

Cazia lifted her hand and let Mother touch the gem. "Sometimes the gem will translate words literally and I can only understand their meaning by the way you say them. When you say 'touch the ground' you mean 'die,' don't you? Well, you won't be surprised to hear that my people don't talk about death as touching the ground. So, I have to ask you what you mean by 'world-breaking.' We don't use that term."

Switch. "You can make fire come from your hands. You created this gem. You make magic. That is what we mean by 'breaking the world.' Magic comes from outside, and you must break through boundaries to bring it here. We long believed that the only creatures capable of world-breaking were lower beasts, like sand diggers and belly crawlers. Magic, we assumed, took the place of intellect."

Cazia's hand jolted back from the gem. Mother fluttered her wings, then touched the stone. "Magic is controlled by intellect, by abstract thought and visualization. We don't need to be able to fly to do that."

Switch. "There is much we need to learn. What can I offer you in trade for the translation gem? I will need it to speak to and control the bugs. If they also have language as you say, there are arrangements to be made."

Cazia felt a little chill at that. Switch. "The gem is not for barter. However, in exchange for the information I have already given you, plus the general location of the Tilkilit queen's burrow, there's something I want from you." Mother bowed her head. Cazia assumed that meant she was open to a bargain, rather than agreeing to perform an unspecified service. "I want you to provide us transport down from the cliff to the outside of a human structure that I designate."

"What?" Ivy gaped at her. "Cazia, you—"

Kinz laid her hand on the princess's elbow. "No, Ivy. No, it is all right. I knew she was making to this and I think she is correct. What is more, if I can bear it, you can. Assuming the bird is willing and can keep her promises."

Mother withdrew her foot and Cazia touched the stone. "The bird would never break a promise, no matter how much weight it carried. I would not be leader of my people if I broke my word. What's more, I suspect I am not speaking to the leader of *your* group, correct? Your companions openly question your decisions. Worse, what use is the location of the leader of the bugs if I do not have the stone that would let us parley?"

Switch. "That's a lot of questions," Cazia said. "First, the queen has a way of speaking without words or language. When you're close enough, you will understand. Second, our group has no leader; each of us comes from a different nation . . . Do you understand *nation*?" Mother fluttered her wings. "A nation is a very large group of people, usually made up of hundreds or thousands of different families."

Switch. "And you represent these different nations?" There was something careful in the way Mother said that.

Switch. "Three of the nearest," Cazia said.

Mother did not take her foot off the stone while she exchanged calls with Auntie, who was still hovering on the updrafts just beyond the edge of the cliff. It was so strange to hear those screeches and shrieks and know there was complex meaning there. Finally, they switched. "I will fly you out into the valley to the location of the bug queen, then my sister and I will carry you down into your own lands."

Cazia didn't like that idea very much; she tried to introduce the idea of a map to Mother, but the concept of a pictorial representation of the landscape was utterly alien to her and she seemed to actively resist any explanation of the idea. It was only when Kinz stepped forward to explain the drawings were another kind of language that it began to make sense. Even Auntie flew closer and settled on a rock to watch the herder draw a map of the landscape of the Sweeps directly in front of them.

Mother did understand the concept at last, although she seemed to think it was poor coin to offer in trade. Cazia thought Auntie was more enthusiastic about it, although it was hard to judge tone from the way the birds squawked. Still, Kinz drew the river that they had floated down to escape, the fallen tree, and a few other landmarks that Cazia hadn't noticed, finishing with the meadow where they'd spent so many idle days. Kinz was certain the hole to the queen's chamber was just beyond the northern edge.

After that, Cazia explained where she wanted to be taken.

Night had fallen. "We should stop using the gem soon," Cazia interrupted to say. "The magic is dangerous if we overuse it."

"It is time," Mother said once they'd switched. "We can drop you close to your destination in the darkness where we will be safe from the tiny darts your people shoot at us, and you will be well outside the hunting range of the belly crawlers. At the sunrise gathering, I will forbid the hunting of your kind. I suspect the discussion will be . . . complicated. But no matter. Someday, we will have to parley again. I suspect there is much we could learn from each other."

Switch. "I would like that, too. Thank you." Cazia pocketed the jewel.

Mother carried Kinz and Ivy while Cazia had to fly alone with Auntie. At first, the huge eagles wanted to grab the girls in their talons, but they would have none of it. Kinz thought it would be better to ride on their backs the way her people rode okshim, but Ivy absolutely refused to ride clinging to their slippery feathers.

In the end, the girls wrapped their arms and legs around the birds' ankles and sat on their curled feet. It was uncomfortable for everyone, but the birds did not complain aloud and Cazia managed, somehow, not to scream in terror when Auntie plunged off the side of the cliff and spread her wings wide.

CHAPTER FIFTEEN

T HEY PLUMMETED A TERRIFYING DISTANCE. WRAPPING HER ARMS tightly around Auntie's lower leg, Cazia shut her eyes and prayed to Monument to help her endure the terror of knowing that they had been betrayed and that these two huge creatures were about to shake them loose and smash their bodies into the mud.

Then Auntie began to level out. It was a strain, but Cazia managed to hold on to the bird's leg, and soon they were gliding out over the Sweeps, the dark lands below flitting by so fast that she couldn't make out any details.

All they had to go by was bare starlight—the moon had not risen yet— but the gnarled tree branches swept below her like giants reaching up to snatch her out of the sky. She knew that, if she fell, not even soft mud or water would be cushion enough to give her safe landing.

Fire and Fury, it was the most exhilarating thing she'd ever done.

Mother, Ivy, and Kinz were ahead of them, barely more than a dark shape moving against the starlit landscape. Cazia tried to see if the girls were still holding on, but it was impossible to tell. She tried to convince herself that she should assume the best.

Grateful am I to be permitted to travel The Way.

They flew, on and on. Cazia's terror faded quickly but so did her strength. Her arms began to ache, her butt became sore, and her leg muscles started to cramp. She was tempted to shout for the birds to land right away, but they had made a bargain and she thought they might take it as an insult if she changed their terms.

Besides, there was something about the birds that did not invite talk. They were utterly silent as they glided over the Sweeps. It was a marked difference from the back-and-forth squawking and cooing they had made on the cliff top. Was this their hunting behavior? It seemed so.

On and on it went. Cazia felt a slight tingle in her hands and legs and it only took a moment to realize that she was sensing magic. Auntie had magic inside of her, somehow. For all their talk about "world-breaking," Mother and her people were creatures of magic themselves, even if they didn't know it.

Cazia's eyes quickly adjusted to the dark, but she still wished they could have made this trip during the day. What sights she could have seen! It couldn't have been easy for Auntie to carry a weight on only one leg, and Mother didn't exactly have a balanced load, either, but they didn't slow until they came within sight of the torchlight above the Alliance watchtowers.

Mother widened her wings and slowed herself, dropping down onto a patch of dry ground bristling with clumps of tall grass. As soon as she touched down, Ivy and Kinz fell off of her legs and rolled away; the older girl kept silent but Ivy let out a moan of relief.

When Auntie did the same, Cazia unwrapped her legs before they even touched the ground. She had to drop a few feet because Auntie had no intention of actually landing. As determined as she was to stand upright, her legs buckled.

Both of the birds turned westward into the wind and began flapping hard, gaining altitude quickly. One let out a piercing cry that seemed to echo off the Southern Barrier, but Cazia couldn't tell whether it was a note of annoyance or a friendly "Until next time!"

None of the girls wanted to be the last one on her feet, so they all stumbled out of the darkness toward each other. The moon had just begun to rise.

"If we had made any sense, we would have waited until morning," Kinz said. "I wish I had thought of it myself, but I did not. Normally, we would be made safe in the tree or in the cleft of the rock. But it is too late to camp now."

Ivy waved toward the glowing torches to the south. "I would rather sleep in a bed tonight. If we start now—and do not fall into a hole or something— we might reach the gate before the midnight. Do we really want to sleep on the ground without even a cloth to lie on?"

No, in fact, they did not. The girls started their trek across the uneven terrain. It quickly became apparent that only the flat little hills actually offered dry footing; everything in between was full of squelching, boot-clutching mud.

They traveled by hopping from one relatively solid bit of land to another; Cazia was the first to slip and fall in the mud, but her embarrassment evaporated when Kinz did the same not long after, then Ivy, then Cazia, then

Kinz, and after that, she no longer kept track. It was dark and the ground was treacherous.

Their progress was slowed by Kinz's insistence that they stop often to check for predators. There were almost certainly eagles out there who hadn't gotten word of a truce yet, and grass lions, while they usually hunted during the day, had been known to take prey at night.

Cazia wished Kinz had been able to bring her pointed stick off the top of the cliff. The only protection they had was her spells, which would be useless in an ambush. Worse, she had no iron darts. The only spell she could fight with was her fire spell, which would be clearly visible for miles in this flat, open landscape.

"Cazia," Ivy said, interrupting her thoughts, "I wonder if you would let me borrow that little gem of yours."

The question caught her by surprise and her answer was sharper than she intended. "Why?"

The little girl didn't seem to notice her tone. "For more than fifty years, the people of Indrega have had an arrangement with the serpents of the northeast, but we have always dealt with them through crude sign language. We can not set treaty terms, can not negotiate borders, and we can not easily explain our laws. It has led to complications, as I am sure you can guess. A serpent nest on private farmland. Pets devoured without compensation. That sort of thing."

"Make to keep your voices low," Kinz scolded.

Ivy spoke in a whisper. "If my family had a gem like yours, we could simplify things."

"And it would strengthen your family's status in the Alliance."

"Indeed it would."

"Is that safe?"

Cazia's question seemed to flummox her. "What do you mean? How could it not be safe?"

Together, they looked over at the fires of the watchtowers. They were farther than Cazia had thought at first, but they were making progress toward them. "A whole bunch of okshim is one thing, but . . . How sturdy is your Alliance? The three of us trust each other a little bit—maybe things are not great between Kinz and me, but she saved my life and maybe I saved hers, too; I can't remember."

"You did," Kinz whispered. The moonlight lit her silhouette, but her expression was hidden in shadow.

"Oh, good. So, we have our conflicts but when things get rough, we mostly trust each other, as long as I don't overuse my magic. When Mother spoke to me—"

The half moon showed enough light to see Ivy tilt her head. "Mother?"

"Didn't I say that out loud to you? Those two birds were Mother—the one with the nest—and Auntie. They never told me their real names, assuming they have names. Anyway, when Mother spoke to me, you couldn't understand anything she said, but you trusted me to look after all of our interests."

"Ah!" Ivy's exclamation brought a sharp hiss from Kinz, but she quickly lowered her voice. "I should have thought of that. I haven not lived among my people for more than a year, but as a member of the royal family, I should have considered this. The Winzoll have always been jealous of Ergoll power—in fact, the Winzoll king tried to offer the daughter to the Italgas in my place, but she vomited on his emissary. I hear she took a purgative right before she met him. I wish I had thought of that. Not that I, you know—"

"I know," Cazia said. "I know very well."

"And the Toal," the princess continued. "My uncle used to say that they like to think of themselves as eldest brother to the other nations of the Alliance. My own people . . . I hope you understand why I say this, but my own people are in some ways the weakest member of the Alliance. Our lands are in the west, you see, and while warriors come from all over to fend off Peradaini incursions, it is our lands where most of the fighting is done. We are a hard people, but not numerous."

"What then?" Kinz asked. She crouched beside them. "Will you make five gems?"

Ivy gasped as though she was about to declare that a wonderful idea, but Cazia broke in. "What would happen to me if the Alliance found out I was a scholar?" *Wizard.* She wasn't a scholar any more. She was a wizard. She just didn't like to say the word aloud.

"They would celebrate you," Ivy answered. "They would feast you, then give you a comfortable house and a guard to win your favor."

Kinz shook her head. "You would be the prisoner. Maybe you would live in one of their houses, maybe it would be the cell, but you would never be permitted to cross the Straim again. This watch post is commanded by the Toal. They would spirit you away, and Ivy would be sent south to her people. Maybe I would be allowed to accompany her, but I would certainly not be allowed to help you."

"We would keep it a secret," Ivy said, "until we reached my father. I would never allow you to be taken prisoner. I do not treat my friends in that way."

Cazia didn't doubt her sincerity. What she doubted was Ivy's ability to impose her will on her elders. As capable as she'd proven herself to be, she was still only a twelve-year-old girl. "What story do we tell about our trip into Qorr?"

Kinz spoke up. "We do not tell them that Cazia can make magic. The tunnel we climbed up the cliff was already there, made by the Peradaini scholar sometime last winter. We saw the bug people but did not make to fight or speak to them."

"Oh! But I shot one with my bow."

Kinz laid her hand on Ivy's shoulder. "You killed one, but only one. We found the Door in the Mountain but the bugs captured us. We escaped the same way we actually escaped, found the stone towers but not the magic lever, scaled the cliffs, and climbed back down the same tunnel."

Cazia nodded. "We leave out anything we learned from Chik or Mother. We leave out the spell that the Tilkilit Queen wanted me to cast."

"We leave out the name of the Tilkilit."

"Yes. Exactly." Cazia took a deep breath. "What about Alga?"

Kinz's younger brother Alga had accompanied them northward across the Sweeps, but the girls had sent him away before they started up the cliff. If he'd done as his sister told him, he would have already passed through these watchtowers; who knew what stories he might have told?

"Gah," Kinz said. "If he came this way, he might have told them you are one of the Cursed."

Cazia had forgotten about that pleasant little term. The herder people thought all magic was a curse.

"You should simply lie," Ivy said. "Say that he pinched your bottom and you punched him. We will say that you knocked him into the mud and he was furious about it. If he is there, I will mock him in front of the other warriors. He will be discredited. Definitely."

I can't go into Indrega. Cazia couldn't deny it any longer. Those fires atop the watchtowers meant cooked food, soft beds, and clean clothes, but she would be enjoying none of it.

They'd gone into Qorr to find out whether the eagles were part of a coordinated attack with The Blessing, and the answer had been unclear and confusing. Mother said they'd been tricked by the gods into coming here. Obviously, they weren't part of a coordinated assault on Kal-Maddum, but had they been driven here as part of a more subtle plot?

Mother and Auntie would have fluttered their wings at the suggestion that they were someone else's pawns in an invasion, but that was how it seemed to Cazia.

What's more, there was something at the back of Cazia's mind that she knew she was missing—something important—but what was it? She tried to remember everything Mother, Chik, and the Tilkilit queen had said, but whatever was there, tickling her subconscious, she could not identify it.

Still, Ivy and Kinz could bring the news of the Qorr to the Indregai people. She couldn't risk passing through those gates and never emerging again. There would still be tyrs out in the empire who needed to know what she knew.

Tyrs like her father. Tyrs like Tejohn Treygar.

They stood and began moving toward the watchtowers again, hopping from dry place to dry place. "However," Ivy said, "you should be aware of some differences between my culture and yours. People will make fun of you."

"I have met Indregai before," Kinz said sourly.

"It is our way to establish dominance through wit. Anyone who mocks you is trying to put themselves above you. As foreigners, you are excused from these contests by custom, but it doesn't always work that way. Depending on the situation, that might be something you simply have to endure—my father the king has the right to mock any of his subjects—or that you have to challenge immediately. Sometimes, you can tease your superiors to show that you have some fire in you, but it is usually a bad idea to best them. However, I think that, as my companions, you will be treated with special deference."

The princess was speaking with a self-satisfied preciousness that Cazia had never seen from her before. They were about to venture into her world now, and she clearly planned to make sure they would be impressed.

As they walked, they found surer footing, in no small part because they were heading slightly uphill. What had been mud before was now an easily avoided streambed or pond. Ivy continued to talk more boldly as they came nearer the firelight, cataloging the various sorts of jokes and teasing they could expect, and what it all meant.

It was all very complicated and Cazia was only half paying attention, but she was amazed once again by the amount of information the kid retained. No tutor Cazia had ever studied under could convince her to learn little details—except Doctor Twofin, of course—but Ivy had learned enough from her uncle in just a few years to become a tutor herself. Really, it was astonishing.

Cazia didn't intend to stay long enough to trade barbs with anyone. All she needed from the Toal were supplies. Water she could create, but she couldn't do the same with food. A bedroll would also have been welcome, and so would another of those wide-brimmed hats that were waxed against the rain. She definitely needed a new knife and would not have turned down an actual spear.

All of those things would be available on the other side of the gate ahead, but once Cazia was through, she couldn't see a way to get back out with them. In the Sweeps, she was free to do as she pleased. Inside the wall was Alliance territory, where Ivy was Princess Vilavivianna. If the little girl wanted Cazia to stay close to her, she could probably make it happen.

There was still a bit of dried fish wrapped up in the cloth across Kinz's back. All she needed to do was wait. Ivy would tell the guards who she was, the gate would open, and Cazia would ask for the last of their supplies then make her goodbyes.

Of course, she'd tried to leave the princess behind once before. Cazia hadn't intended to bring the girl into Qorr, but there had been little choice. That's why it was important to wait for the gates to swing open. Mahz and her clan had no interest in forcing Ivy into safety, but Alliance soldiers certainly would. Besides, Cazia was pretty sure she could convince Kinz to carry Ivy inside if it came to that.

She half hoped Kinz would come with her. It was silly to think so, since the older girl clearly didn't like her and would probably be anxious to find her brother down in the peninsula, no matter how tense their last parting. Still, Kinz was more familiar with the Sweeps than Cazia was, even if it was just a matter of pointing out edible weeds.

As she was working her way up a somewhat steep hill, she felt Kinz's hand on her shoulder. For a moment, it felt as though the older girl was rapping on her bone with a hard knuckle, but there was an immediate sensation of having something torn away from her. *Anti-magic stone.* Cazia lost her balance and fell halfway down the slope, bruising her hip on a jutting stone.

"I am sorry!" Kinz said, hurrying toward her. "Did you not hear me say it was time?"

"I didn't. I was lost in my own thoughts."

Kinz helped her up and apologized again. She sounded completely sincere. Cazia limped after Ivy. Fire and Fury, now she was going to be without her magic for at least a day.

Cazia's eyes were aching from lack of sleep when they finally came within earshot of the watchtowers.

"Fort Whune," Ivy said.

The gates were shut and the walls—made out of raw logs—where higher than any she'd ever seen. Still, even though she knew the Alliance didn't have scholars, she'd expected stone. Monument sustain her, but she was tired.

Would it make sense to pass the night inside the walls and trust to her ability to slip away later?

Cazia saw a commotion on the wall and took hold of the translation gem with her right hand.

"Turn back!" a woman shouted from atop one of the towers. "The gates will not be opened before dawn. Turn back a thousand paces."

Ivy stood on Cazia's left, with Kinz on the other side of her. As royal retinues went, it wasn't much, but they weren't trying to impress anyone. "Attention, lackwits and restless owls!" Ivy called at the top of her thin voice. "I am Vilavivianna, princess of Goldgrass Hill and the daughter of the Ergoll king, Alisimbo of Goldgrass Hill. I order—"

There was a sound like the twang of a bowstring and something flickered through the firelight. A familiar buzzing sound grew louder. On impulse, Cazia stuck her left hand in front of the princess.

An arrow pierced her palm.

Chapter Sixteen

Tejohn caught his breath when he saw them. Soldiers. Before his time at the temple, he would not have been able to see them at this distance. Javien would have had to describe the clash. Now he could crouch behind a tree partway down the hill and watch.

The little squad did not have archers or skirmishers, which didn't surprise Tejohn at all. There was no reason to field soldiers kitted for mobility against grunts. The squad lifted their shields and slammed them together—the clash echoed through the valley—then they raised their spears high. They were short spears—the kind Tejohn had always fought with. What they lacked in range they made up for in maneuverability.

The grunt bounded over the fence and skidded slightly on the wet grass. It huffed three times, then roared.

Tejohn realized he was gripping the tree so hard that the rough bark dug painfully into his fingers.

Helpless. It was one thing to be down there with them . . . Not that he knew them at all. In fact, they would probably receive a reward if they dragged him back to the city bound and gagged. Still, humans were fighting grunts and he wanted to be there with them. He laid his hand on the knife at his hip, his only weapon. The fight would be over by the time he could sprint down the slope, vault the fence, and climb the hill on the other side, but a small, foolish voice inside him urged him forward anyway.

The soldiers had the high ground and they meant to make use of it. All five spears pointed unerringly at the grunt, swaying from side to side to follow it. The shield wall stuttered to the right, trying to keep the beast from flanking it.

It didn't work. The grunt was too fast. As it raced around their flank with the speed of a grass lion, the soldiers tried to turn with it in a hinge maneuver, but now the steepness of the hill worked against them. They couldn't shift fast enough on the dew-wet ground and a soldier at the end of the line slipped in the mud. He sprawled on his backside, the woman beside him turned to help, and then it was too late.

The grunt rushed the two nearest spears, ducking under their points at the last instant. Then it was inside their defenses. It grabbed the bottom of a man's shield and wrenched it upward, knocking him and the man beside him to the grass. They hadn't even fallen fully to the ground before the grunt had bitten down on the first man's calf.

He screamed, and the sound had more despair in it than pain or terror. One bite. That was all it took.

The spear on the ground had just enough time to reach for his short stabbing sword before the beast struck him mercilessly on the side of his helmet, stunning him. Then the spear in the middle went on the attack.

He was good, Tejohn could see. His footwork was expert, even on a slope. His point control was solid and his shield steady. If the man had come into the palace gym, Tejohn would have invited him to demonstrate his technique for the prince.

It wasn't good enough. The grunt weaved from side to side. When the man's attack came, the beast slipped it and caught the haft in its left hand, snapping it like a reed. Then it grabbed the man by the wrist and dragged him away from the others. He struck it with the edge of his shield just as he lost his balance; the sound of the blow was powerful enough that Tejohn could hear it from where he was hiding. It didn't matter; the grunt bit down on his hand and backed away.

The last two spears had recovered their footing but were now downhill from the beast. Tejohn could see that they were perfectly competent fighters: their spears were steady, but they took too many little steps. Both of their points followed the creature as it circled them. Again, they tried to pivot on a hinge as the beast flanked them. The woman had to raise her spear over the helmet of the man beside her, and that's when the grunt rushed them.

Again, it feinted around the spear point and bowled into the soldiers. Before they'd hit the ground, the woman had received a bite on her ankle and the man took one on his shoulder.

The grunt backed away, circling them. The first soldier, who had taken a wound on his leg, had cast away his spear and drawn his sword. He faced the grunt on one knee, shield and weapons at the ready. The third fellow, who had anchored the center of the line, threw down his shield and drawn his sword in his off hand, holding it like a big knife. He looked ready to make a suicide charge.

He didn't. Neither of them did. The grunt watched them carefully, barely moving, while their sword points wavered. Finally, they lowered their weapons, burying the points in the dirt. The woman knelt and turned her sword to her own stomach, as though she intended to take her own life, but she wouldn't—or couldn't—push the point home.

The grunt crept carefully forward and, with the gentle touch of a mother caring for an infant, bit the stunned soldier's forearm.

They had lost. Five to one—and it wasn't even one of the larger creatures—but it hadn't been enough. Fire take the whole world, how could they defeat an enemy like this?

The grunt took hold of the stunned man's collar and began dragging him off to the right, toward the road. The others stood uncertainly, looking from one to the other as though one of them might be able to save them. The beast dropped the injured man and raced around them in a circle, growling and roaring at them.

The soldiers threw away their weapons and let themselves be herded toward the road.

"Monument sustain me," Javien whispered. "We have to get away from—"

"Follow me," Tejohn said. They moved uphill, keeping to the trees as much as possible, then went into the farmhouse.

The place had been torn apart, which was no surprise at all. Tejohn picked through the torn cloths, burst straw mats, and shattered crockery. Javien found three small unbroken jars of pickled compote, which they crouched by the hearth to eat. Tejohn thought it was very similar to the compote they served in Peradain, nothing at all like the smooth, sour paste he remembered from his youth.

"We shouldn't linger here," Javien said as he finished his breakfast.

"They won't be back. Didn't you see it piss on the wall outside? It was marking its territory. It won't return today." Tejohn heard the certainty in his own voice and he wondered where it came from. He was no expert in grunts.

Those soldiers should have been able to defeat that grunt. Failing that, they should have been able to drive it away. Even a bear or grass lion would retreat from a line of spears. But this . . .

In war, soldiers would line up in squares and charge each other, stabbing and shoving to break the other side's formation. They were trained to move forward or brace to hold their position. The grunts, though, were incredibly mobile. If humans were going to win this war, they were going to need new tactics.

Tejohn glanced at the doorway, half expecting to see a grunt standing there, teeth bared. Part of him hoped to see it, so that he could throw himself against the creature with nothing but his knife and whatever strength Fury gave him.

Which would be suicide. A dismal recklessness had come over him— even his rush to enter this house came from his urge to be pulled into a fight.

But today was not the day for noble, hopeless battles. Maybe someday, when he was sure he could never see his wife and children again, had no hope of retrieving the spell Lar asked him to find, and could never stop the spread of the Blessing, but not today.

"They're closer to Ussmajil than I thought," Javien whispered. "Beacon Veliender believed the creatures were still farther south, barely penetrating Raftlin lands. The Raftlin holdfast still stands—or it did, before we left the city."

"The grunts are not an invading army. They aren't interested in capturing towns and lands, ruling over farmers and shipping home all their wealth. And they're not stupid, either. They're . . . "

The beacon stared at him, waiting for him to finish his sentence. Tejohn could feel the man's attention on him.

"Finish your meal," he finally said. That dismal recklessness was becoming keener, like the tip of an iron spear. It was time to *do* something. "Then change out of that red robe. We have to take a detour in our mission."

"We can not," Javien insisted. "You saw what happened to those spears. If humankind is to have any hope at all, we will need that spell."

Assuming it exists. No, Tejohn was not going to give voice to the nagging doubt that had dogged him since he had set out from Fort Samsit so long ago. "We do. But we also need to know as much about our enemy as possible."

The faint, misting rain continued as they crept down the hill toward the site of the little battle. Again, they kept to the trees, straining their ears to hear the sound of a grunt moving through the grasses, but there was nothing. They could have been all alone in the world.

The soldiers had thrown aside their weapons and gear as they'd been led away, leaving them lying in the grass. Tejohn pressed a scabbarded sword and belt against Javien's chest until the young man took it, then strapped one on himself.

They were made of poor iron but they were better than the knives at their belts. It felt good to feel the weight on his hip again. The tall, rectangular shields were heavier than he liked, but workable. The spears were fine—sturdy but unremarkable—but none of the helmets fit. He dropped the last one back into the grass. Better to have no helmet than one that could twist and cover your eyes.

The beacon could not be convinced to take up a shield and spear; Tejohn didn't push it. The man was a scholar and a priest. He probably didn't have the strength to hike all day with them.

Tejohn stood and stared out toward the road. The grunt had dragged the soldier through a stand of wheat, leaving a clear trail to follow. It was headed generally south-southwest. Did the thing have a den? A nest? He had to know.

"We can't!" Javien whispered as he followed Tejohn toward the road. "We should turn north!"

Tejohn ignored him. Five soldiers had fought bravely and fallen. He needed to see what had happened to them. They hadn't been killed, and he was fairly certain they weren't being held prisoner in the way he thought about it.

He had to know what the grunts did with their "unborn young." If that was recklessness, so be it. As long as he didn't let himself be drawn into a fight . . .

They followed the trail of broken wheat stalks to the road. There was no one to bring in this harvest, of course, nor any of the other crops on the other farms around them. If the grunts kept quietly dragging farmers away, there would be starvation during the winter, spring, and—worst of all—summer of next year.

Assuming he could stop the grunts somehow and return human beings to this land.

They lost the trail once they reached the road. There was nothing to mark a dragged body, and no footprints in the packed stone road. They continued westward for a little while, knowing it was dangerous to travel so close to the ditches. It was Javien who noticed a bloody mark on the gatepost of a farm on the south side of the road. One of the soldiers must have leaned against it when they entered.

"The rain isn't—"

Tejohn hushed him. With the wheat stalks so tall and so close, a grunt might be hiding in ambush just a few feet away.

The gate stood wide open. Tejohn crossed the road and stepped through. The path that lead uphill was rutted and damaged, and there were a few curving breaks through the stalks higher up the hill.

It felt wrong. They both backed away, moving into the ditch beside the road. The house wasn't visible beyond the curve of the hill, but they could see the peak of a barn roof above the stalks. The blood on the post was fainter now. The misting rain was slowly washing it away.

Tejohn signaled the beacon to follow him farther along the road. The farm on the next plot of land was also packed tight with wheat stalks, but the gate was shut. This farm sat higher on the hill than the one the grunts had entered. They climbed over the gate and moved, crouching, up the path. Near the crest of the hill, they saw the farmhouse—it looked as empty as the one where they'd broken their fast—and a barn.

There were no grunts in sight and they couldn't hear anything but the drizzle falling on tall grass. Tejohn crept forward, then at the edge of the field, he dashed across the open space to take shelter behind a cart.

The musty scent of piss was strong here. They circled to the west-facing side of the barn and found a broken door. It was quiet inside, and the gray daylight did not shine far in. After glancing at the space beneath—like many storage buildings this close to the Waterlands, it had been built so the wooden floor would be two hand-lengths above the ground—Tejohn hefted his shield and spear, then moved into the doorway, knowing he'd be silhouetted by the light. If there was a grunt inside, it would be coming for him now. Right now.

Right now.

Nothing happened. Tejohn let out a sigh of relief and stepped up into the building, the priest close behind. It stank of death. They stood together in the dark room, letting their eyes slowly adjust, while unseen rats scurried at the edges of the room.

"Monument sustain me," Javien said. "Rats."

Tejohn almost laughed. "That sound reminds me of my childhood. My father waged an unending war on the rats in his fields. Take it as a good sign, beacon. If the grunts had a habit of coming here, the vermin would have fled long ago."

"So, what are you planning? Do we hide here until the rain passes? Until nightfall?"

Tejohn didn't answer. He moved carefully from bay to bay, doing his best to step quietly on the planks and avoid touching anything. As he passed around a tall rack of shelves, he saw the faint glimmers of light from the broad front door. It stood partly ajar, the crossbar lying broken in the gray light of the gap.

This end of the barn was better lit, and Tejohn's eyes adjusted quickly. A rope on a pulley hung over the bay from a connecting tie, and a pallet still dangled from a hook way up on the collar beam. Grain sacks had been stacked against one wall, and an empty oil lamp hung above the door.

At his feet lay the dead body of a farm hound. It had been torn apart and devoured.

"Oh!" Javien exclaimed. He crouched beside the corpse. "Poor thing. Poor old thing."

Tejohn found a box of bronze nails beside a hanging rack of bronze hatchets, hammers, tree saws, and a scythe. "Can you fire darts?"

"Yes," Javien answered.

"Good."

"What are we doing here?"

"If you were a soldier, I'd give you three lashes for asking questions. Since you're not, I may not be so gentle. Come with me."

Tejohn led him to the broken front door. Together, they crouched low and peered through the gap.

The open ground ahead sloped away from them, giving them a view of the small hillock atop the next farm. The barn looked similar to the one they were in, but the farmhouse itself, which they couldn't see from the road, was the largest they'd seen yet. "Someone had a big family," Tejohn muttered. Just the thought of it made him nauseous.

A blue-furred grunt came around the side of the house and stalked through the front yard, walking on all fours like a long-armed bear. It looked in every direction, as tense as a sentry in enemy territory, which it was. It settled onto its haunches and sat still in the rain. Tejohn wished he could be closer to see if it was sniffing the air, listening, or looking—or some combination of those. Unfortunately, as amazing as his new eyes were, there were limits.

Tejohn chuckled to himself. He'd been cured of nearsightedness so severe it had practically been blindness, and he was already wishing for more.

"That's the same one, isn't it?" Javien said.

"Doubtful. It's standing guard over something inside the house. I don't think it would have gone scouting for more . . . converts without leaving someone in place. I think there must be at least one more. At least."

"We should tell someone. We should hurry to the next guard post and tell the King's spears what we've found. They could return in force—"

"We just saw one grunt defeat five soldiers without taking a scratch. How many soldiers do you think they'd need to face two grunts, or three or five? How long do you think it would take to gather the force they'd need? Don't forget that those five soldiers will be grunts themselves in three days."

"And who knows how many more people are inside that—"

The grunt in the front yard barked once, sharply. Tejohn and Javien saw a second beast step out of the doorway—he hadn't noticed that the farmhouse door had been torn off and thrown into the garden. Did the grunts hate doors? The creatures moved warily toward each other, and if they grunted or growled, it was impossible to hear over the patter of the rain.

While they gestured sharply and snapped their jaws, a little girl appeared in the dark doorway. She couldn't have been as old as two, and she wavered like a drunkard as she stumbled into the mud of the yard.

Both creatures turned and roared at her, waving their arms above their heads. The child, startled, fell onto her rear end, and an older child of six or seven scooped her up and carried her back inside.

A deadly, icy calm passed over Tejohn. He was not going to leave children at the mercy of The Blessing's next hunger pang. He could not turn away. Not now.

CHAPTER SEVENTEEN

"**W**OULDN'T IT BE BETTER TO WAIT UNTIL DARK?" JAVIEN INSISTED for the tenth time.

"Do it," Tejohn said. "Now."

Javien began the hand motions to cast the spell. Tejohn immediately remembered Doctor Rexler making the same motions, his fist full of darts; someday, someone would have to make a chart of each spell so that soldiers could recognize them while they were being cast.

Except that Javien didn't cast the spell. He made an error somewhere and nothing came of it. "Fire and Fury," he muttered. "Let me try that again."

"Mistakes like that could get both of us killed," Tejohn said quietly.

"I know. I know." He started again. This time, his hands trembled slightly.

Tejohn briefly considered withdrawing. He knew he shouldn't even be risking this battle when his mission was so vital, but he felt he had no choice. Only a month or two ago, he would have walked away from the children he'd seen in that house, and the captured soldiers, too. He would have followed orders.

There was no one to give him orders now. The Italgas were gone. Others called themselves kings now, but Tejohn felt nothing for them but sharp contempt. He'd even cast aside his own title, *tyr*, as a relic of the fallen empire.

He had lived in the Palace of Song and Morning as an honored friend to the royal family, and he had lived in the bare, drafty barracks of a servant. That swing from one extreme to the other had freed him from the small voice in his head that said, *This is a mistake,* over and over. He knew it was a mistake just as he knew he had to do it.

The priest managed to cast the spell correctly on the second try. "Whew," he whispered after the rock flew from his hand. "I haven't had much practice with that one."

His hands were still trembling slightly. "Will you be able to cast the other spells without fail?"

"I think—"

His answer was interrupted by the sharp crack of the stone striking the roof of the farmhouse below. Tejohn had originally planned to use the bronze nails, but the rocks would be harder to see in the air and on the ground.

From the moment the noise sounded, the grunts went a little crazy. The beast inside the house charged out and leaped onto the roof, ready to challenge whatever he found there. The other grunt raced from a position near the fence line to the field behind the house, where the stone had skipped. The owners of the property had planted barley back there, and from the lack of furrows, it seemed the creatures had not explored it much.

The grunt on the roof peered out over the barley while the other barreled through it.

"Now," Tejohn said.

He and Javien rushed out of the barn into the tall grass. The grunts had broken a trail through the wheat on this property, too, and the two men ran across the exposed side of the hill until they came to it. Tejohn shoved the priest into the furrow, then pressed his head toward the ground. They needed to stay very low if they were going to make it to the bottom of the hill unseen.

As expected, the grunts were riled, but as they roamed the back fields searching for the source of the disturbance, Tejohn and Javien ran to the edge of the crop at the bottom of the hill. The fence was only twenty feet away, but the men crouched quietly, waiting.

The rain had worsened somewhat by the time the grunt passed. It was exploring the entire property now, and from his hiding place among the stalks, Tejohn watched it pass along the fence. He waited, counting his breaths the way he'd been taught as a green recruit. At two thousand, they broke from cover, hopped the fence, and slipped into a ragged, curving furrow on the other hill. Enemy territory.

From their high vantage point on the neighboring farm, Tejohn had studied the crooked paths the grunts had plowed through the field. The rain, falling even harder now, masked the sound of their footsteps as they crunched across the broken stalks. They came to the first turning, then the next, then continued straight across the field until the furrow curved back on itself, heading uphill toward the farmhouse and barn. This was the one he needed to take.

He approached as near as he dared. The end of the ragged furrow met the muddy yard at an oblique angle, about twenty paces from the farmhouse itself. An axe, a woodpile, a flatbed cart, and a stone well stood between them.

The barn was closer to the wheat, but not much closer to the end of the furrow. Tejohn was a little dismayed by the distance he had to cross, but this position would do. It would have to. The doors stood wide open at this end, too, just like the smaller entrance he'd seen from the far hill. The gray daylight showed scattered straw on the floor and a few toppled wooden shelves. Good.

He lay about six paces from the end of the furrow, where he hoped the stalks were thick enough to hide him from the grunt patrolling the yard. He was about to decide they were not and move backward when a grunt passed.

Its back was to him, of course, which meant it had already looked at his hiding place and missed him. Tejohn saw the ridges and plates on its back and his breath caught. He hadn't been prepared. If it had rushed him while his shield was beneath him—placed there so the rain wouldn't drum on it—and his spear on the ground, it could have torn him apart and devoured him, or worse.

By the time the grunt went around the corner of the building, Tejohn realized he had forgotten to time it. He lay absolutely still until the beast passed again. The second time, it took the grunt one hundred forty-two breaths to circle the farmhouse. The third, it was one hundred and fifty-one.

After the third, Tejohn crept forward until the farmhouse door came into view. It stood wide open, just like the others, and a grunt passed in front of it.

"Now," he whispered to Javien.

The beacon came up out of the mud and sprinted out of the furrow toward the farm. He was exposed there for no more than three breaths, but those moments made Tejohn's skin prickle with sweat. If one of the grunts spotted him . . .

They didn't. Javien reached the side of the farmhouse and ducked behind it out of sight of the house. Tejohn moved back to his safe spot and waited for the signal.

After what seemed like much too long, Javien came back into view and the near corner of the barn. He was ready. Tejohn watched the grunt disappear around the corner of the house again as it made its endless, tedious circuits, then took a pair of pebbles from the inner pocket of his robe.

Sliding up onto his knees, he counted to sixty-five, then threw them with all of his might. He'd been nearly blind his entire life, and chucking stones was not something he had a lot of practice with. Still, it was an open barn door, and Song knew he would get what he deserved if he missed.

He didn't. One of the pebbles struck a wooden shelf and skipped upward to rebound off a wall. The other hit the wall directly and bounced several times in the bay against wood and iron. A clay pot shattered.

Javien had already begun the hand motions for his spell when the grunts' roars began. Tejohn threw another stone, then dropped flat to the dirt. He could hear the grunts splashing toward the barn as his third stone struck something metal.

Both grunts charged inside with the speed of an arrow in flight. Tejohn scrambled to his knees, then his feet, feeling as plodding as an invalid. A terrible furious pounding echoed from within the building as the creatures threw themselves against the small back door. Tejohn sprinted across the yard, his shield and spear in hand.

This was the most dangerous part of the plan. Javien's orders were to stay out of sight until the beasts were well trapped. If they escaped, he was to slip away while they tore Tejohn to pieces.

They had to be quick. Tejohn sprinted, leaning so far forward, he nearly stumbled. He'd hoped the rain would hide the sound of his charge, but the two beasts pounded on the back door as if they were trying to tear the whole building down. They were making so much noise, he could have driven a herd of okshim at them and caught them by surprise.

Tejohn crossed the open doorway to the other side of the barn. The interior was so dark, he couldn't see anything inside, and his skin tingled at the idea that one of the grunts might leap upon him while his shield was out of position.

It didn't happen. They were clearly still furiously intent on battering the back door open. Tejohn laid his shield and shoulder against the door and—feeling it tremble as the grunts pounded the other end of the building—began to swing it closed. The hinge creaked. His boots squelched in the mud. His stomach fluttered in stark terror. The grunts did not notice until he had blocked off almost all of their light.

Just as he wondered where the priest had gone—and if he'd fled in terror—the young man was there, hands in motion. Tejohn jammed his spear point into the mud at the base of the door as the first of the grunts threw itself against it. The whole door buckled and the spear point bent so far that the shaft bulged outward and touched Tejohn's collarbone.

He threw himself against the bottom of the door, adding his weight to the spear. A moment later, a broad pink block of stone appeared beside him, dropping into the mud so close by that the edge of his gray robe was trapped beneath it.

The grunts' assault on the door was deafening. Their claws slipped through the gaps in the wood and the stink of their breath blew across his face. Fire and Fury, they were close.

The stone was big, but Tejohn wanted bigger. It was two hand-widths high, three times wider than that and maybe ten times longer: enough to block the door, but there was so much wobble, he thought the wood would split. "Another."

Javien shut his eyes and began the spell again. His hands were visibly trembling, and while he managed to cast it, the second stone was even smaller than the first. It fell atop the first one, the same dimensions of length and width but not nearly as tall.

Tejohn tore his robe standing out of the mud, then stepped back. The assault against the door didn't let up, but the door wobbled slightly less. Slightly. It wouldn't hold for long.

Javien's eyes were wide and terrified. His courage was close to breaking, and if Tejohn asked for another stone block from him, he might not get anything else. "Now."

He started a different spell this time, and his hands trembled so terribly that he had to stop in the middle and start again. Tejohn stepped toward him and laid a hand on his shoulder. Whether that reassured him or not, the second attempt succeeded, and a gout of flame appeared from between his hands.

The priest bent low and held the fire against the corner of the barn where the wood met the stone foundation. It caught immediately, and he began to walk along the side of the building, playing the flame on the wood and the narrow gaps between the slats. They'd agreed to light this side first, since the direction of the wind should have left it driest, but nothing about it looked dry to Tejohn. The rain that had masked their approach worked against them now.

Still, the magic fire was hot; it steamed away the water and sent tongues of flame up the side of the wall. The grunts continued to pound on the door in the same frantic way, but their roars had a note of fear in them now.

Tejohn rolled the hay cart to the door and upended it to brace the top part of the door. Then he fetched an armload of kindling from the woodpile for the back door. It had already been blocked by another piece of granite—that had been the priest's first task, the one he'd had to complete before signaling. He piled them against the wood, wondering what good it would do when Javien brought his flame to this part of the building.

Oil. He needed oil, but there was so little in the property next door that he hadn't bothered to bring it. The wheat stalks were wet enough that they might smother the fire instead of feed it, and—

A sudden flare from inside the barn made Javien stumble backward and fall into the mud. The flames roared from inside the building, veils of firelight shining through the gaps in the wood onto the misting rain.

The grunts became hysterical with fear, and the pounding against the wood stopped. Tejohn saw flame growing on the wall opposite the one the priest had lit. Something inside—oil, tar, something—had burst and spread the fire throughout the building.

As Tejohn helped Javien out of the mud, the grunts began to scream in pain and terror. They were terrible sounds, and no matter how much he hated those creatures and their Blessing, the cries they made as they burned to death made him sick.

He and Javien had been lucky. Every plan depended on good fortune to some degree, but Fury and The Great Way had favored them.

"Grateful am I," he said, "to be permitted to travel The Way." Javien repeated the prayer just as the grunts fell quiet.

The barn burned bright and hot in the light rain. In normal times, every soldier and farmer in the valley ought to be able to see that and come running. Tejohn wondered if anyone would come today.

He and Javien turned to the farmhouse. The shutters had been thrown open and the windows filled with faces. The soldier who'd tried to fall on her sword was there, her expression blank. The others looked much the same.

Tejohn laid his hand on his sword and hefted his shield. "Is there a third creature inside?" None of them answered. "Is there a third grunt inside the house with you? Come out!"

The soldiers looked at each other as though he was speaking a foreign language.

Javien turned toward him. "My tyr, if another of The Blessing was inside the house, wouldn't it have charged us by now? Or tried to free its brothers?"

"I would think so. So, why are they refusing to come out?"

Tejohn started for the doorway, his shield high and his short sword low and point-forward. The older couple crowding the doorway retreated from him, pulling the little children with them.

There was no grunt inside. Tejohn had to stop himself from sighing in relief.

Inside were the five soldiers, including the one who had been struck senseless—he appeared to have managed a miraculous recovery once the curse was upon him. There was also an older couple with the gray hair, sun-wrinkled skin, and ropey muscles that come from a lifetime of farm labor. Behind them was a stout young woman of about thirty. She had charge of three children: a boy and girl too young to be out of dresses, and the six-year-old girl Tejohn had already seen.

The farmhouse was one large room, with a pit of sand in the center where the owners cooked their meals. There were leather balls in one corner and a pair of cloth dolls in a crude wooden raft. Children's toys. An ancient trident hung above a workbench, which Tejohn assumed to be a spoil of war. Tridents came from Espileth, in the Simblin lands, and no Simblin would have been permitted to settle in Finstel lands.

Tejohn tried to figure if the old couple were the owners of the house or if it might have been the stout woman. Not that it mattered now.

"You'll have to do it," the female soldier said. "We five swore an oath to each other that we would not let the creature's curse take us, but now that we are here, we can do nothing. The curse stays our hand; we can't harm ourselves or each other."

"I'll make it clean and quick," Tejohn assured them, "if you'll let me."

"Thank you," she said. The other soldiers thanked him, then the older couple. The stout woman said, "Blessing," then clenched her fist in frustration. The curse was growing strong inside her, saying its name.

"We'll have to take the little ones away first," Javien said, "before you transform and hurt them."

That startled them. "We couldn't hurt them," a soldier said. Was this the skilled fighter? Tejohn couldn't recognize him. "We couldn't hurt them any more than we could hurt each other."

No.

Javien didn't understand. "Not now, no, but if you change suddenly, you'll be mad with starvation. That's how it works, yes? Once you stop being human, you won't be able to help yourself. We need to get them away from you before that happens."

"You don't understand," the old man said.

The stout woman bent to the little boy sitting listless by her feet. "They have been blessed just like blessing." She lifted the hem of his dress.

There was a nasty red puncture mark on his thigh. He—and all the children—had been bitten, too.

"This doesn't make sense," Tejohn blurted out. "They're so small! What sort of grunt could they get from a tiny child?"

"A full-grown one," the old farmer said. "They're all full-sized. The first to be bitten on our property was a debt child who worked in our farm. No more than nine, she was, the lazy little thing. She was all *bless bless bless* at the end, and when she changed she just split apart. A full-sized monster burst out of her."

Tejohn suddenly felt terribly cold. "What happened to her? To this grunt?"

The old man nodded toward the fire still burning outside. "You just put her out of her misery."

I killed a child, Tejohn thought. *I killed a child. A grunt. A child. I knew the things had been human once, but a child?*

His legs felt weak and his head swam for a moment. He, of all people, had just murdered someone's child.

And he was going to have to do it again.

CHAPTER EIGHTEEN

THE PAIN WAS SHARP AND SUDDEN. CAZIA CRIED OUT, HER VOICE echoing through the chill night air. Harsh laughter sounded from the walls.

Ivy caught hold of Cazia's wrist, bumping the point of the arrow and levering two knuckles apart. Cazia cried out again, which brought more laughter from the darkness to the south. They sounded like wild dogs, and Cazia was suddenly aware that her cries of pain would be like a beacon to the predatory beasts of the wilderness.

"What is it?" Kinz asked, sounding very annoyed.

"An arrow!" Ivy exclaimed. "They shot an arrow at us. Cazia saved my life."

A second buzzing noise came toward them; the girls ducked low and scrambled away from the wall. They heard impacts against the ground around them; the guards were shooting more arrows.

They scrambled through the muddy, uneven terrain. Ivy wouldn't let go of Cazia's arm, and it was difficult for her to keep her balance in the darkness.

"What are they making to do?" Kinz demanded. "I understand Toal. You told them who you are. Are the Ergoll at war with the Toal?"

"No!" Ivy said, sounding almost desperate. "No, they can not be. The Alliance has ways of dealing with disagreements that come well short of war, and Kelvijinian would never allow us to waste our strength that way, not when we have so many enemies pressing in on us."

"Then what happened?"

Cazia stopped running. She had to pry her wrist out of Ivy's grip. "That's what I want to know. Why are Alliance troops shooting at a member of the royal family?"

"I do not know! Oh, Cazia, I am so sorry! Those men would have killed me if you had not acted." Ivy grabbed her hand again and held it up. "What made you do it?"

"I'm not sure." That, at least, was true. "I saw and heard something, and I just . . . I'm not sure. What are the chances that I can find a sleepstone nearby?"

"Bad," Kinz said. "Peradaini devils never make them this far east. Er, I am sorry about that. It is an old habit."

"Fire take it," Cazia snapped. "I don't care if you call me a devil. How far to the nearest sleepstone?"

"On foot? With an injury? Twenty days. Maybe more."

"No, Cazia, we can not." Ivy's voice was hushed. "That would take us too close to that fort—What was the name of that place again?"

Monument sustain her, the princess was right. "Samsit."

"Yes, Fort Samsit. The grunts were running wild there three months ago. Do you think some of them have come north? Into the Sweeps?"

"Yes," Cazia said. There might be grunts just a few hundred paces away right now, stalking the wilderness, trying to find the source of her screams. "Yes, I do. We need to find cover. We don't want one of Mother's people to swoop down on us out of nowhere before she's had a chance to spread the word. And we don't want a grunt to come upon us in the dark."

The half-moon had risen high enough for Cazia to make out a stand of trees on a low hill to the east. They made for it quietly. The jeering from the fort had stopped, probably under orders.

Kinz said something about wanting to climb into the trees, but the trunks were narrow and slender—not much for climbing, even if Cazia could use both of her hands. They would have to take their chances with the grunts, grass lions, and whatever other beasts hunted the night.

They sat without talking for once. Cazia wished fervently that they could risk a fire. She was hungry and dispirited, and her hand throbbed. Had they really risked their lives in the Qorr Valley just to be attacked by her own— well, she shouldn't call them her *people*. They were Indregai Alliance soldiers, and they were technically her enemy. What's more, they were apparently in the habit of shooting at little girls, so Fire could take the lot of them.

Still, after her clashes with The Blessing, the Tilkilit, and whatever Mother's people called themselves, it made her heartsick to come so close to actual humans again only to be driven away.

Ivy moved close and rested her head on her shoulder. "Is this uncomfortable?"

She had settled on Cazia's uninjured side. "No, it's good. I'm sorry that we're still stuck out here."

"It is just one night." She nestled in as though she wanted to sleep. "Did I thank you for saving my life? Thank you."

"That's what I promised you, remember? Back in Samsit before we fled into the wilderness. I promised to protect you."

"From the tyrs," Ivy answered. "Not from my own people."

Cazia shifted her injured hand. It didn't lessen the pain at all. "Maybe I should have been more specific."

They laughed together, quietly. Ivy held out her hand to Kinz, who shifted to the trunk they were leaning against and settled in on Ivy's other side. "I should keep watch," she protested.

"Why?" Cazia said. "We have no weapons and no magic. If a grass lion comes upon us now, there would be nothing we could do."

"Grass lions make their hunt during the day," Kinz said. "We should worry about other things."

There was a tension in her voice that Cazia couldn't place. "I'm sorry I said *wilderness*. I know it's your home, but . . . Habit. It's just stupid habit."

"We should make to put our differences aside," Kinz said. "We must. Whatever crimes have been committed in the past, we must turn away from them. If we do not, all of our peoples will be overwhelmed."

Crimes. Cazia tried to shift her hand again but the pain was too much. Ivy, her "little sister," had nearly been murdered, and now Cazia was badly hurt with no access to healing magic. The whole situation made her feel so helpless, and so filled with useless frustrated rage at the soldiers on the wall of the fort. Was this how it felt to be attacked by Peradaini soldiers?

What if they'd shot a second arrow and killed Ivy? Cazia squeezed the girl's hand, trying not to imagine the grief and burning desire for revenge she would feel.

Kinz had a right to call them crimes, and she had a right to her anger and hate. And to think Cazia had made a fuss over the words *tributes* and *taxes* in a world full of wounded, grieving people. "Yes." She couldn't say more for fear of being sick into the grass.

Ivy said, "Agreed. Should we take out the arrow?"

"No," Kinz answered. "If you are sure we will be allowed into the fort at sunrise, we should wait. Arrows make to be tricky. If we did the wrong thing, that hand might be made the amputation."

"Little sister," Cazia began nervously. She almost didn't want to have this conversation because she was afraid of what she would learn. "Little sister, what treatments do your people have for injuries like mine? Will they be able to heal me?"

The way the princess hesitated before answering scared Cazia more than her answer. "We do not have healing magic, obviously. All we can offer is clean bandages, tinctures, and herbs, plus some exercises that will help you regain your strength. I—Cazia, are you worried that you will not be able to do magic again?"

"I am. I'm very worried about that." That ended their conversation.

In the end, they slept. Cazia did not expect to sleep, but they all did. Cazia's injury woke her several times.

They rose with the sun. Cazia felt as though she hadn't rested at all, but at least she had been able to pass the night in slumber rather than sitting up fretting. She stood carefully; her hand felt as though it had swollen around the arrow shaft like a clenching fist. If the pain had been bright and sharp last night, now it was dull, throbbing, and awful. Pain like this could make her hate the entire world.

"Oh!" Ivy exclaimed. They turned together and saw what she was pointing at. Piles of tiny stones had been arranged on the ground not four paces from where they'd slept.

"Inzu's Breath," Kinz exclaimed, then rushed forward.

"Wait!" Cazia called, and the girl halted. "The lakeboys do this, don't they?"

"They do. The next night they make the attack. Very dangerous."

"But delicious," Cazia said, remembering the last time they'd had a conversation about the creatures Cazia's people called *alligaunts*. She moved toward the piles. She'd seen this briefly before they'd crossed into Qorr. That time had been right at the water's edge, but this one was at least fifty paces from the nearest streambed.

"It is a display and threat," Kinz said. "They are stones like cairn stones. I could not make to explain this to you the first time."

Cazia didn't say *because you were pretending we didn't speak the same language.* They were putting the past behind them.

They didn't look like cairn stones, though. They were little piles, starting with one pebble atop another, then three leaning together, then four with a fifth balanced on top. The next had seven stones in a jumble. It was just as she remembered it. She moved to the last pile and counted thirteen stones.

"Some animals swallow stones," Ivy said. "They help with digestion—until they pass them out."

Ugh. Pass them out? Cazia had handled the stones. "No," she said. "These came from a streambed, not some animal's guts. Look, there's a pattern here."

"The pattern is a threat." Kinz began kicking over the piles. "This is my land. My people know how to deal with these things. We must make to move away or be attacked tonight."

"I know what you are thinking," Ivy said. "We could talk to the birds and to the bug soldiers. Why not the alligaunts, too?"

"Exactly."

"No," Kinz insisted. "We know these creatures. They have been here for many generations. They do not have the society. They do not think. They only hunt and kill."

"And make odd patterns."

"It is the threat." Kinz's expression was obstinate. "The way for them to make mark of their territory, like the dog that lifts its leg."

Ivy turned south toward the fort. "It does not matter. Today, we take Cazia into the fort to be cared for. And break our fasts. And to send word to my father and mother."

They started across the muddy ground toward the rough timber gate. "Remember to tell the altered story." Kinz said. "We may be separated when we make to tell what we have done."

"The soldiers at Fort Whune are Toal." Ivy took hold of Cazia's good arm to support her. "They are staunch allies and good fighters, but they are also arrogant."

"Elder brothers," Cazia said. It was hard to focus on the uneven ground and Ivy's words; her injured hand was too huge in her mind.

Ivy said, "More than that. They believe themselves to be the seed of the Indregai peoples, and often treat other kings like my father as if they were the grown sons. Do you see what I mean? Equals in power but not wisdom or respect."

Cazia gave her a look.

"I know how it sounds," Ivy said, her cheeks flushing red. "I do. But I can speak for you if we are among the Ergoll. I'm still very young, but my voice will be heard. If nothing else, they might feel indebted for the good you have done for me, and my mother has always indulged me if I pester her enough. But we must convince them our story is true or you will not be free."

Cazia took the translation stone from her pocket and tossed it away. She should have traded it to Mother after all. "Now I have no darts, no robes, no enchanted gem. Anything that would identify me as a devil is . . . Kinz, touch a Tilkilit stone to me again, please."

She did. Kinz and Ivy kept glancing back as they walked. Cazia wasn't sure if they were mentally marking the spot or fighting the urge to run back for it immediately. Whichever it was, they kept a steady pace toward the fort.

When they were close enough, Cazia was surprised to see that the fort's defenses were more complex than they'd seemed in the darkness. The walls were rough timber, yes, but where they joined the mountainside was steep rock. Also, a slowly trickling waterfall ran down the eastern cliff face into the muddy ground before the wall. The current wasn't strong enough to sweep away their enemies, but it did fill a broad, deep pool lined with stones.

A *moat*, Ivy called it. It was forty feet wide, and the only way to cross it was to stand on a stone platform that protruded over the water and wait for them to lower the *drawbridge*, a gate with its hinges at the bottom.

What's more, the walls and drawbridge were topped with small bronze spikes no longer than Cazia's little finger.

Midway up the wall, she spotted tall slots between the timbers where archers could take their shots. Atop the wall they could see six archers and the odd blank white banners that the Alliance troops preferred.

"Ivy," Kinz whispered harshly, "do not get ahead of us."

The princess did not take that advice. As they walked out onto the promontory, one of the archers shouted before Ivy could speak. Cazia couldn't understand their language, of course.

The comment brought another round of raucous laughter. Cazia saw movement in the arrow slits. If one of the archers atop the wall bent their bow at Ivy, they would have warning enough to flee. If one of those hidden behind the wall shot at them, they would not know it until the arrow was on its deadly flight.

Ivy called back to them, and Cazia wished she had kept the translation stone. She couldn't understand anything except for the full version of the princess's name. The guard and the princess shouted back and forth several times.

Kinz finally noticed Cazia's distressed expression. "They do not believe her," she explained. "They are saying we make fine servants for fetching back their arrow, but they are demanding payment before they allow us inside."

Of course they were. Cazia looked off to the east. Could they simply flee down the Sweeps all the way to the ocean? Would that bring them to safety, finally?

After several exchanges, one of the archers nocked an arrow. Without shields or cover of any kind, the girls would have no choice but to run away. Again.

The princess was in no mood to retreat again, it seemed. When she saw the archer, she raised her voice and began shouting short, sharp phrases.

Kinz turned a mournful expression toward Cazia. "Now she's insulting their courage, their ancestry, and their entire clan."

Cazia held her injured hand close to her chest. She expected more arrows any moment, but they never came. The archer never bent his bow, and within a few moments, a man with a white plume sticking out of his bronze helmet came to the edge of the wall. He shouted something that almost sounded respectful. Ivy shouted back, and the drawbridge began to lower.

"You see?" the princess assured them. "We simply needed to convince them we were people of importance."

They were admitted at spearpoint. Ivy continued to speak to everyone around her as though they were her subjects and she expected them to welcome her. They didn't. Still, it was good to be out of the wilderness.

However, it became immediately clear that they had not been brought inside the fort itself. Beyond this first wall was another moat, this one spanned by a slender bridge. South of that was a tumbledown expanse of boulders and a low stone wall manned by men with extraordinarily long spears. Even the Ozzhuacks didn't carry spears that long. The boulders were very like the stones just outside the walls at Fort Samsit, except no one had cleared a path through them; only a flimsy wooden walkway allowed them to cross.

It made sense. The narrow wooden span across the water and the stones could be withdrawn—or burned with soldiers still upon it. A Peradaini square would be unable to cross that uneven ground in formation. It would have been impossible for them to hold their shield wall while scrambling from rock to rock.

No wonder the Peradaini kings had found it difficult to invade the peninsula. Cazia had never seen a fortification with more than one layer of defense; the Toal might not have had access to scholarly magic or iron weapons, but they made do with ingenuity.

The girls were marched across the walkways in single file, with soldiers in front of them and behind. The wood buckled alarmingly, but it held. There was no gate at the low wall ahead, but a wooden staircase was lowered for them.

Beyond that was another high stone wall with numerous arrow slits. This had a traditional gate, and it swung open to allow them through.

The inner yard of the fort was like the one in Samsit or at the gates of

Peradain: soldiers drilled, servants carried burdens, cleaned, or rushed about on their daily errands, someone barked orders, someone cracked a lash over the heads of okshim to move a cart southward toward the inner gate. The only differences were the colors the soldiers wore, the stone walls made of mortared black stone instead of the pink granite blocks scholars created, and that Cazia couldn't understand anything anyone said.

The first thing that happened inside the courtyard was that they were all forced to kneel in the dirt and remain utterly still. "I do not know what they want," Ivy said. "This is not the usual way the Toal treat guests."

Except it was clear that they were not guests. Not yet, at least. The man with the tall white plume emerged from a doorway with a second man in tow. This new fellow had deep brown skin, like Cazia's, and long black hair. His face was worn and he looked so exhausted, she thought he might fall over.

Scholar. She wasn't sure why she thought so, but she did. He certainly wasn't wearing a scholar's robes; he was dressed in Indregai white. Still, there was something about the roughness of his hands and the wariness in his manner that suggested he was a mining scholar.

The man with the plume—Cazia really had to learn what that big feather was supposed to indicate, so she knew to call him "watch commander" or "archery target" or whatever his rank was—pointed at the three girls. The exhausted man held his hand just above Cazia's shoulder, then Ivy's, then Kinz's.

"Nothing," he said, surprising her by speaking Peradaini.

"Try again," the archery target ordered.

He did, physically touching them this time. "There's nothing," the exhausted man said again. His voice was without tone or inflection. He appeared to be too tired for emotion. "I sense no magic in any of them."

He was dismissed. Cazia fought the urge to call out for him to stay, if only so she could hear people talking her language. She also had a vague urge to rescue him somehow.

When they had a chance, Cazia was going to touch a Tilkilit stone again; that was the only reason the scholar couldn't sense the magic in her, and she wanted to be ready in case there was another spot inspection.

One of the soldiers took the iron crown and the circlet from inside Kinz's robes and brought them to the commander, who clutched at them greedily. Ivy protested but Kinz shushed her.

The girls were then escorted across the yard into a cool, dark wooden room. The only light came from a slot cut into the wall just below the ceiling. There was a long table set with bowls of broth and loaves of bread, and beside that was a set of three cots.

"A cell!" Ivy exclaimed to them. "They have put us in a cell!"

Kinz did not have any qualms about their accommodations. She went directly to the long table and drained a bowl of red broth. Cazia did the same, but the bread smelled of sweet wine and she found that she couldn't eat it.

Ivy was yelling through the door in her same high, imperious tone. Kinz turned toward Cazia and said, "She is calling for a doctor."

Cazia was thrown for a moment until she realized that "doctor" had a different meaning outside the empire. The heavy door eventually swung open and a gray-haired woman bustled in with a leather bag. Ivy insisted on examining the contents and was clearly not pleased. After a brief discussion, the old woman went away.

"They think you're my girls," the princess said. "My servants, I mean. Never let anyone address you as *girl* or *woman*; once that insult takes hold, you'll be a servant. At least, they'll treat you like one, which is much the same thing."

While they waited for the "doctor" to return, Ivy taught them the words they should listen for: *girl*, *woman*, and *servant*. Then she taught them the word for *man*, in case they wanted to insult one of the men. It seemed that it was important to show your status by bad-mouthing people, she explained, then began to go through the complicated rules surrounding wit, jokes, and ridicule.

The whole thing make Cazia's pain-addled head spin. "Do they speak Ergoll?" she asked, just to change the subject.

"Oh, no," Ivy answered. "They speak Toal."

Cazia felt a flush of embarrassment. "Princess, how many languages do you speak?"

"Toal *barely* even counts. It is like speaking Ergoll with a mouthful of pebbles, if you leave out all the nuance and beauty."

The doctor returned. She cut the arrow shaft and pulled it out of Cazia's hand. The pain was so intense that she blacked out for a short while, waking to find her swollen hand soaking in a bowl of nasty-smelling black liquid. The doctor was speaking in soothing tones, but Cazia didn't understand a word of it.

"She is saying it does not appear infected," Ivy said. She had gone even paler than usual. "But this fluid will clean the wound. Does it sting?"

Cazia's mouth felt as though it was full of glue. "No worse than getting shot with an arrow."

"She is going to make a poultice and wrap it tight so you do not lose too much more blood. She wants you to eat and drink more broth before you sleep again. And you have to keep this clean."

Ivy exchanged a few words with the doctor in an irritated tone, then said, "Just take *common sense* precautions about keeping it clean." Clearly, the doctor had said something insulting, but Cazia felt too weak and wobbly to care.

The old woman finally removed Cazia's hand from the bowl of nasty, stinging water, then poured diluted wine over it to clean it. Cazia looked down at the injury—Great Way, it looked so small. How could so much pain come out of such a tiny hole?

More blood welled up out of it, and the doctor laid a bundle of green herbs against the wound and began to wrap it in bandages. The cloth smelled of the same nasty black stuff.

Every piece of Indregai cloth she'd ever seen was as pure white as it could be, except the dressing for her injury.

She began to laugh. The old doctor looked at her with surprise and fear, as though Cazia was about to whip out a knife and begin killing. That only made her laugh harder.

"It is okay." Ivy was beside her, holding her good hand gently, and Kinz stood in front of her with her hand on the back of Cazia's neck. Suddenly, the laughter evaporated and she felt tears running down her cheeks.

No. She must never cry. She was a Peradaini scholar and tears meant she would have her fingers chopped off. Her ruined, useless fingers.

The doctor knotted the bandage and stood. She gathered up her things and headed for the door.

"I don't understand," Cazia said. "It still hurts. How can she be finished if it still hurts? It feels like I'm wearing a glove on this hand; can't she make it better?"

"Oh, big sister," Ivy said. "You are not in your empire any more."

They made her eat a loaf of bread and drink another bowl of broth, then she was permitted to sleep. Sometime in the middle of the night, she was woken by five women with long bronze knives who wanted them all to strip. They did and were thoroughly examined. Cazia had barely enough energy to be envious of Kinz's long, fit figure while also wondering at the awful scar above her left hip, then it was over. She dressed and fell back into a fitful sleep.

The next day, the pain was worse. Was this how people dealt with injuries outside the empire? No wonder the Peradaini had conquered so much of Kal-Maddum. Great Way, the whole world should want to be Peradaini.

She lay in her cot and spoke to no one, not even the soldier who had come to interrogate her in her own language.

For years, she had feared the punishment for being hollowed out: to lose the use of her fingers and with it, her magic. In one unthinking moment, she had saved her friend's life and lost forever the ability to cast spells. She did not regret the sacrifice and would have made the same choice again, but without her magic, she wasn't Cazia Freewell any more.

Nothing was never going to be right again.

Chapter Nineteen

THEY STAYED IN THE CELL FOR FIVE DAYS AND WERE FORCED TO STRIP
for a search every night. They all understood the Toal were afraid of
allowing grunts through their defenses, and respected the precautions they
took, no matter inconvenient they were.

For Ivy, it was a different issue altogether: she insisted that it was dangerous to allow disrespect to go unchallenged or it might become worse.

Still, there was nothing she could do about it, so she endured. As for Kinz
and Cazia, they were content to be provided as much food as they could eat
while doing as little as possible for a few days.

And there was the matter of the Tilkilit stones. How many scholars did
the Toal have? How useful would the stones be here, at Fort Whune? More
importantly, would they be distributed until a way could be found to make
more—if that was even possible?

Ivy assured them they would not. Precious items like Kinz's iron
crown—when stripped from prisoners—would become the property of the
commander here, for good or ill. Luckily, Kinz was able to hide the stones in
her clothes; if only they could have hidden the crown as well.

The doctor arrived every morning to inspect Cazia's hand and change
the bandage. The Captain of the Wall (that was the title of the man with the
plume) arrived every afternoon to chat with them about where they had been
and what they had seen. He spoke in Peradaini; Ivy and Kinz answered in
Peradaini. Cazia barely took part in the discussions, even when addressed
directly. Her hand was becoming worse every day, she thought. The fingers
screamed in pain if she so much as brushed a piece of cloth against them,
and the palm had no comfortable place to rest.

When Cazia said as much, Kinz admonished her. "Your fingers. Your palm. You must not talk about them as though they belong to someone else. Trust me. Your body must remain yours if you are going to care for it and become strong."

She chose her words more carefully in the future, although her feeling hadn't changed. The hand. Her magic. Would she trade the whole of the left hand for the ability to cast spells again? She was certain that she would.

Every morning, Kinz touched her with an anti-magic stone. The scholar had not returned since that first meeting, but they were afraid he would.

Absurdly, Cazia was most unhappy with the food. None of the girls liked eating bowls of mush, but Ivy claimed it was very like the food she had eaten when she was small, and was fitfully nostalgic about it. Cazia found it unbearably bland; with the pain, the isolation, the boredom, and the constant fear that they might be executed, the miserable paste they ate twice a day made her want to weep.

The Captain of the Wall introduced himself every time he entered the cell, in a strangely formal style that annoyed Cazia deeply. He was a bit of a puzzle himself; she'd thought that everyone on the Indregai Peninsula looked like Ivy: red- or yellow-haired and fair-skinned, with a flush of red beneath their cheeks when the sun was hot or they worked too hard. However, while the Captain was indeed fair-skinned, his hair was long, glossy, and as black as Kinz's own.

On the third day, it occurred to her that she was supposed to be distracted by his manners and good looks. She wasn't. His pale complexion reminded her of goat's milk, and the very thought of it made her stomach flip. Little Spinner, turn him away, he must have been close to thirty! His every attempt to engage her failed.

Finally, on the fifth day, he asked her to sing a song.

"We hear rumors of the power and skill of the musicians of your empire, but I have never heard the work. Would you sing a song for me?"

The idea was ludicrous on its face. Cazia was tempted to take a bowl of broth from the table and dump it over his head. Still, Ivy and Kinz thought it was a fine idea. When they saw that Cazia wasn't enthused, they encouraged the Captain to go first.

He did, and it was awful. Not that his voice was bad—it was fine and clear—but the song itself would have bored Peradaini children. *La dee la dee la dee la dee* was the entire melody, with a brief *leelee dee* thrown in here and there. He sang it for much too long, but when he stopped, he said he'd cut it short. It was a walking song, he explained, used to help people find their way in the days before map-making.

Ivy and Kinz wanted to hear the one she'd sung for them on the mountain. Didn't she remember the one?

She did, of course. *River Overrunning.* The song that had made Old Stoneface—Tyr Tejohn Treygar, she corrected herself, since he wasn't an Enemy anymore—famous. Did they really want to hear it? She wasn't much of a singer, Song knew.

She sat up and took a deep breath. When she'd sung for the girls in their tunnel, she had been on the verge of being hollowed out. Perhaps she'd gone over it. In any event, she'd felt a certain detachment from the grief that every ruined scholar feels. Her hollowed-out grief had come from some other place, from something awful that existed behind her magic.

None of that was available to her now. She had only the grief of her lost magic, and with it the loss of everything she had ever hoped for her life.

She began to sing without planning to start. How long had it been since she'd thought of Old Stoneface, the man who had tried to hurl himself to his death to save the prince and all of his friends, her included? It was such an odd thing to remember at a moment like this.

Lar had told her not three months before that Peradaini songs were made of symbolism, and as she sang about being helpless while loved ones were washed away, she realized this was a song about war.

Suddenly, she was singing about more than just the loss of her magic. There was also Tyr Treygar and Lar himself, both surely lost to The Blessing. There was Bitt and Tim and Jagia and Pagesh and also her own brother, dead by her unknowing hand. Song preserve the memory of all they had known, because Fire had taken them and Cazia was alone among strangers in a crumbling world.

When the song was over, the captain only stared at her, openmouthed. His face was paler than it had ever been, and his helmet, which he normally held on his left knee, had nearly fallen to the floor. For the first time ever, she thought he looked handsome. Without his careful manners and knowing, patronizing expression, he seemed like a genuine human being. Cazia suddenly wondered what it would be like to kiss him.

She turned toward the wall and lay down. The Captain stood, took his leave, and locked the cell door behind him. *Enemy,* she thought unkindly. She'd hoped to put that instinct behind her, but not yet. Not yet.

The door swung open. This time, it was an older man with dark circles under his eyes and thinning red hair. The older man dragged that same Peradaini scholar into the room and pushed him at Cazia.

"You look like you've slept and eaten," Cazia said to him. It was true; he looked almost healthy.

"I won't lie to them for you no matter how polite you are," he responded. He laid his long hand on her shoulder—Great Way, he was so warm, he felt almost feverish. He kept it there, his eyes shut tight. After a moment, he lifted his hand. "Nothing," he said to the red-haired man.

"How can it be nothing?" the older man demanded. His voice boomed in the stone room. He must have been the one in charge; an underling would have been taught to control his tone. Also, the princess was right; he spoke Peradaini as if he had little stones in his mouth. "How can it be nothing?"

The scholar shrugged. "It's not magic. She hasn't been trained. She's never cast a spell in her life. I could tell if she had."

The old man glared at the scholar, who only shrugged again.

Ivy stepped forward. "It is a song, commander. Not a magic spell. Only a song." She looked at the scholar, who seemed to be uncomfortable with her attention. "Is there a form of magic that can make a man weep? Or that can break someone's heart?"

The scholar turned toward the commander. "There isn't. It's the truth; magic can only affect the physical world."

"Well," the old man said. He ran his fingers through his thinning red hair. "Well well well. I wonder if I could ask you to sing again, young lady. There will be a feast tonight with quite a few Toal nobles present. I'm sure they would be fascinated to learn more about this Peradaini song."

"You'll let me out of my cell?" Cazia asked. "So I can sing for the entertainment of your guests?"

"Obviously. You would also be invited to dine with us, if you impress us."

"After one of your soldiers shot an arrow through my hand? An arrow that would have killed the princess?"

The commander didn't hesitate. "Obviously."

She turned to the scholar. "What are the odds that you have trained in healing magic?"

"Answer her."

The scholar nodded. "I worked in a mining camp. I can make blocks, crumble them, create water . . . "

But Cazia had already turned her back on them both. She pulled her legs onto the cot and faced the stone wall. "Go away."

"If you think there is a need," the commander said, "I can provide you with a lash to pay back the man who shot the arrow at you. If you think there is a need, I can see that you punish him right there at the feast, with everyone to see. If that is what you want."

Yes! "Go away. What good would it do to whip a soldier, even one who shot at a group of unarmed girls? He's your man, isn't he? If there's someone who should be whipped like an untrained dog, it's you. Bring me a lash and I'll use it on you."

He could have done anything to her in retaliation. Her bandaged hand was right there on her hip, completely exposed. All he had to do was touch it to punish her. All he had to do was knife her in the back.

Instead, he began to shout in his own language, but the princess cut him off. With three sharp words that Cazia couldn't understand, she brought silence to the room. Once that was accomplished, the princess began talking in a low, rapid-fire voice that sounded very much like a little girl who thought things had finally gone too far.

The commander tried to break in, gently, but Ivy wouldn't have it. After a few moments, Cazia stopped paying attention.

She had lost the use of her hand. Unless she could find a sleepstone where she might be safe from the grunts, or a medical scholar willing to work on her, she was going to have to rely on *her own body* to heal this wound, like she was a savage or something.

Fire take her, she could not be giving in this way. She had been locked in a cell and brought food like a prisoner. She had nothing to do; she couldn't even talk to the other girls for fear of eavesdroppers. The Toal had done everything they could to make her helpless.

But she wasn't helpless. She didn't have her magic and she couldn't speak the language, but she was still the same girl who had terrorized her tutors back at the palace, who had crossed into the Qorr Valley and flown out again with the help of the giant eagles. She was Cazia Freewell, daughter of the man who had nearly stolen an empire.

She was never going to be helpless again.

Cazia rolled over and stood, then looked from Ivy to the commander. "I'm going to talk to you in Peradaini right now. It would be polite to hear responses I can understand."

"Of course; I'm sorry," Ivy said, but Cazia didn't let her finish.

"Don't apologize, little sister. This isn't my country and I can't expect everyone to talk my language all the time. However, for this conversation, it would be nice."

"Of course."

Cazia looked straight into the commander's eyes. "You put us in here because you thought we might transform into The Blessing, right? You were afraid we would become grunts."

"I did," he said. "We will hold you until the end of the month—"

"It takes three days for a person to change into a grunt. That's it. Three days."

"Whenever a man or woman of Peradain tells me a fact," the commander said, "I assume the opposite is true."

"Have you at least sent word to the princess's family that she is here?"

The commander bowed to Ivy. "I have many duties to attend to." When he turned to Cazia, he gave her a beady, condescending smile. "It is time for me to have myself whipped. I have decided to run my command—the post it has taken me thirty-five years to earn—on the advice of a teenage girl."

"It's time for you to let us head south, so we can take Vilavivianna home."

"Peradaini girl, perhaps you should next ask for more food so that I will starve you." He turned his back and walked out of the room, the scholar following close behind. Cazia watched them both, hoping that at least her fellow countryman would look back at her. Neither did.

Fine. The scholar had new masters. He'd told her as much. And why should he help her? So he could end up in a cell, too? Or worse?

Kinz went to the door and gently, slowly pulled on it. It was barred from the outside. "We have been stuck here too long. I do not want to be trapped in this room when The Blessing make to attack—or the Tilkilit, for that matter."

"They do not believe me," Ivy said. "It is only clear to me now, but the commander and the soldiers do not believe I'm Alisimbo's daughter. They must think this is a Peradaini plot to overthrow the Alliance. I do not think they have even sent a runner south to tell my family I'm here."

The little girl's face was stoic, but Kinz and Cazia stepped forward and took hold of her hands. "We have to find a way. We will. I'm not sure how, but we will."

"How?"

Neither Cazia nor Kinz had an answer for the princess's question right away. They talked over their options for the rest of the afternoon. The doctor, who had already come that day, was always wary when she came in, and so were the servants who brought their food twice a day. What's more, they knew that any escape might earn them a whipping. Kinz was adamant that they could not do that to the servants, and Cazia felt she owed the doctor too much. Making that old woman take a lashing would have been a betrayal.

If anyone was to be blamed for their escape, it had to be the soldiers.

The Captain was not wary but he was watchful; Cazia thought he could be overcome if they rushed him as soon as the door opened. Kinz would grab his legs, Cazia would shove him, and backward he would go.

The other girls weren't keen on the idea. To Cazia's surprise, Ivy liked him very much, and Kinz glanced sharply at the floor at the mention of grabbing his legs. Great Way, had they falling for that smarm?

Cazia, who had always been the expert at watching everyone around her, had been too wrapped up in her own problems to notice.

Eventually, night fell, and when the three female soldiers arrived to search them, the girls were already crouched by the door. They had tossed aside their jackets, leaving only their underclothes on.

They were so quiet they could hear the bolt drawing back and the women outside talking about their next hunting trip. As the door swung outward, Kinz bolted toward the gap.

She was the oldest, the largest, and the strongest, and she struck the lead guard full in the stomach with her shoulder, lifting her up and flinging her back into a second guard.

Ivy was right behind her, moving as quick as a sparrow. She dodged low under the grasping hands of the third guard and, as the woman bent to catch her, Cazia slammed into her armor.

Cazia hit her with her right shoulder, but it still jarred her left hand so badly that it felt like someone had stuck a twig into her wound and wiggled it. The idea that she could outrun all the guards, every step jarring her hand with a dull throb, seemed suddenly impossible, but she couldn't stop. If she hesitated at all, Ivy and Kinz would as well, and they would all be caught.

The first two guards lay in a tumble of bodies, but one of them had the wit to catch hold of Kinz's ankle. Before the older girl could break free, Cazia ran between them, trampling the guard's forearm. The woman cried out, but she sounded more in shock than pain. Then Kinz was free and they were all following Ivy along the wall toward an open doorway made of rough logs.

It was a laundry. The princess had assured them she'd seen it on the way in. They ducked beneath the outermost line of hanging clothes and moved into the darkness.

Behind them, they finally heard voices raised in alarm. "These!" Ivy shouted, pointed toward a line of clothing that looked like a blanket with a hole in the middle. Kinz yanked them down and they pulled them on, barely breaking stride.

Cazia saw the thick coil of rope handing on a peg—a line for hanging wet clothes, supposedly—and collected it. "Got the rope!" Then they followed Ivy up a flight of stairs.

A chime began to ring from somewhere nearby. It was dull, flat, and high, coming in double strikes. *Ting-ting! Ting-ting! Ting-ting!*

Even their alarm bells are primitive. Cazia shook that off. The whole fort would be on alert in moments, and they were unarmed. Ivy had insisted that they not take the guards' weapons or seriously hurt anyone; she thought it would only escalate things.

Cazia clutched at the coil of rope, ignoring the pain in her hand. Every moment made her heart beat harder, which made her hand throb even worse. She couldn't stop. They had no time to rest, and if she fell behind, they wouldn't have the rope they needed to climb down the southern wall.

How Cazia was supposed to climb down a rope one-handed was another issue entirely. The other girls didn't seem to have noticed that it would be impossible for her.

So she ran behind them, determined to keep up but knowing that if they were successful, she might never see either of them again.

An old man wearing a blanket just like theirs appeared on the landing with a torch in his hand. His cloth was cinched with a rope belt but the girls' were not; Cazia was suddenly certain that he would call an alarm.

Ivy spoke to him in a high, panicky voice, pointing back behind them. The old man waved the three of them by him and raised his light, peering down the stairs into the darkness.

At the end of the next flight, they came to a dim, curving corridor. There were no more stairs upward, so Ivy waved them to the right and ran with her. *Ting-ting! Ting-ting! Ting-ting!* "We have to keep heading south until we find stairs that lead up the wall."

Ahead, a man leaned out of a doorway, a candle in his hand. Ivy kept running toward him, and Cazia could see that he was not dressed in the same blanket with the hole to poke your head through. He wore a traveling tunic that came down to his knees, soldier's boots, and a coil of greenery woven through his blond hair. He was no servant; he was dressed for the road.

Ivy didn't break her pace as she approached him, but one look at his expression made Cazia's guts go sour with fear. *He is not fooled.*

The man stepped out of the doorway all the way, blocking the corridor. He had a gleaming bronze stabbing sword in his other hand.

Ivy pulled up short; Kinz and Cazia both rushed to stand in front of her. They showed him their empty hands.

The man's head quirked to one side and he said, unmistakably, "Vilavivianna?"

With great surprise, the princess said, "Goherzma?"

Cazia heard heavy footsteps coming from behind them. Hurry!

The swordsman tried to stammer out a question, but Ivy cut him short with a quick entreaty. He immediately bowed, stepped back, and allowed them to rush into the room. He shut the door behind them.

They were safe. Or they had been trapped.

CHAPTER TWENTY

Did it matter that he hadn't known? Did it matter that she was so much older than his own children, both the one who had died so many years ago and the three who were supposed to be hiding safely in the distant East?

No. No, none of that mattered. One of the grunts he had trapped and burned had been a little girl. He had murdered a child.

Tejohn felt a wave of dizziness overtake him; the world seemed to have turned into an empty white void. He had killed mothers and fathers, brothers and sisters, sons and daughters, but they had always been adults—or at least old enough to take up arms. But a little one? The image of his own child rushed back to him, lying in the mud beside his back door, all split open and spilled out like a butchered animal.

"My tyr?" Javien said. "Tyr Treygar, are you all right?"

"I'm not a tyr," he answered, as though that was important. He thought he should feel suicidal right at that moment, but that would have been absurd and melodramatic. This wasn't about him and his honor. It was about that child.

Spilled grain crunched under the boot of a square-faced soldier as he stepped toward them, and the world suddenly reappeared. Everyone was looking at Tejohn as though he was the one in trouble.

"Are you really Tyr Tejohn Treygar?"

If this soldier spoke a word of admiration to him, Tejohn would strike him dead on the spot. No one was going to treat him like a hero—like a famous man—not today.

"It were my words that hurt him," the old farmer said. "I have to be the one to straighten things out. Tyr Treygar, if that's who you are, you didn't kill a little child. Not even a debt child. I saw her change into that creature—the three of us did, right here on the floor. Her body tore apart like the clothes of a werebear in a little child's story."

"It's true," his wife said. "The creature killed her, and then it ate her. You didn't harm that little child. She was already gone."

"As far as any of us is concerned, we died the moment we were bitten. It's like we have poison in us, but the poison won't let us hurry to our own preferred end."

The stout young mother spoke up. "Can we be cured on a blessing stone? A bless . . . *Bless*—"

"A sleepstone?" Tejohn asked. She nodded gratefully. Javien turned to Tejohn, a look of warning on his face, but he knew better than to tell the others that the man was a medical scholar. "I've tried that. A sleepstone only makes the transformation come on stronger and faster."

The woman looked down at the children at her feet and began to weep. The two smallest had curled up on a burlap sack and fallen asleep, while the six-year-old crouched beside them, her eyes wide.

Javien stepped forward. "I know I'm not wearing my robes of office right now, but I'm a beacon. If you need help to ease the children out of this world without pain, it is my duty to provide that help."

Tejohn grasped his elbow. "Javien . . . " What had he planned to say? He couldn't imagine.

"Back home, it was my duty as a beacon to slaughter spring lambs for the Festival of the Tides." He said this as much for the mother's sake as anyone's. "I can do it in a way that is utterly painless. They don't have to die in pain and fear when the curse takes them. They can leave The Way peacefully, in your arms."

"Yes," the woman said, and who else had any say in the matter? "I would bless that. Yes." She looked down at the little ones again, and her cheeks shone with tears.

The female soldier stepped in front of Tejohn. "You promised us a quick, clean death, my tyr. If I had to take a sword thrust, I'd prefer to take it from a Finshto hero. Will you keep that promise?"

"Outside," Javien said, as though the answer to that question was already a given—and of course it was. "I will look after the mother. Try not to make a noise that will wake the children."

Tejohn turned and went out into the muddy yard. The rain still fell in the same misting drizzle, but no one seemed to mind. They strode out toward the woodpile, partly because there was nothing else to catch their attention but the brilliantly burning barn fire.

"I want to go first," said a soldier that had not spoken before. He looked terrified.

"Me and the wife were bitten first," the old man said sulkily, "but it's all right, I guess."

Tejohn set his shield and spear against the wall of the house, being careful to keep his eyes downcast. He didn't want to see what was happening inside. When he turned to the others, he felt oddly defenseless, as though he was going into battle unarmed.

The man dropped to his knees like a defeated soldier awaiting execution. He looked terrified. Tejohn came close, drew his sword, and knelt with him in the mud.

"I'll keep quiet for the little ones," the soldier said. "I promise."

"Do you want to say a prayer?"

"I finished all my praying."

Tejohn thrust the point of his sword up into the man's heart. It was quick and clean, but it was clearly not painless. As the man slumped to the side, Tejohn eased him into the mud.

One of the soldiers began to whisper urgently to the others, and the woman with him began to talk to him in quiet, reassuring tones. Tejohn watched the man closely as he wiped off his sword. If the fellow bolted, he would have to run him down or all of this would have been for nothing. But could he catch a fellow more than twenty years his junior?

"I guess it's for us next," the old farmer said. "If you don't mind, I'd like to do it over there, with you behind us. That hill over there is our property, and if I can't die on it, I'd like it to be the last thing I see."

"Of course," Tejohn said, watching the soldiers out of the corner of his eye. The soldier at his feet had a knife at his belt. Tejohn took it and tested the edge. Good.

The farmers walked hand in hand to the corner of the muddy yard, not far from where Tejohn had crouched while waiting for Javien's signal that he'd blocked the back entrance.

"There it is," the old woman said. They looked out at a field of barley on the next hill over, then turned toward each other and held their faces very close.

"Grateful am I," the man said, "to be permitted to travel The Way."

"Kelvijinian," the woman answered, as though they were sharing an old joke, "I return to you."

It was a quick knife thrust for them, straight to the heart. The old man grunted, but it was a low, brief sound. Then it was done.

Tejohn turned toward the others. There were four more of them, and he was already trying to decide what would be the most humane way to end their lives.

It was nearly dark when he finished. The rain had picked up and the droplets made the fire hiss. Tejohn stood staring at it a moment, wondering how he had come to this moment in his life, with the innocent blood of allies on his sword, when Javien emerged from the house.

"No one has come about the fire," the priest said. "If nothing else told us there was something terribly wrong here, that would be it. Farm folk do not leave fires unfought."

"Let's move them inside," Tejohn said, "so we can start another and go back to our task."

As Javien moved toward the nearest soldier, he said, "I've covered them with a cloth."

Tejohn was grateful for that in ways he couldn't express. Together, they carried the bodies inside, then took from them anything of value, which turned out to be seven iron-bladed knives; they didn't have a speck between them. While the priest poured oil around the main room, Tejohn carried armload after armload of firewood inside.

Someone had worked very hard to chop all that wood. It felt like a crime to waste all that effort.

Night had fallen by the time Javien cast his little fire spell at the doorway of the house. The flames spread quickly. They stood partway down the hill and watched the house burn. Tejohn thought he ought to say something to the young priest, but nothing seemed appropriate. Javien appeared to be utterly composed, as though his role of beacon protected him from self-doubt.

For himself, Tejohn held his spear and shield close. He needed them now in a way he wouldn't have been able to articulate if someone had asked. They were like a connection to his old self, the one that had never become a king's shield, a servant, a captive in the dungeons of Ussmajil, or an executioner.

They returned to the farmhouse on the high hill where they had spied on the grunts. It was still empty. Tejohn filled two bowls with water while Javien lit the hearth. Then they washed very, very thoroughly.

As usual for late summer, the larder was not well stocked, but they managed to find small meals. Neither ate much. The roof leaked a little but they were glad for a dry corner. Tejohn lay in the darkness and wished he could be far away with his wife and children, living somewhere in the east. He'd sent them away almost three months ago, and he'd expected to be with them again by now. He longed to see his children again.

But there was nothing he could do about it. Even if everything went perfectly, he would not see them again for a long, long time.

In the dark, when they were supposed to be sleeping, Tejohn could hear the priest weeping quietly. For once in his life, his hand did not fall to his knife. For once, he knew there was no reason to fear a scholar's tears.

In the morning, Tejohn used a bit of rainwater mixed with wood ash to clean the waterfall insignia off his new shield; he wasn't a king's spear and had no interest in impersonating one. Then they scavenged everything they could from the larder—including half a dozen stale sourcakes—and returned to the road. It was still raining. The house and barn they had burnt had already been reduced to charred foundations, but the wheat field was mostly untouched.

The old soldier and the young priest continued on their way, heading toward the west.

CHAPTER TWENTY-ONE

JAVIEN INSISTED THEY HURRY. HE WANTED TO TRAVEL LIGHT, SLEEP as little as possible, and waste no time with talk. Tejohn understood and agreed. The sooner they accomplished their task, the sooner they could turn the war against the grunts around. Maybe then they would feel like heroes instead of butchers.

If they were lucky. If they managed to make their way to Tempest Pass alive, and if the spell was there, and if Ghoron Italga—once the heir to the throne of Peradain and now little more than a scholar hermit—was willing to teach it to them.

That was a lot of "ifs" to contend with. The only certainties they had were that they had just committed murder and that no one on the road was going to welcome them.

At the first village they came to, they faced a local militia with a line of spears and three archers. Not only were strangers not welcome there—even beacons wearing their red robes—but half the militia followed them eastward on the road, and away from Salt Pass, to make sure they didn't try to circle around and approach the village from the north or south.

Of course, once they were alone again, Tejohn and Javien *did* circle around, but they kept well clear of the village. They found a little stream they could follow and, feet wet for an entire day, tramped northward among the rocks.

Near the end of the day, a farmer spotted them and, with grudging politeness, asked them to get out of the stream. He pointed with his bill toward a deer path, promising it would lead them to a ferry.

Tejohn had the feeling the farmer wouldn't have been so polite had they been unarmed.

Javien was quite disturbed to hear that they would need a ferry. His maps suggested there were no large rivers or lakes nearby, but it turned out there were. The next morning, the path emptied onto a road and they saw a lovely little freshwater lake. It was too small for most maps but long enough that it would have taken a day to pass around it.

The ferrywoman demanded double her usual fare. No one was crossing southward these days, she said, and who would pay for her trip back home?

Tejohn told her he would pay her two sourcakes for the crossing, and she agreed so readily, he realized she would probably have taken half of one. As she hauled on the rope to pull the ferry raft across, she informed them that her cousin out west wouldn't even come near the lakeshore until his passengers had stripped to their skin to prove they had no bite marks, patches of blue fur, or bare eyeballs poking through their chests. Rumor had it that the grunts could look out of a person's palm, or back, or bum, and see who nearby was worth the eating.

The road they were on would take them to the pass they wanted, she assured them, although why they would want to venture so close to dangerous lands, she couldn't imagine. Best head for home and keep well away from the Bendertuks to the west. Rumor and better than rumor said their troops were running wild on the border, killing anyone who so much as looked at them funny. Tyr Finstel's spears and bows were all to the south, driving away grunts, so Tyr Bendertuk was having his way with the Finshto common folk.

On the far shore, Tejohn handed over the two cakes, then promised to keep away from the border. He also warned her that Tyr Finstel had crowned himself King Shunzik, and she ought to take care to call him that, just in case.

"That news itself is almost worth the price of the crossing," she said, although she didn't hand back the food. Instead, she took the tiniest pinch from one and ate it as if it was the first meal she'd tasted all day.

Tejohn and Javien watched her haul herself back across the water. "It'll be better in the fall," Tejohn said. "There will be less hunger once the harvest comes in."

"Assuming anyone is here to eat it."

We'll make sure of that, he wanted to answer, but it seemed like a hollow promise.

Javien changed back into his red robes, looking in dismay at Tejohn's gray. The priests' red was supposed to ease their passage across borders; they could not reach the pass without crossing into Bendertuk lands.

Once he had put on his red, as he called it, the young priest became much more talkative. He suddenly had a hundred questions about the grunts. Did they mate or did they only spread by biting? Were they male and female? Did men transform into male grunts, or was there no correlation?

The priest seemed to have an alarmingly nonchalant attitude about changing gender. Certain swamp animals in the Redmudd homeland were known to switch from male to female, he claimed, and there was no reason he shouldn't expect to see it in more complex creatures, especially magical ones. Tejohn admitted that he hadn't thought to check and hoped that would be the end of the conversation.

Javien also wondered what they did in environments where they took over. How did they find balance? Even if they transformed humans only and not lower animals—something he was not convinced of yet—their appetites would turn their habitats into wastelands.

"That makes sense," Tejohn interrupted. "Say that someone wanted to conquer the Evening People; they would unleash The Blessing in their homeland and let the curse spread until the land was emptied. The grunts would transform or devour everything, then die off themselves. How long do you think that would take? Two generations? Three? It's war by proxy. The grunts do the fighting and then vanish, leaving open land for the taking."

"That would be an ingenious plan," Javien said.

"It's dishonorable," Tejohn said sourly. "It reeks of cowardice. The only real question is this: did the power behind the grunts intend for their attack to spill over into Kal-Maddum, or was that an accident?"

"Either way, if their magic is that potent, I wouldn't want to face them."

Tejohn grunted in response. If their enemy, whoever it was, didn't have the courage to march out to face those they intended to conquer, they deserved a spear to the guts. The best way to deal with a scholar—or wizard, or whatever these things were—was with a piece of sharp metal, expertly applied.

Near the end of that day, they crossed the top of a hill and came upon a little girl squatting at the side of the road. She held out her hand, mutely begging. She looked to be no more than eleven, and half starved.

"I'm sorry, little one," Javien said. "We have a long way to go and little enough for ourselves."

"Nonsense," Tejohn said. He crouched beside her and unwrapped a sourcake. She reached for it, but there was some reluctance in it. "Of course. You don't want this." He withdrew the cake and broke a piece of meatbread from the heel of the loaf. The girl waited for him to offer it, then snatched it from his hand.

"My . . . friend," Javien said, rightfully cautious about using honorifics. "We don't have enough for ourselves, let alone every hungry child we find by the side of the road. The Way is full of hardship as well as comfort."

"Yes, it is," Tejohn answered. "However, the road will sometimes have a lookout. Is there safe passage, little one?" He took out the smallest of the iron knives he'd taken from the bodies at the farmhouse.

The blade was short and slender, the wooden handle cracked, but the girl's eyes lit up when he held it out to her. She laid her hand on it, but Tejohn didn't let go. "Is there a safe path?"

She nodded at him, then led them partway down the hill they'd just climbed. Pulling aside a branch, she revealed a deer path into the woods. It didn't look promising, but the girl made a motion like a swimming fish and smiled at them.

"Left, right, then left?" Tejohn asked. She nodded, looking around as if fearful she might be caught. He gave her the knife and watched her run to the top of the hill.

The deer path was so narrow, he had to sling his shield onto his back. The priest followed him into the trees. "Bandits?"

"Common enough," Tejohn said. "In the summer months before harvest, some folk will ease their hardship by crouching by the side of the road, bow in hand. They're usually reasonably polite about it, but sometimes you meet someone with a taste for killing."

"I'd rather avoid that, if I could."

"And I'd rather not have our food and weapons stolen."

The path led through swampy lowland, and they had not emerged from the thickets when the sun went down. They slept in trees without a fire and, in the morning, emerged onto the road near a village wall. There were no Bendertuk soldiers in sight, but they were questioned vigorously at the gate before they were allowed inside. The beacon was a portly fellow who talked quite a bit about the bad harvest of the previous year. He also asked a few vague questions about how the two visitors had come to town. When he found they had not taken the road, he scowled as though he'd lost a business opportunity.

Javien hated the man from the first and raged about him for half the day once they returned to the road.

The next village was too small to have a beacon of their own, but the people there were happy to feed and house them once Javien agreed to marry one couple and divorce two others, asking only for donations of meatbread in payment. Both men heard endless complaining about the cost of the local beacons' services, even when they didn't have to travel.

The next village had grown beyond its walls and offered sleeping arrangements inside its growing temple. The village after that had been sacked and burned to the ground by Bendertuk spears. The village after that refused to allow them through the gates. The village after that was in mourning.

And so it continued, for day after day, as they approached the mountains of the Southern Barrier.

Chapter Twenty-two

The room was not the most lavish Cazia had ever seen, but it was a huge step up from the last few months. There was a frame stretched with soft boq skins that served as a bed, and a row of chests and wicker baskets that held clothes and other essentials. It reminded her of the belongings they'd found in the ruined camp out in the Sweeps. Great Way, that seemed so long ago.

Goherzma—apparently, that was his name, as unlikely as that sounded—stayed in the corridor. Cazia heard heavy footsteps approach, then a conversation in Toal, then the footsteps retreated. The girls crouched silently in the room, keeping well back from the windows.

The door shut again, and the man returned. He slid his sword into a sheath in a wicker basket by the entryway, and looked over the three girls.

He bowed again, more deeply this time, and Ivy stood up straight. The two of them exchanged a fair bit of chatter. Cazia couldn't follow it, but the man gave her a single dark look, which she didn't like at all.

He was older than she'd first thought, possibly forty or more. He had the arms and shoulders of a fighting man, but there was a doughy layer around his middle that suggested retirement, promotion, or soft duty. His face and hands were unscarred.

"The princess," Kinz whispered, "is telling him how we were made prisoner here and how we have been treated. Apparently, her cousin is inside the fort."

"Probably enjoying that feast," Cazia said. She spoke in a normal tone, which made the swordsman look sharply at her again. Let him. She was not a thief or a spy and she would not whisper like one.

Kinz stopped whispering but she did not speak at normal volume, either. "They are discussing the wisdom of summoning him immediately or waiting for him to return on his own. If the alarm does not stop, he might be quartered in the hall for the night. Now Ivy is telling the man to fetch her cousin right away. She does not want to wait."

Kinz stopped translating when the servant made his reply, his tone full of warning. After an uncomfortable delay, Kinz said, "He—"

"That's all right," Cazia said, laying her uninjured hand on Kinz's so she wouldn't have to translate something rude. They had put their conflicts behind them. "I know what he said." She couldn't expect a soldier to be happy to host a Peradaini, even in times like these.

"Do not rest on the bed," Ivy said in Peradaini. "It is my cousin's and it would give the wrong impression. That bench by the window would be better if you keep out of sight. Anyway, I have told Goherzma your names and that you are my friends, not my girls. In a moment, he will fetch my cousin and then we will not have to climb down the south wall or any other. We will be able to walk through the gate in the broad daylight with full bellies. And there is a bath in the other room; would you mind if I go first?"

"Of course not," Cazia said. Could she let her injured hand touch bath water?

"I already had the summer bath," Kinz said, "when we jumped in the river."

The princess laughed happily as if she were joking, then drew back a tapestry to reveal a short passage into another room. Ivy lit a second candle and went in. Kinz shifted as though she wanted to follow. "Should we accompany her?"

Cazia moved to the bench and sat. Her hand had never hurt so badly, even when the injury was fresh. All it took was the movement of running and the pressure of her quickened heartbeat to set it *throbbing*. "They would assume we were her *girls*." Kinz nodded and sat beside her.

Left alone with the Ergoll servant, Cazia and Kinz fell silent, watching him take a few things from a travel pack and distribute it among a few baskets. He was silent, almost sullen, but it wasn't until they heard Ivy's happy splashing from the next room that he spoke to them.

By her expression, Kinz did not recognize the word, but Cazia did. The serving man pointed to the basket beside him and snapped his fingers. It was a gesture of command, one that would not have been used by anyone short of a chief of servants, and even then only if he were very unhappy with a servant's work.

Cazia stood. The man glanced at her, then looked back at his task. Cazia walked toward him, not the basket he'd pointed to, and said "man" in Ergoll, just as Ivy had taught her. He glanced at her in surprise.

She slapped his face.

Doughy middle or not, he still had a fighting man's reflexes; her fingers barely grazed his cheek, but it must have stung.

His eyes suddenly went wild, and he did just what she expected: he slapped her back. Cazia turned her face with the blow to lessen the impact. Great Way, he was strong. If he'd taken her by surprise, he might have broken her cheekbone.

Still, the pain in her face was not nearly equal to the pain in her hand. "Tell him something for me," Cazia said. "Compliment him on the softness of his hands. Tell him that being slapped by him is like gently resting my head on a soft cushion of down."

Kinz hesitated. "Are you certain? If he makes the alarm, we could be thrown in chains. Or hanged."

"I'm sure. If we don't make a stand here, we will be scrubbing floors and washing Ivy's underclothes for the rest of our lives. I'd rather be hanged."

Kinz translated, and all the apprehension had vanished from her voice and expression. The man seemed surprised and a little impressed by her boldness, but when he began to respond, Cazia slapped him again.

This time, his reflexes failed him and the blow took him full on the cheek. Kinz began speaking again without prompting, and from her tone, Cazia could tell she knew not to try to console the man or ease the hurt to his pride.

Goherzma looked chagrined, glanced at the doorway where Ivy had gone, then let out a deep sigh. He bowed to them both, said something in a low voice, and went out the door. When he was gone, Cazia tried to bar it with her one good hand, but Kinz had to help.

Kinz had that mischievous smirk again. "He said he would return quickly with his master."

They retreated to the bench. Cazia was so *tired*. "That might not be the last time this happens. I hate to admit it, but we might get the same treatment every time we meet someone, from the royal family to the kitchen help."

"We are both too dark for the Indrega," Kinz said simply. "But there is no disguising that you are from Peradain. It's not just your brown hair and skin; unless we can find you the long wig or the pretend husband, there is no hiding that hair."

Cazia ran her fingers through it. Of course it was a mess; she'd just spent months in the wilderness. "What does having a husband have to do with my hair? I need a comb, not a suitor."

Kinz gave her a sly look. "You cut it. You have probably cut it your entire life. Among my people—and the princess's—girls do not cut their hair until the morning after their wedding."

"Oh. I thought you and Ivy just liked it that way."

"We do. For now."

Cazia would have laughed, but Kinz suddenly got a faraway look in her eye. *Who would have cut her hair after her wedding? Her mother? Her aunts? Who did she have to cut it now?* "Maybe I should just find a hat."

Kinz looked dubious. "No matter what, it will be difficult to travel far together in Indrega. We may have to make pretend to be servants to the princess just to smooth things over. For her and for us."

What she said made sense. Once they made it into Ergoll territory, Ivy could demand they be treated with respect, but until then, they risked a lash from everyone they met. As much as Cazia wished it would be otherwise, she . . . *they* were surrounded by Enemies. Again. Discretion would be wise.

Cazia had never been called wise. "Fire take that idea," she said. "If I'm going to walk down this side of the Straim, I'm going to do it as a free citizen."

Kinz gave a one-shoulder shrug, and they fell silent after that, listening to the double gong of the alarm and the splashing from the next room. Cazia had nothing to distract her from the pain in her hand.

Ivy finished mere minutes before someone tried the door, so she was there to respond to the angry complaint that came from the hall. She and Kinz unbarred the door, allowing Goherzma to enter with another man close behind.

He couldn't have been more than thirty, tall and slender, with a pale, mournful face and straight black hair braided like Kinz's. The left side of his neck and shoulder—what showed through his tunic, at least—was dimpled and yellow-white. A burn scar? His white uniform was crisp, clean, and perfect.

Ivy called out a string of nonsense syllables that might have been his name, and he shouted, "Vilavivianna!" at which the two of them fell into overlapping chatter in Ergoll. Kinz looked as if she was about to try to translate it, but Cazia shook her head slightly. She didn't need to know what Ivy said to her family.

After some time, Ivy came over beside Cazia and laid a hand on her shoulder. "Cazia Freewell, this is my cousin, Belterzhimi of Shadow Valley, the Warden of the Western Frontier." Cazia stood and gave a polite little curtsey. How funny. It had been so long since she'd last curtseyed, and yet here she was doing it without a moment's hesitation.

"It is my great pleasure to meet you," Belterzhimi said. "I am told you promised the princess that you would return her safely home."

"I did," Cazia said. He stared at her very intently, as though there was no one else in the room. It gave her goose bumps. "We're almost there."

"I would be pleased to accompany you. Is it true that you are of royal blood?"

She almost said, *I was the prince's cousin.* "Cousin to the prince," she said, a little inelegantly. "But that does not matter very much among my people."

"It matters here," the young man answered, then he bowed a little. "How is my Peradaini?"

"Very good!" she answered a little too enthusiastically. He smiled gratefully at her. Cazia felt herself blush. The smile didn't seem to suit his face, although she was still glad to see it. "I wish I spoke Ergoll that well."

"Thank you. I have been practicing among the refugees from East Ford. When you come to Goldgrass Hill with us, we will reunite you with your people. I am sure they will be pleased to share news." He turned to Kinz. "My man tells me that when he confronted you, you both stepped in front of the princess to shield her. Yes?"

Kinz answered him in Toal. Cazia noticed with some dismay that he gave the older girl the same intense look he'd just given her. Was he this way with everyone or was Kinz—older, taller, and more beautiful—that much more enticing?

Cazia suddenly felt extraordinarily tired but didn't want to insult Ivy's cousin by sitting. "Big sister," Ivy said, "are you all right?"

It was just a wound to her hand. Cazia hated to admit it, but it really was tiring. "I'm fine."

"I am cutting my visit short," Belterzhimi said, "obviously. My cousin has been found safe! We will head south in the morning. Do you have any packing?"

Ivy tugged at the blanket she was wearing. "We could use some fresh clothes. And the commander took two iron artifacts from Kinz. They are proof of the adventures we have had! Can you see to it they are returned?"

"I will speak to him. We will purchase clothes in the market as we leave. The Ergoll have been fortunate these last few months, but never more so than this night. Let me finish my duties with the commander this evening, smooth things over with the alarm, and we depart at dawn. Sleep, cousin. Sleep, friends."

Ivy dragged Kinz to the tub, despite the older girl's protests. Goherzma rushed from the room and returned shortly after with the commander. There was a lot of talk after that, another visit from the doctor, a change of bandages, a stack of new sleeping clothes for the girls, and a sincere apology from the great big archery target. Ivy's response was haughty, while Kinz—her hair freshly washed and unbraided—and Cazia hung back to let her handle it.

Belterzhimi insisted they were to have their own room. "You understand, I hope, why I can not host you," he said in Peradaini while he looked at Cazia's head. "I mean no insult or disrespect." Ivy nodded and led Kinz and Cazia to an empty room at the far end of the corridor.

"He couldn't *host* us?" Cazia asked. "Is that because of my hair?"

"Of course!" Ivy answered. "You are a foreigner, so it does not matter to you, naturally, but an unmarried girl with short hair would scandalize my people. When I first came to Peradain and saw eight-year-olds on the street with bobbed hair, I thought your entire civilization was depraved!"

Kinz cleared her throat. "Do you think it will be made hard for her?"

"That is a good point," Ivy said. "We could get you a widow's wig for the trip. I'm sure my cousin would not mind."

A disguise. Cazia knew it was a sensible idea, but she rebelled against it anyway. She was Peradaini, and Surgish, and quite close to the prince of the Italgas. She knew their songs and their magic. She was herself and she was not ashamed.

"No wig," she said. It was mostly pride that made her refuse. Whatever common sense there might be in one argument or another, she did not want to hide among Enemies.

They slept comfortably on a frame bed stretched with downy-soft boq skins, until a soft-voiced servant called outside their door at dawn. The three of them were loaded onto a cart with four okshim rigged to the front, and they waited patiently for Ivy's cousin and his man as they finished whatever business they had with the commander in the last moments before first light.

Cazia did not expect to be traveling with a cohort of soldiers. There were a dozen archers and thirty spears—*spearmen*, Ivy insisted, even the ones who were women. Also, at the very perimeter of the group, there were serpents.

They looked strange in the daylight. The dead ones she'd seen in the demolished camp had been dull-colored, but alive, they were as bright and colorful as polished jewels. Their scales shone like rainbows and their long snouts moved slowly from one human to the next, tongue flicking in and out.

"Beautiful, are they not?" Ivy asked. The way she was smiling, Cazia might have thought she'd painted them personally, but she and Kinz couldn't help but smile back.

"But deadly," Kinz added. She seemed a little tense.

"Oh, yes. They are very powerful allies."

Could they talk? They circled the camp like well-trained guard dogs, but Cazia had decided she was not going to underestimate the beasts of Kal-Maddum any more. Sometime soon, when she had a safe, secret place of her own, she would make a translation stone and spy on them a little. Ivy had asked for one, but Cazia needed to satisfy her curiosity.

Outside the gate was the market. It looked like every other market Cazia had ever seen, except the canvas tents had all been dyed white. She wanted to wander out among the stalls—how long had it been since she'd been among crowds of ordinary citizens?—but despite all her brave talk, she was nervous about the way she'd be treated.

Not that she was given the choice. Ivy and Goherzma both requested that she stay in the back of the cart among the supplies. She was a little embarrassed at the gratitude she felt toward them both.

The cart picked up its pace again, moving through town—if muddy paths and log cabins could be called a "town," no matter how much it sprawled—then into the forest. Cazia, Ivy, and Kinz were given clean white clothes like the others wore. They changed under the tarp on the jolting cart, and Kinz helped Cazia without being asked. They really had put their conflicts behind them. *The Little Spinner never slows.*

The clothes were surprisingly comfortable, and Cazia was happy to receive a wide-brimmed hat that allowed her to tuck up her hair. Great Way, it wasn't even particularly short.

The road started due west at first, and they came within sight of the Straim for the first time.

"This is not the riverhead," Ivy explained, pointing out at the churning lake that filled the space beside the Toal fort, the town, and the mountain range. "The Straim actually begins somewhere in the Sweeps, running beneath the land. Here is where it emerges into the sunlight on its path to the sea."

"The river is underground?" Kinz said, astonished at the idea.

Cazia had never even heard of such a thing. She thought about powerful currents pulling her down into darkness and she shuddered.

"It is!" Ivy seemed proud, as though it was her personal accomplishment. *She loves her home.*

The lake was not large, but the southern end had collapsed into a long, rocky slope. The slope ran for nearly a thousand feet, then widened into the broad, deep river itself. The girls leaned against the rail, watching the water crash and flow. The cart turned away from the sight too soon, moving deeper into the deep green forest.

Belterzhimi and Goherzma joined them in the cart shortly after, and they pulled the tarp overhead to block out the rain. Cazia told him the story of their escape from Peradain. She even talked about the Festival, the portal, and the fact that it was long shut and wouldn't open again for a generation. She talked about saving the prince, saving Ivy, about Pagesh being left behind, and about the time they spent regrouping in Samsit. She told him about the death of her brother, about the quest the prince undertook for a spell powerful enough to defeat the grunts, about the way they changed, and about rescuing Ivy from the fort.

She told it all, except that she made herself seem like little more than baggage. It was the other scholars who fought from the flying cart over Peradain. It was an archer who shot and killed her own brother, transformed into The Blessing.

When she reached the point where they met the Ozzhuacks, Ivy interrupted. "The rest is for Mother and Father. I hope you understand."

"Unfair!" he cried in a playful way. "It is not fair to tell a man half an adventure."

"Think how fun it will be to pause at this exciting moment."

"I hate waiting." He gave Cazia a measuring look.

"Cousin," Ivy said carefully, "since you have not returned the iron artifacts that were taken from Kinz . . . "

"Ah yes," he said, and it was clear from his expression that they were gone. "Already melted down and traded away. The metal was astonishingly pure and strong, even higher in quality than the metals we take from the Peradaini." He bowed his head to Kinz. "The Toal owe you a debt."

"I will collect it," she said.

"We had a boy come through here a few months ago," Belterzhimi continued. "He said he had left the princess with two companions, and that one of them was a Peradaini scholar."

Of course he did. "That's not us," Cazia said with a shrug. "The Toal commander tested us several times."

"Did he?"

Kinz lay back and stared at the sky. "I wish I was the scholar. I would make cook fires with the wave of my hand, cover the muddy road ahead of me with smooth stone, and trick every chieftain I met into giving me their okshim."

"You would also live as an honored guest of the people of Goldgrass

Hill, sharing a home almost as luxurious as the princess's. You would not even have to wave a hand to light a fire; you would simply command your woman to do it."

Cazia stared at the turning wheel, but she watched Belterzhimi out of the corner of her eye. He had been looking at her when he'd last spoke. Not intently, as he had before, but looking just the same. She pretended not to notice.

"I do not think I would make to enjoy that," Kinz said vaguely. "It might be nice for the short while, but I would miss the outdoors, traveling on the backs of the herd, chasing the children."

"That does you credit, I think. May I make a confession? I have a fascination with the flying carts. How are they flown?"

Kinz shrugged. "Magic," Ivy said.

"How else could people fly but by magic?" Belterzhimi asked reasonably. "But how do they work? Must the occupants will themselves off the ground? Is a blood sacrifice required?"

"Their scholars did it merely by thought," Ivy said. "Did you know that many scholars learn only a few spells?"

Her cousin nodded. "The Toal learned this just recently."

"When we escaped Peradain, the cart was flown by a scholar who seemed to have been specially trained. The other scholars with us didn't know the trick."

The color orange—a bright orange. The feeling of stepping into a deep puddle unexpectedly with your left foot. A square where the right side breaks midline and collapses into an isosceles triangle. Cazia had heard the "trick" once and she would never forget it. Not that there was any reason to admit that now. "The scholars were very secretive," she said, "even among their own people."

"I see. Miss Cazia Freewell, have you been looking after your hand?"

Cazia was startled by the change of topic. "I— Yes. I keep the bandages clean."

"That is good but it is not enough. You should also be moving your fingers as much as possible. It is necessary for you to regain the full use of your hand."

Was this some sort of trick? "Is that possible? I didn't think it was."

"Perhaps not the *full* use of your hand, I must admit, but if the wound stays clean and does not turn into an unmoving claw, you will only have some weakness there. Maybe stiffness, too. When you are old, it may ache with bad weather. But you must remind your hand that it is meant for work.

Only then will you be tying knots and carrying staves at the end of summer."

I could cast spells again. The idea that Cazia hadn't lost her magic flooded her with joy and relief. Suddenly, the pain didn't seem so terrible.

She was about to lunge forward and hug the man when Belterzhimi sighed. "Girls, I must ask for your forbearance. I was up all night finishing my business at the fort, and I must get a little sleep before we make camp tonight."

"Of course!" Ivy hopped out of the cart; Kinz and Cazia followed. Belterzhimi bowed his head to them, then laid a blanket over his eyes. His man did the same. Within moments, they were very still and breathing deeply.

The three girls walked behind the cart through the afternoon, Cazia flexing and unflexing her fingers as best she could. It hurt. It hurt quite a bit, actually, but she didn't stop. She could get her magic back, and all it would cost her was pain.

Still, she was vaguely embarrassed by her urge to throw her arms around Ivy's cousin. First of all, she barely knew him. Second, they were both reclining in the cart in full view of everyone. Third . . . Honestly, she wasn't sure what the third one was, but it probably involved the shock and revulsion he would certainly feel if she tried it, and the horrendously polite way he would be forced to push her away.

Why had he asked so many questions about the flying cart?

"Ivy"—Cazia kept her voice low so they wouldn't disturb the sleeping men—"why does your cousin look so sad?"

Ivy's eyes widened with surprise. "Ooooo! Cazia has a crush on Belterzhimi!"

She and Kinz teased Cazia for a little while but seemed to get the hint when it became too much. They walked the rest of the afternoon in silence, surrounded by stone-faced spearmen and women with unstrung bows who gave Cazia murderous looks. There were servants, too, and others whose roles were hard to define. No one spoke a language she could understand, so she spent the whole day trying to decide if she was making her hand better or worse by flexing it. It didn't matter how it felt. She trusted Belterzhimi's advice implicitly, and of course she did not have a crush on him. That was ridiculous.

Near the end of the day, a huge spatter of mud struck her back. No one knew who had thrown it, and while camp was being arranged, she had to scrub her jacket one-handed. She was determined to keep her clothes as neat and white as everyone else's.

On the second day, the harassment became cruel.

CHAPTER TWENTY-THREE

No MATTER HOW MUCH CAZIA SCRUBBED, SHE HAD NOT BEEN ABLE TO remove the shadow of the mud stain on her jacket, and of course, the princess had noticed as soon as they started walking in the morning. The last thing Cazia wanted was for the insult to receive royal attention, but now it was too late.

"Stay close to me," Ivy said. "I'll see that they treat you with respect."

"That's all right," Cazia said. *I am not helpless.* "I don't need a babysitter, and I've faced scarier things than cowards who fling mud at people's backs."

She didn't say it quietly, and as she hoped a pair of servants—or something, who could tell?—began whispering as if they understood.

Good. Cazia had lived among sneaks and backbiters her entire life. She knew how to deal with people like that.

Before the usual buns were distributed at midday—the Ergoll ate lunch on their feet while walking, which seemed sensible to Cazia, although the food was unbearably bland—a pair of girls approached Kinz and began speaking in Toal. Cazia had learned to tell the difference overnight; Toal sounded like a monotone while Ergoll had a lilt to it. Not that she could understand a word. But the girls encouraged Kinz to follow them to the front of the column.

Then, while they ate, Ivy's cousin asked her to join him on the western side of the group to talk privately about family matters. The princess didn't want to leave Cazia alone, but Cazia insisted it was fine.

And it was. It would have to be. Cazia slowed her pace, letting the cart— and the bulk of the crowd—pull ahead. Walking with the princess, she liked to stay close to the center of the retinue. Not directly behind the cart, of course, because of the little surprises the okshim dropped, but close. She honestly wasn't sure how dangerous the forest was; Belterzhimi's soldiers were obviously there to stand off a Peradaini incursion, which was clearly not going to happen. As for the grunts, the Straim was the widest, deepest river in Kal-Maddum; if armed, skilled boatmen had difficulty navigating those fast, treacherous currents, The Blessing ought to find it nearly impossible.

Maybe there were bandits or something, but Cazia figured it was safer not to ask about it. Someone would surely take it as an insult.

As Cazia fell behind, spearmen passed her. They moved in pairs with long, flexible weapons and round wooden shields covered in bronze on their backs. Instead of swords at their hips, they carried small knives. The looks they gave her made it clear what they thought of her, and they sometimes muttered nastily in Ergoll.

It wasn't Enemies outside the camp that she had to fear. It was the ones within.

But if the men stared with stony contempt, the women looked at her with undisguised hatred. Narrowed eyes, curled lips . . . Cazia was sure they would put an arrow in her back if they thought they could get away with it.

Of course, they probably could. No matter how furious Ivy became, Cazia doubted that her killer would be actually hanged for the crime, considering the history between her people and theirs. Not that it would matter to Cazia once she had been Fire-taken.

It occurred to her that, for once, she was going too far and risking too much, but she dismissed it. No retreat. Not from this enemy.

An archer came from behind and bumped her, hard, knocking her toward the center of the road. She had to hop and dance to avoid the sticky piles of okshim flop, which made the archers laugh. She couldn't understand what they said, but it didn't matter. These weren't the ones who had flung mud on her.

Eventually, she fell back far enough that she was alone on the road. The oak trees grew close to the path, and the morning drizzle dripped from the leaves in fat drops. Only her broad white Toal hat kept them off the back of her neck. It did not take long for them to come to her.

There were four, all women, all carrying unstrung bows and wearing the asymmetrical sleeves of Indregai archers. The one in the lead had shorn blond hair—she had a husband somewhere—and broad, muscular shoulders. She was as tall as Kinz and almost as muscled as Colchua had been. There was a bit of swagger in her step, which the others didn't match. *The leader.*

The woman stepped two paces away from her, then curled her lip while she looked Cazia up and down. She appeared older than Belterzhimi, and, while the other three women were younger, they were adults. All older than Cazia herself.

The big blond took a switch from the hand of a woman beside her and flicked it sideways. Tiny specks of mud spattered across the front of Cazia's jacket.

"Finally," Cazia said, "someone gets up the nerve to confront me to my face."

"You are spark." The smallest and wiriest of the three women could speak her language, if not very well. She lifted her arm and pretended to flick a piece of dirt from her sleeve. "Spark."

"You mean *speck*. If you're going to insult someone in a foreign tongue, take care you don't compliment them instead. *Speck, not spark*."

The small woman said something in Ergoll, and the big one flicked her wrist, laying a stinging stroke on Cazia's upper arm with the switch. "No carrect," the little one said.

Did they think she'd never been beaten with a switch before? "*Correct, not carrect*." The blond struck her again, this time higher on her arm. The sleeve of her jacket absorbed some of the blow, but not much. "*Speck, not—*"

She didn't get to finish. The blond let fly with the blows, swinging with her full arm now. They hurt, but her tutors had beaten her harder when she was eight. She curled her arm to protect her injured hand and one of the strikes—the eleventh or twelfth—caught her across the cheek.

One of the women caught hold of the big blond's arm, stopping the attack. Apparently, there was a limit to what they would do: leave evidence of their bullying.

Cazia touched the bright, burning spot on her cheek where she'd taken the blow. Her fingers came away bloody. The big blond shook off her friend's grip and glared at Cazia.

She glared right back. Fire would take her before she cringed before these cowards. She stepped close to the big woman—so close she had to crane her neck back to stare at her—and gently pinched the hem of that archery jacket with her bloody fingers.

There was a sudden inhuman screech from somewhere behind Cazia. All five of them turned toward the sound, but there was nothing to see but gray skies, heavy trees cover, and blowing rain. It sounded far away, but not nearly far enough.

It sounded again, a grinding, hissing sound like dying metal. Cazia glanced back at the Ergoll archers. Judging by their expressions, she could tell they had never heard it before, either.

Cazia snapped her fingers and pointed at their bows. She'd meant for them to string their weapons, but the women lifted them and began to withdraw.

That wouldn't do. Cazia clapped twice, sharply; they looked at her in surprise. She pointed at the one who had grabbed the big woman's arm then pointed back up the road. "Alarm."

Then she pointed at the three remaining: the small one who could barely speak her language, the second slender one who looked like she wanted to be invisible, and the big one who'd beaten her. Then she pointed at their unstrung bows.

There was a third cry from between the trees. It sounded as if it was getting closer, but that might have been her own fear. Of course, she herself had no weapons at all, not even a knife at her belt. The fingers of her left hand wouldn't flex far enough for her to touch her index finger and thumb together, so she could not manage several of her spells. No fire, no blocks, no crumbling stone, no shooting iron darts, not that she had any.

She bent down and picked up the switch the big woman had dropped, then started toward the sound. The Ergoll archers did not follow. Monument sustain her, were they soldiers? Were they not supposed to be the outer guard for this retinue?

Something in her expression must have goaded them, because three of the women began to string their bows. After a mumbled conversation, the smallest one ran back toward the cart to raise the alarm. Brilliant. Cazia wanted to send one with the longest legs and keep the one who could almost talk to her, but they had to do things their own way.

The messenger vanished around a bend in the road before the women had their bows strung and arrows nocked. They started northward toward the sound, and the Ergoll archers let her stay at the front, like bait.

Fine. Maybe it would have been better to wait for more soldiers, but Cazia was sure she knew that sound. Not that she'd heard it before, not exactly, but it had the same up/down quaver of the roars she heard from The Blessing.

Could the grunts have crossed the Straim? If one had, it would need to be killed quickly. As quickly as possible.

She lifted her injured hand and flexed it again. Fire and Fury, there were so many spells she would be unable to cast still. She could put out a fire if they came across one. She could probably purify a small amount of water . . . Actually, she had never thought to use that against another living creature;

was it possible to "purify" a creature's blood, turning it into water? Should she cast it toward the heart? The legs? The head?

Another scream echoed from between the trees, but now it was coming from the northwest. It was off the road in the trees. Would she be able to lead it to the open, where the archers would have a clear shot? It was pretty to think the Ergoll would actually shoot at this whatever-it-is *before* it tore her apart, but she wasn't going to bet her life on it.

Still, if a grunt had made it to this side of the Straim, running away wasn't going to do much good. It would only catch someone else, and then she'd have two grunts to run from.

She climbed the little slope at the edge of the road and slipped between two trees. One thing she'd learned in Qorr was that the quietest way to walk through woods was on exposed tree roots, and the grass had been chopped low by countless caravans and military carts to feed the okshim. She hopped from one trunk to another, then had to jump a muddy patch to reach a third.

The archers didn't seem to be following her. Fine. She held the switch in her good hand and flexed the injured one. Maybe she could touch her fingers together without the bandages. With her teeth, she began to worry the knot on the back of her knuckles. The cloth didn't want to give, and her hand still hurt like mad.

There was another cry, and this time, it sounded astonishingly close. While it carried a sibilance that the sounds of the grunts never had, she was more convinced than ever that she had guessed right. Somewhere nearby was one of The Blessing.

A chill ran over her whole body. *Why am I doing this? I don't even have a knife.* The familiar sense, last felt just before she started toward Qorr Valley, that she was putting her life in danger largely because she could not imagine things going all that badly, was upon her again. It was a failure of imagination, obviously. Someone with a better head could envision all the ways this might go wrong and would run back toward Vilavivianna and all the Ergoll spears and bows.

Of course, then she would be asking for help from her Enemies, and Fire could take that idea.

Then she heard grass rustling behind her. Her bullies were close behind. So be it. She *definitely* couldn't turn and run now, not while they were looking. Besides, she wasn't planning to actually do any *fighting*. The closer she came to the source of the noise, the more obvious that seemed, blood purifying spell or not. She just wanted to confirm that the grunt was there, make note of where it was, and sneak back to tell the soldiers. As she tugged and loosened her bandages, she reassured herself that she was only spying, not looking for a fight.

Cazia kept hopping from the base of one tree to another. As she got farther from the road, the grass was thinner and thinner—in some parts of the forest floor, the ground seemed to be made of nothing but fallen, rotting branches.

She heard faint but ragged breathing, so she crouched low before peering carefully around the tree trunk. There was nothing to see, but she got the sense that the thing making those awful noises, whatever it was, had to be close. Just ahead, she could see that the trees suddenly stopped. Was she at the edge of a meadow? As she crept forward, she heard the sound of flowing water.

The Straim. She was coming very near to it. Then she heard another strange, grinding cry, and she suddenly recognized that it was a cry of terrible pain.

The tall grass near the riverbank rustled, making the hairs on the back of her neck stand up. The next time they moved, she saw it happen. There was a huge fallen tree lying near the slope of the bank, and the grass was shuddering back and forth above it. Whatever was there, it was just on the other side of that fallen log.

Cazia circled to her left, trying to imagine that she could get a little more distance from the source of that noise. Whatever it was, it was close, and frankly, the thought thrilled her.

The knot on the back of her hand suddenly tore free and the bandages around her palm unraveled. A quick test showed that she did have more mobility without it, maybe even enough for a dart spell. Now if only she didn't have to use it.

She came to the bottom of the fallen tree, where the roots had been torn out of the soil, and crept around to the water's side. The trunk was so thick that, had she stood up straight, the top edge would have been as high as her nose. Not that she stood up straight. Carefully, she peeked though the broken roots. There was nothing to see. The Fire-taken grass was too high.

I have to know. There was nothing to do but climb up the exposed roots. She retreated to the opposite side of the trunk. Wind and rain had washed the dirt away from the exposed roots, but it was still treacherous footing. If a rotted hunk of wood snapped . . .

It didn't happen. Cazia carefully crawled over the top of the trunk.

On the far side of the trunk to the left, she saw a space where the tall grass had been broken and flattened. She moved toward it a little, then saw a sudden flash of rainbow colors as something thrashed just barely in sight.

A serpent. She'd almost forgotten that the Indregai serpents had joined the troops, traveling at the very edge of the convoy. It seemed to be alone.

From where she stood, only the tail and perhaps a third of its body was visible. It still had the beautiful sheen of colors on its scales, but near its tail, she could see something sticking out of it, as though it had burst through its skin.

Feathers. They were blue-black feathers hanging from its tail in irregular clumps. She didn't know much about the Indregai serpents, but she knew they didn't have feathers.

A bird call caught her attention and made her turn around. It was the three Ergoll archers. Cazia waved them closer. Fire take them, why had they sent away the only one she could talk to? The big oaf's spite was going to get them killed.

The three women moved closer. Cazia pointed to the other side of the trunk, then made a serpentine motion with her arm. Then . . . how was she going to explain "feathers" with only hand gestures?

Before she could figure it out, the women hurried away from her, blundering through the tall grass with all the grace of an okshim herd. They'd understood it was a serpent on the side of the trunk, and as far as they were concerned, that was all they needed to know.

She watched their faces as they broke through to the edge of the flattened grass. There was dismay and alarm, but none of them rushed toward the creature the way they might have hurried to an injured human. No, they hung back, clearly worried but unwilling to risk going close.

There was no point in hiding now. Cazia came up onto her knees in full, peering over the edge of the trunk at the entire serpent. It was shuddering, and about a third of the way down its body, its scaly skin was grotesquely swollen. Had it swallowed something big, like a half-grown boq? Maybe the feathers on its tail—actually, behind the fringes of its head, too—had come from its last meal.

Or maybe it was about to lay an egg.

It opened its mouth and let out another cry. Monument sustain them, Fire pass them by, there was nothing natural in that noise, and the expression on the Ergoll women's faces confirmed it.

"You should kill it," Cazia said, her voice soft.

The women couldn't understand her words, but they understood her meaning. The big blond lifted her bow and drew. Cazia immediately rolled away from them, hearing the unmistakable sound of an arrow striking solid wood as she dropped to the forest floor.

Warning shot. If the archer had been aiming at her, it would have passed over the trunk. Still, she had—

There was a sudden tearing sound, as though wet cloth was being torn. That same tremulous screaming returned as well, along with cries of horror from the women. Cazia rolled over to see if there was a gap between the bottom of the log and the forest floor that she might peer through, but she had no such luck.

Then she heard screams. Terrible, blood-curdling screams. One of the women cried out in Ergoll, and the other two ran around the end of the log and sprinted through the high grass toward the road.

A moment later, a long serpentine figure passed over Cazia. It was dark, like a shadow, and it flew on three pairs of long, slender wings. Cazia was unable to breathe for a moment. *That thing is going to kill me.*

But it didn't. It moved through the trees, six feet above the ground, after the fleeing archers. It didn't even look like it was flying; it was moving so slowly, weaving back and forth and languorously beating those wings. It moved as if it was swimming through the air.

Magic. Ivy and the others had to be warned. This serpent had been transformed by The Blessing. Cazia rolled to her feet, rustling the grass around her.

The flying serpent turned to look at her.

Fire take the whole world, couldn't she have waited just a few breaths more? The creature began to circle around, weaving through the trees, and Cazia bolted into a hard run.

She circled the fallen log and found what she'd expected: one of the archers lay atop a bloody mat of broken grasses. Cazia ran toward her—Great Way, her arm was gone at the shoulder—and was astonished to see that she was still clinging to life.

She bent low over the woman and stared into her eyes for a moment. It was the one who'd stopped the lashing Cazia had just been taking. Her eyes fluttered and fell closed.

Cazia snatched a handful of arrows from the quiver at the dead woman's hip. Five. It wasn't enough, but the flying serpent had navigated its turn and was weaving through the air toward her. There wasn't time for her to cast a spell; it was too close.

She turned and ran through the grass, following the river downstream. She began the hand motions for her dart spell—arrows were an imperfect substitute, but they would do in a pinch, assuming they held together.

No, she had to clear her mind and go through the mental visualizations, too. She started again, quickly, adjusting the spell on the fly to shoot all the arrows at once. The pain in her hand was real but distant. She could touch her middle finger to her thumb, then her little finger.

The spell built up within her—Great Way, it felt so powerful.

There was a hiss from behind her. It was too close! She bolted to the left, moving into the trees. Then the spell was almost ready. She spun around, lifting the arrows.

The serpent swooped down on her, jaws gaping. Cazia leaped back, stumbling over a tree root and falling backward as the cluster of arrows flew from her hand.

She rolled over, the root digging into her ribs and shoulders. *Keep moving*, she told herself, but there was no way she could be fast enough to avoid those gaping jaws.

The bite never came. Cazia stood, moving to put a tree trunk between herself and the creature. There was silence. She glanced down at her injured hand and saw that it had begun to bleed again. The flying serpent could have been all over her already, but all Cazia could hear was the rush of the Straim, just two dozen paces away.

She peeked around the tree trunk and saw the creature lying still on the ground. The back half was hidden in the tall grass, but she could see the first two pairs of wings sprouting from its back.

There were two arrows stuck into it, both through the mouth. One had struck just behind its fangs, passing so far through the end of its snout that Cazia could see the fletching. The other had struck farther back, with the point emerging from the center of its skull, just behind the eyes.

Dead. It was as dead as the archer beside the log, as dead as Cazia's brother. She snatched up a stone and threw it at the creature's head. It bounced off; the creature did not respond.

Cazia moved closer to examine the thing. Its wings were ridiculously small—barely larger than a crow's—and could never have supported its weight alone. The thing had to stay aloft through some sort of enchantment. She held her hand near the foremost pair of wings—she didn't have the nerve to touch it yet—and confirmed it. There was magic in it.

The beautiful rainbow colors of the serpent's scales had become an even blue-black, the same as the long, curling feathers that covered them. Its head was more slender and streamlined than the uncursed serpents, and it didn't have the same red frill. The jaws opened wider, but the fangs seemed smaller.

Great Way, the thing was huge.

She'd survived because of a lucky shot. She hadn't been able to aim, hadn't had time to plan, hadn't even brought a weapon of her own. She'd known how dangerous Kal-Maddum could be, and she'd sought out that noise anyway. Was she suicidal?

Never mind. She'd think about that later, if she had to. There was too much to do first.

CHAPTER TWENTY-FOUR

B Y THE TIME THE SOLDIERS CAUGHT UP TO HER, CAZIA HAD REMOVED the arrow that had pierced the end of the feathered serpent's snout and broken it. She had also fetched the dead archer's bow.

Near the woman's body she found something she hadn't expected: the serpent's scaly skin. The brilliantly-colored scales slowly lost their color while she watched, turning the same dull white as a marble block, while the head turned black and brown. She knew all snakes shed their skins, of course—her tutors had shown them to her—but those curled, translucent coils hadn't been gory with torn meat on the inside. The grunt had emerged out of the serpent's flesh, not just its skin.

What's more, she'd heard it screaming as it had transformed. Obviously, the process wasn't quick or pleasant.

Colchua. Cazia stared for a long time at the knife on the dead woman's belt, but in the end, she decided not to take it. She laid the bow across her, too.

Goherzma led the group of soldiers who found her, finally. She pointed out the corpses, explained that she'd used the archer's weapon and had gotten lucky. She then claimed to have stabbed it a second time just to be sure.

She was led to a copse away from the main group and forced to strip under the watchful eye of six female soldiers. The beating the archer had given her had just begun to get real color around the red welts, but the soldiers found no bite marks.

They gave her permission to dress and return to the main group. By this time, Kinz and Belterzhimi had caught up to them, and she had to repeat her story. Kinz explained that some of the soldiers wanted her killed on general principle, but Belterzhimi wouldn't allow it.

Eventually, a half dozen serpents joined the crowd. Ivy's cousin tried to communicate the situation to them in hand language, but they did not seem to have any way of responding. Finally, the serpents signaled for the humans to follow them. It took most of the day, but they led them to a quiet little hollow on the eastern side of the road. Sprawled inside was the rotting corpse of a grunt.

The fur was dark blue, which meant it had been human once. Whatever else they might have learned from it was lost to the local scavengers. Birds, forest dogs, tree-nesting rats, and who knew what else had torn it apart.

"The serpents signal that they destroyed this creature days ago," Belterzhimi said. "One of them bit through the beast's skull."

The wind shifted, bringing the stink of rotting flesh to them all. Cazia turned away. "Shouldn't they have told you?"

"They do not talk to humans unless they must," the man answered. "It is not in the nature. No matter what anyone says, they do not like us much. I will do my best to explain to them the dangers these creatures pose, once you have explained it to me. As thoroughly as you can. We had long believed that the grunts did not swim."

He said it as though it was an accusation. Cazia let it pass. The truth was, the earlier excitement had left her too exhausted to argue. "The transformation isn't immediate."

"So you think this fellow was bitten, then crossed the water before he could change."

"It's not their normal behavior. When I saw people who had been cursed in Samsit, the grunts watched over them like nannies."

"There could only be one like this." Belterzhimi waved a broad hand back toward the hollow. "The serpents hunt by the smell as well as sight, and if there had been several of these creatures, we would be getting a tour of the corpses."

Unless the serpents had all been killed or transformed, and no human anywhere knew about it. Belterzhimi's expression was grim; she was sure he had the same thought.

"We will need more patrols along the shoreline," he said. "Unfortunately, the Toal and the Ergoll do not have enough soldiers for such a task. Even if we neglected the fields all summer and autumn to muster our people, we could not do it."

Goherzma bowed. "Should we call up the Peshkoll?"

"And the Winzoll." That seemed to surprise the servant, but he only nodded. "No one can now deny the danger we face. Soon, we will be invaded from the west and the north. There is no time for delay. If you would excuse me," he said directly to Cazia, "but I must be rude to you again." Without waiting for a response, he began to give orders in singsong Ergoll.

Kinz stopped short when she heard them. "What is it?" Cazia asked.

"He is diverting the unit away from Goldgrass Hill," she answered. "He has made orders that we are to go directly to the Temple of the Mountain Tower." Cazia shrugged to show that she didn't understand. "He is taking us see Kelvijinian, Tyr over the Sleeping Earth. Their god."

By the time they returned to the road, the okshim cart had caught up with them, and Ivy with it. "This is outrageous!" the girl exclaimed as soon as Cazia and Kinz close enough to talk. "I was physically restrained from coming to your side! Do they think I am helpless?"

"They think," Kinz said, her voice flat, "they will be made to suffer terribly if you are hurt in their care."

"Hmph." Ivy lifted a bow out of the cart. "At least they allowed me to borrow the dead woman's bow. It is a little taller than I would like, but I can make it work. I wish you had left me more arrows, though. Did you . . . ?"

Cazia said, "Lucky shot."

"Of course."

Cazia lowered her voice. "Your cousin is planning to go to the Temple of the Mountain Tower."

"Ooo!" The girl's eyes widened with delight. "He must be planning to call up all the clans."

"Does he have the authority to do that?" Kinz asked.

"Of course he does. I told you he is Warden of the Western Frontier. If he thinks the need is great enough, he can call for spearmen and archers from all the clans, even ask for more serpents, although that is a chancy thing to request. It is a great responsibility and a great risk."

Cazia couldn't resist. "What sort of risk?"

"If he calls warriors away from the homes and farms needlessly, he will become a laughingstock and will be stripped of the position. Then he would be challenged to a series of duels, until he failed. It would be terrible. Some would like to see that very much. An Ergoll has held the Western Frontier for over twenty years; my uncle once told me that the other peoples wanted the chance at honor."

"Especially the Winzoll," Cazia said, remembering Goherzma's look of surprise. She felt a little sick when she imagined Belterzhimi sadly facing a line of men with spears, all waiting to duel.

"Yes, obviously," the princess answered. "Even though they are nothing but a pack of lazy priests."

"Then why is he going to the temple? Does he have to pray for permission or something?"

Ivy looked at her crookedly. "Of course not. The Indregai peoples are spread across the entire peninsula. It would take many days for a messenger to reach all of them—if they could even make the trip safely. We do have bears and bandits and wild dogs, you know. Bad enough we will have to wait for the soldiers to muster and march into place. No, he's going to the temple to entreat Kelvijinian to spread the call."

Cazia and Kinz looked at each other. "In what way?" Kinz asked.

The princess sighed as though they were exasperating her. "Kelvijinian is the god of the sleeping earth. He can make his presence known throughout Indrega. Well, throughout Kal-Maddum."

Cazia blinked at her for a few moments. "Little sister, do you mean he could appear anywhere, see anything, and carry a message to anyone, if you asked him properly?"

"Of course, Cazia! *He is a god.*"

There was a sensible, diplomatic response to that statement, but it was as far beyond Cazia's skill to think of it as it was for her to swim out into the ocean. "I have to go with him," she said finally. "I have to know what's happening in the west. And I have to contact the tower in Tempest Pass."

Lar would not be there, no, but Stoneface might. And Lar's uncle. She'd managed to bring five Tilkilit stones out of Qorr, but she had no idea what to do with them. There had to be someone who knew what would be best.

"Right! We will all go!"

That sounded like a fine idea in theory, but Belterzhimi was not enthusiastic. He insisted that Ivy continue southward to rejoin her parents, and for once, Cazia was on his side. She never said so aloud, of course, but Ivy—Vilavivianna, actually, since it seemed right to be more formal—had a family that loved her and an important role to play among her people. Cazia had neither, really. It was one thing for Cazia to make this detour, but Ivy ought to be heading home.

Still, the princess was on her side, and Cazia tried to impress upon the commander the importance of finding out what was happening in the west. Scholars were the key to defeating The Blessing, and if they could send a message to Tempest Pass, they might be able to get the help they needed. *Magical* help.

Belterzhimi asked again about flying carts; he was very concerned about patrolling the western edge of the peninsula. Cazia suggested it was very likely there were carts and drivers in the west.

That sealed things for her and Kinz. For the princess, it became more complicated. Kinz quickly stopped translating, explaining that they had begun insulting each other.

Rule by wit, Ivy had called it, but in truth, it was mainly name-calling and condescension. Kinz began to blush furiously whenever Belterzhimi spoke at length, and Ivy's face became pale. Cazia couldn't understand what they were saying, but it was clear the little girl was not winning her cousin over.

"She has to come," Cazia finally interrupted. They turned their faces toward her. "Your soldiers are brave, but you don't have many of them. How many can you afford to send south with her? How many will you take to the Temple? Even with the numbers you have, two or three grunts might overwhelm you."

The Warden did not like that. "A girl of the slouching, grasping west will have little understanding of the warriors of Indrega. We—"

Cazia held up her hand and he fell silent. His expression was just beginning to grow angry; she wanted to touch his hand to calm him, but she didn't have the nerve. *Please don't become an Enemy.* "I'm not one of your people. I don't insult others to gain advantage, and I'm not trying to insult you now. I've seen grunts fight human soldiers. Have you?"

Belterzhimi sighed. All the anger seemed to drain out of him and he looked sad again. "Thankfully, no. We have captured refugees from the other side of the river, but I have not even seen a grunt until today."

"I should be dead right now," Cazia said softly. Monument sustain her, it was true. She'd taken a wild risk and had barely come out of it alive. "It was just stupid luck that I struck home against that creature. But I've seen them in action, and so has the princess."

"They are terrifying," Ivy said.

"Fast like grass lions, hard to kill like bears, utterly fearless, but they're smart."

"A few hundred of them," Ivy added, "overran the entire city of Peradain in a single day."

"Less," Cazia said. "Even less. The point is, if you split your forces now, you will either leave the princess exposed on the rest of her journey or you will leave yourself and the rest of us exposed. I don't want to taunt you or insult the warriors under your command. I'm just trying to give you the information you need."

He sighed again, then slapped his thigh. "Telling me you mean to speak no insult, only truth, is one of the oldest ways to insult someone, but I believe you mean it honestly. All right. She must accompany us."

Ivy cheered and threw her arms around her cousin's neck, then hugged Kinz and Cazia together.

"But," Belterzhimi continued, "if I am to take you, you must tell me the whole story of your journey. Hold nothing back."

Ivy's face lost its excitement. "Mother and Father first."

"We are not going to your parents, and I will not wait. You will tell me the entire story or I will send you home afoot with a pair of guards, and let the danger wash you away, if chance fails you."

Then it was time for them to leave his campfire so he could attend to other things. Ivy pulled the other girls away from the main group of soldiers into the woods. A trio of serpents lay curled around a tree, watching them, but the humans were out of earshot.

"Do we have to . . . " Kinz said.

"You will just have to get used to them," Ivy said, a little more tersely than she needed to. "We are going to have to tell our story to my cousin."

Cazia remembered how much she wanted to do exactly that when she was in Qorr Valley. Of course, she had been hollowed out at the time, but the whole point had been to spread the word about what they'd discovered. They'd held off because Ivy had demanded it, but they weren't sure why. "Isn't he exactly the sort of person who should know what we found?"

"Yes, but he will not believe us." She sighed, glanced at the serpents, then bowed politely to them. The creatures lifted and dipped their heads in return. Cazia felt goose bumps run down her back. No matter how many times the princess assured them those creatures were allies, she couldn't help but fear them. "And that's risky."

Kinz's expression showed she was confused, but it suddenly became very clear to Cazia. "Because they will mock you."

"'Mock' is the wrong word," Ivy said. "There is no good word for this in Peradaini. The worst thing a ruler can do is lie about the achievements, because it makes them a target for laughter. For snickering. It is like giving a knife to your enemy. I can tell the story to my mother and father and make them believe it. It would take time and effort, but I could. I do not have the same influence with Belterzhimi, and he is unlikely to give me much credit. It would be easier if we were boys, I'm afraid."

Kinz sighed. "Even among my people, that would be true."

"If no one believed our story, it would follow me for the rest of my life. I could never become a respectable member of the royal line, never command others, never be anything but a joke. That is why I wanted to bring the iron crown and spiked circlet back."

"We have the Tilkilit stones," Kinz said.

"But to use them as proof, we would have to reveal that Cazia is a scholar."

A wizard now, actually. "Fire and Fury. Ivy . . . If I have to, I—"

"We will not do that," Ivy said. "No matter what. I refuse to take my place among my people at your expense. Either of you. Not after everything we have been through together. However, if he refuses to believe *anything*, he might order you two to be whipped."

Cazia gritted her teeth. It was one thing to be beaten with a switch; a whip was another. It would cut her open and she would have to heal naturally, of all things. "Your cousin might suddenly find himself less handsome if he tried it."

Kinz made a face. "You think he is handsome? But he is always making the tragic expression, as though making practice for future misery."

Cazia wanted to say a dozen things all at once, about sadness being a sign of wisdom, deep feeling, and generosity, but her thoughts were too tangled up and it was impossible. Instead, she only blushed.

Both girls laughed and hugged her. It was so embarrassing! Not that it mattered. He was so much older than her and certainly married or something.

Not that she spent much time thinking about him. More pressing was the princess's dilemma and Cazia's secret. Would she sacrifice her freedom for Ivy? Obviously, yes, but if there was a way to avoid it, she would.

They camped right there by the road for the night. Cazia was asked to tell the story of killing the flying serpent over and over again, moving from one campfire to the next, while the soldiers listened in thoughtful silence. They would never like her, but a little bit of respect suddenly seemed possible.

The caravan was up and moving before dawn, heading back north for part of the morning, then taking a narrow road that led them north east. Unlike the Ozzhuacks' okshim, the Indregai's didn't seem to mind being turned this way or that.

The way was steep and quickly became steeper. The road became a path, and they had to follow its winding way around lakes and boulders. The trees seemed to draw in closer with every step, and Cazia soon fought the urge to climb one just so she could look over the canopy at something farther than twenty feet away.

Belterzhimi said it would take six days of hard travel to reach the temple, and it did. It was a sudden change when it finally happened. They trudged around yet another curve carved into the side of a hill, and there they were,

CHAPTER TWENTY-FIVE

As Tejohn and Javien came to the base of the Southern Barrier, they had some difficulty finding the road that would take them through Salt Pass. Javien was certain it was farther west and insisted they push forward. Tejohn wanted to backtrack before they crossed into Bendertuk territory. He had already scraped the paint off the Finstel shield he was carrying, but if they met a Bendertuk patrol, they would be fortunate if they were only robbed of everything they had.

Fortunately, they happened upon traveling merchants held up at a crossroads by a broken wagon wheel. Their little group was too small to be called a caravan—only a dozen wagons or so—but they did anyway. Their leader was a woman who called herself "Granny Nin." She insisted they call her "Granny," even though Tejohn thought she couldn't be more than ten years older than him.

After Javien introduced himself, Tejohn gave his name as Ondel Ulstrik again.

The first thing they did was trade one of the fallen soldiers' knives for a new coat of paint on Tejohn's shield, along with a spot in the wagon. Granny assured them they would pass through Bendertuk territory without incident, since she had many friends and relatives on that side of the river and always did fine business there.

Friends were the secret to doing business, she exclaimed, and she had so many! She couldn't wait to get up into Salt Pass to see her friend Iskol, and after that they would venture into the Sweeps to trade with her friends the miners and herding clans.

Tejohn tried to warn her that there might be few customers in the Sweeps this year, considering how much trouble was spreading, but Granny wouldn't hear of it. She knew how people were. They always needed something, and she was there to trade.

They crossed a bridge into Bendertuk territory without any hassle at all. Granny was as friendly with the soldiers as she'd claimed, and they let the wagons pass without incident. Tejohn thought about the spear and shield Granny had insisted on loading into a wagon; walking without it through enemy lands made him feel as though he'd been stripped naked, but he did it and he survived.

For sixteen days, they walked through the northwestern corner of the Bendertuk lands, following roads that became steeper with every passing day. Everyone in the caravan except Granny took their turns following the wagons with a broad wooden shovel—okshim patties couldn't be left in the road. What's more, a pair of young boys had little wagons of their own, into which the shoveler loaded the dung. Then the boys ran to the front of the caravan and dropped it for the okshim to eat.

Yes, Granny assured him, it was revolting, but the beasts would starve if their grasses passed through their bellies only once. What's more, even the fresh grass cut from the side of the road had to be mixed with dung first; otherwise, the okshim might think themselves in charge of the pack and become unruly. There were tricks to leading a caravan, she insisted, and not everyone knew them. Tejohn better understood his father's decision to tend sheep and pull his own wagons.

Javien stopped at every village and performed weddings, said prayers, or more often, granted divorces. The temples had been emptied at the beginning of summer, they were told, and every beacon in the land had been summoned to the Bendertuk holdfast.

In the past, Javien had been happy to accept food and lodging for himself and Tejohn in payment for his services, but Granny explained it would be unfair to expect newlyweds or penniless divorcing miners to host the whole caravan, so at her suggestion, he asked for a small bit of coin, of which she took a reasonable share.

The young priest didn't seem to mind. Javien was careful never to be seen crying in his bedroll, although he did awaken with terrible dreams more than once. He spent his days talking with the merchant families, sharing stories, jokes, and gossip in that easy way that always made Tejohn a little envious.

For his part, Tejohn manned the shovel when it was his turn, ate with the group, but otherwise kept to himself. The others knew only that he was a farmer turned soldier and assumed he was the priest's bodyguard.

Eventually, the roads became so steep that the okshim foundered and the families had to get out of the wagons and push. It was strenuous work, but Tejohn did his part. They camped that night in a wide, tree-lined place on the side of the mountain. Tejohn stood at the edge of the little cliff and looked out over the treetops. He would have thought it lovely if it hadn't been in Bendertuk hands.

Granny Nin came up behind him. "This is the last grove of good hardwood until we cross into the Sweeps. It's all scrub pine from here."

"I like pine," Tejohn said. It occurred to him that he hadn't yet seen a stand of evergreens with his new eyes. There were so many things he wanted to see. "I like that they're green during the winter."

This made Granny smile for some reason. "I'm pleased to see you coming this far with us. You and your companion have more than earned your keep. I wonder, though, what you will do after we visit my good friend Iskol at the top of the pass. Will you be turning east with us to visit the mines in the Sweeps?"

Tejohn considered his answer. He and Javien would have to split off from her at some point, but would it be better to announce it after they left the pass or before they visited this friend of hers? Would it even matter?

He quickly realized that the delay in his answer was answer enough. She knew he wasn't heading east. "We have other plans, I'm afraid. Not that you haven't been wonderful hosts."

"Hosts!" She seemed delighted with him. "You surprise me again. But I wonder if I might change your mind. This is a bad time to travel westward in the Sweeps. The Durdric are a lovely people, as long as you keep away from the Holy Sons. That will be hard to do at the height of summer."

"There are Holy Sons in the east, too. I've heard tell of raids on mining camps west of Caarilit."

"I would not put much stock in those rumors, my friend. Miners love to tell stories, and those stories grow like weeds in the telling. I put as much faith in stories of Durdric raids in the east as I do of giant eagles swooping down and carrying people away."

"What about the grunts?" Tejohn said evenly. "Do you believe in them?"

"It's hard to say. I believe *something* happened in Peradain, but I'm still not sure what."

"So you don't credit tales of monsters with pale purple fur—"

"Purple?" she interrupted. "I'd heard they were blue."

"One kind is purple. One kind is blue."

Granny Nin smiled kindly. Even when she was being condescending, she had charm. "You see? The stories change and grow. Oh, please don't think I'm being rude. I don't mean to be. It's just that I've heard so many stories in my travels. Mermaids in the high salt-water lakes of the Southern Barrier. The goat people who are at war with them. The secret city of the alligaunts. It's all very colorful and quite hard to believe."

"I see your point."

"Peradain has fallen. This we know. But who did it? Think on this: where do blue dyes come from? The Indrega Peninsula. In fact, you can't make purple without mixing red with blue, yes? And we've recently opened trade routes with the Indregai again after many years of conflict. So let me ask you: which seems more likely, that we've been invaded by blue and purple monsters or that Peradain was sacked by warriors wearing dyed bear fur?"

"Warriors," Tejohn said flatly.

"Perhaps. Another story could be that the Indregai, who have long fought alongside their serpents, have found a new beast to accompany them into battle. Bears, perhaps, with dye splashed onto their backs."

"Warriors and bears."

She slapped him playfully on the arm. "Don't make that face, you." Tejohn laughed. "Is it any more outrageous than tales of monsters? No, the real dangers here are bandits, and the tyrs in this part of the world never let their bands grow too large. We know how to stand up to them and how to drive them off."

Tejohn couldn't let that pass. "I'd like to see that."

They had settled the okshim at the westernmost part of the meadow, where the trees were thinnest, but they had not had a chance to eat. Good. Granny Nin scrounged up eight of them, four men and four women. Grumbling, they took up their unpainted shields and long wooden poles, then formed a shield wall two deep.

"They look fine, do they not?" Granny said. "They're all former soldiers, and the bandits always think twice when they see us."

Tejohn thought they looked adequate. "Bring me my shield and . . . and a pole, I guess."

One of the young lads ran to the wagon to get it, and a crowd began to gather. Javien stood among them, and he was the only one not smiling.

The weight of the pole felt wrong without a spearhead at the end, but he moved his grip farther back. There. The merchants saw that he intended to attack them and, looking a little incredulous, they made ready.

Tejohn glanced at their line and saw instinctively where the weak points were.

He charged toward them, his feet staying close to the ground and moving in little crescents. Just before he came in range of them, he jolted to the right.

Two of the merchants tried to lunge forward and two held their spot. He knocked aside their poles with his shield and the haft of his own "spear," then dealt one a sharp knock on the forehead. She tumbled back into the row behind her. Tejohn stepped back, to the right, then lunged forward again to deal the same blow to the man at the end of the row.

He sidestepped around them, moving onto their flank. The merchants tried to reform their line, but they were too slow. The man on the end of the line held his shield high enough to protect his head and Tejohn gave him a jab on the inside of his thigh just above the knee.

He kept moving to the right, knocking away their attacks with his shield and striking at their fingers and feet. They could have overwhelmed him, but they were afraid of taking a tap to the head.

"Enough!" Granny Nin called. The merchants stepped back and lowered their poles.

Tejohn gave one last hard knock to the shield of the nearest merchant, and she gave him a sour look. "You don't lower your weapons when your commander calls for an end to the fight. You lower them when the other side agrees to it."

"A fine point," Granny said. She turned to Tejohn. "I'm glad the bandits don't fight as well as you do."

"You should drill them more often," he said. "Start with their footwork. It's not the heroic part of soldiering, but it'll keep them alive."

"I was only injured," one of the merchant's said. He sounded a little peevish. "He only gave me a flesh wound."

"No," Javien said. "He hit you on the inside of the thigh. If there had been a blade on the end of his pole, you would have bled to death by now." The merchant looked like he wanted to argue the point, but a look from Granny Nin silenced him. Javien turned to Tejohn. "You used the grunts' tactics against them."

"What's this?" Granny Nin said, startled.

"Flanking a line or a square is standard tactics," Tejohn said. "If they'd been well trained, they would have adjusted the line."

"Beacon Javien," Granny Nin said, "what's this about a grunt?"

"We saw one fight a line of spears barely a day outside of Ussmajil. They were Finstel soldiers and they . . . Were they well trained, my—friend?"

Fire and Fury, no one could have missed the little delay in Javien's voice before he said *friend*. "They were good enough," Tejohn answered. He threw his pole to the man who thought a cut on the thigh was a minor wound. "They had been well trained and the terrain was on their side, but they couldn't adjust fast enough."

Granny laid a hand on the young priest's shoulder. "You saw them? Truly?"

Javien looked confused for a moment. "Granny Nin hears a lot of stories," Tejohn said, "and is naturally skeptical."

"We killed two of them," the priest said. "We tricked them and burned them to death. And then . . . And then . . . " His face went pale and his hands began to tremble.

"Ssshhh," Granny said. She took Javien's hands and held them in hers. "We're going to talk about this, my friend, but not like this. We'll build a fire, serve a meal, and then we'll talk. Would that be all right with you?"

He nodded. That's what they did. Night had fallen by the time they had all eaten, and the entire caravan gathered close to listen to Javien tell the tale of his and Tejohn's encounter at the farmhouse. He told it flatly, without affect, leaving out only the spells he had cast.

The merchants were understandably upset by the fate of the grunts' victims, but they never doubted the necessity of it, not when the story came from a priest in his red robe. After he finished, two of the older women pulled him aside to talk quietly about what he had done. Tejohn was concerned at first, but when he realized they were going to exchange stories about painful choices they'd had to make, he backed off. As he'd told the Freewell girl a lifetime ago, talking with others who had experienced a similar pain had been the only useful thing that had ever helped his own case of the flinches.

As he settled back down in his spot, he realized that Granny Nin and the rest of the merchants were staring at him. "Why didn't you tell us?" she asked.

"You would have laughed at me," he said, trying not to be cruel about it. "You would have thought it was another folk tale."

"But you were there. You saw it."

Tejohn nodded. "That was the beacon's first experience with grunts, but it wasn't mine. I've seen both of them. The purple ones are larger, maybe twice the size of a man, and they don't have the same bony ridges on their backs and arms. However, they operate the same way; if they're hungry, they tear you apart and eat you. If they aren't, they bite you to pass on the curse, then hold you captive until you change."

"I'd kill myself," one of the young men blurted out.

"You can't," the older woman beside him said. "Isn't that what the beacon said in his story? They couldn't kill themselves or harm each other."

"One thing that few people know," Tejohn said, "is that they talk to each other." All of their attention was focused on him now, and he didn't like it. "I've held a translation stone while they were nearby, and their grunts and roars are actually words. *Bless* and *Blessing* is all they ever say. I think it's what they call themselves. *The Blessing.* What's more, I think it's the curse itself that's talking. Even before you change, the curse starts to take control of you, and it doesn't want you to kill it. It wants you to help it spread."

"Fire pass us by," Granny said. "What times we live in. What terrible times. Tell me about this translation stone. Where did you get it and where is it now? It would be worth a year's lodging in a holdfast for the lot of us."

Tejohn thought back to the day at Fort Samsit when Cazia Freewell made it for him. She had remained behind when Lar Italga set out on his quest, and . . . By now, she was either dead or transformed. "I took it off a corpse," Tejohn said. "And it was taken from me at the gates of Ussmajil."

"Feh. I bet they don't even know what they have. Pity. It would have made us rich, and the rich are always safest in a siege."

There was no point in quibbling over her use of the word "us." Tejohn shrugged and said, "A great deal has been lost."

"Any other terrors you want to tell us about?" Granny's tone was almost challenging.

"Have any of your people disappeared in the night? Maybe you assumed they ran off?"

Everyone in the circle shook their heads. "Is that what grunts do? Snatch people in the middle of the night?"

"No. Grunts aren't stealth hunters. It's the ruhgrit who carry people off. Those are the giant eagles people have been telling stories about. I saw them over Fort Caarilit, but they're mostly in the northeast and in the Sweeps."

There was a commotion over this, and Tejohn met Granny's appraising look. He shrugged. "I don't know anything about merfolk or the lost goatman city, though."

One of the men in the circle blurted out, "What do you suggest we do?"

Tejohn became very still. They should not have been asking him for orders; he was not the one in charge, and he didn't want to usurp anyone's authority. "Granny already has you doing it. Post guards at night. Keep watch. If you meet anyone who says 'bless' or 'blessing' every other sentence, check their body for bite marks or patches of blue fur."

"Because they might already be blessed," someone said.

"*Cursed.*" Tejohn corrected immediately. "They might already be *cursed.*"

"Do you think we could hold off an attack from a pack of grunts?" the young man who promised to kill himself asked.

No. "With Granny Nin's permission, we can practice a few footwork drills in the morning before we set out. Nothing extensive or over-taxing, I promise."

She drained her cup and stood. "Thank you, Ondel"—the way she said his false name made it clear she knew it was false—"You've saved me the trouble of asking."

In the morning, Tejohn showed them how to stand to hold the line, how to sidestep an attack, and how to advance quickly but carefully. If they had been real soldiers, they would have spent hours practicing each until it was habit in even the most trying circumstances, but that would never do here. He demonstrated, they copied, he corrected, and they were done.

Before they started, he had been worried that his lesson would give them unfounded confidence in themselves, but it was clear that wasn't happening. He had unnerved them the night before and they looked haunted.

The day's journey was even harder than the previous, because the road was cruelly steep. After a while, Granny Nin began to sing a slow-paced but cheerful work song, and the whole troupe joined in. Even Tejohn sang along, although the people near him winced when he missed notes, as he often did. Their footsteps kept beat with the tune and they reached the top of the pass shortly after midday.

There were stone markers by the side of the road, indicating the border between holdings. He was relieved to be leaving Bendertuk lands, but where were they entering? The empire was dotted with minor tyrs and small holdings, especially in the mountains and down in the southernmost waterlands.

They came upon a painted sign standing at the place where the road turned directly north and became a gentle slope. It had been freshly painted, showing a white circle in a green field. Within the circle were the dual-finned humps of a serpent or eel as it might appear above the water.

Tejohn thought he ought to recognize it, but he didn't. Prince Lar had been drilled in the banners of his tyrs. Tejohn had been concerned with their spears, shields, and swords, not how they were decorated.

Shortly beyond the painted banner was a curved wall that stretched across the road from one cliff face to another. It wasn't a high wall, but the way it commanded the long, flat slope leading up to it would have created a deadly killing ground for archers and siege engines.

The wooden gate stood wide to receive them, and he saw the pennants flying above them: two humps of a water serpent. It was almost familiar, as though he'd met the local tyr years ago at some function at the Palace of Song and Morning but had forgotten him since.

The holdfast was small even by the standards of petty tyrs: the building was made from lashed logs and stood only two stories tall. The small balconies had been built solidly, like miniature towers, sporting arrow slots in every direction. A few flaming brands and a bucket of pitch would have undone it, but perhaps they thought themselves too small to be worth an assault. The doors of the grand hall swung open and a dozen people hurried out; some were soldiers, some were bureaucrats with wax tablets tucked under their arms.

"Granny Nin!" cried the tallest of them. He was a weedy-looking man with a skin pallor that suggested he hid from the sun. His gray-toothed smile was broad and genuine. "Granny Nin, it is always a pleasure to welcome you."

"Thank you, my good friend. I have a gift for your mighty tyr, but first, you must ask your questions. Ask away!"

"I'm afraid I must. Do you have all the same merchants as last year?"

"Granny Blacktree passed last midwinter, I'm afraid, and her kin weren't interested in keeping up the wagon. So, we are doing without her."

The bureaucrat made a sympathetic face. Tejohn was startled to realize he was wearing shell decorations like the Durdric Holy Fighters he'd fought in the Sweeps. Were they Durdric sympathizers? The man was also wearing an iron ring, which would have been blasphemy to them. "The poor dear. We all liked her."

"But it was hard on her these past few years," Granny said, "so it wasn't a surprise. However, we've also picked up a wandering beacon and his armsman."

The bureaucrat glanced at Tejohn—who had left his spear in Granny's wagon and had his shield on his back—then looked away without interest. To Javien, he said, "Where are you from and where are you bound, Beacon . . . "

"Beacon Javien Biliannish, out of Ussmajil. We are passing through to the Sweeps on a mission for the temple."

But the bureaucrat was distracted by a messenger running out of the hall. The young girl whispered a few words, then bowed. The bureaucrat thanked her, excused himself, then moved toward the doors.

Granny Nin looked surprised to see the man turn his back, and she was even more surprised when the soldiers at the side of the holdfast suddenly lowered their points and rushed forward.

Tejohn stepped in front of Javien and slid his shield off his back. He was reaching for his sword—and cursing his decision to set down his spear—when Granny cried out, "No!"

She was in charge. Tejohn moved his hand away from his sword and let his shield fall to the ground. The soldiers did not shove their steel into his guts, but he saw no indecision in their expressions. When the order came—if it came—they would kill everyone in the caravan.

"What is the meaning of this?" Granny Nin called, but no one was paying her any attention. Two of the shutters on a holdfast balcony banged open, and everyone turned their attention to the gray-haired man staring down at them, tears in his eyes.

It was Doctor Twofin.

To be concluded in THE WAY INTO DARKNESS

Author's note

In modern publishing, there is no force more powerful than word of mouth. If you liked this trilogy, please tell your friends. Write a blog post, post a review somewhere, tweet about it, even mention it during a face-to-face conversation, if people still have those.

And I don't just mean my books; tell the world about *all* the things you enjoy. Make yourself heard. Readers who share their enthusiasm are more powerful than any Hollywood marketing campaign.

Thank you.

CPSIA information can be obtained at www.ICGtesting.com
Printed in the USA
LVOW07s0131140415

434480LV00004B/260/P